**WILD PUF**
**AN EXCEPTIO**

# AN EXCEPTIONAL AURA
## Frances Dolan

Ozwaldo Hawk

All rights reserved; no part of this publication may be reproduced or sent to another via electronic, photocopying or otherwise, without the prior permission of the author

First published in Great Britain 2024

This paperback edition first published 2024

Proofread 2024 www.michelleemerson.co.uk

Copyright © 2024 by Frances Dolan

Copyright © Cover Illustration Anthony James 2024

The moral right of the author has been asserted

Ozwaldo Hawk Publishing

Thank you for choosing to read this book.

Wild Pursuits is a trilogy so if you would like to keep up to date with the series, email *contact@ozwaldopublishing.com*.

You can also follow Frances Dolan on Instagram via *@francesdolanauthor*

## ~ CHAPTER ONE ~

# Mind in a Muddle

Deep within an island, a stretch of water separates two woodlands. Unless you're a keen limnologist, that is someone who studies inland aquatic ecosystems, you may wonder what this particular stretch of water is, for it looks a little too narrow to consider a river and too wide to call a stream. You might try to work it out by holding a stick into it to assess the depth. This method of measuring will reveal that it certainly isn't shallow. In fact, your stick probably wouldn't even reach the waterbed. If this discovery makes you lean towards it being a river, then you would be in agreement with the animals who live in this area. They think it's a river too. But by visiting this water source, it doesn't necessarily mean you'll see them as well.

Do you ever think about all the times you must unknowingly encounter another species? The blackbird not taking its eyes off you as you pass its shrub. The rat peeking at you through your floorboards while you watch TV. The fox leering at you underneath your garden shed, drooling at your half-eaten sandwich.

By the riverbank in question, there's a particular animal who could be staring at you as you gaze at the water and tap pensively on your chin. The odds are you wouldn't see it, but if you fortuitously did, the moment would undoubtedly be short-lived. The animal would vanish into a tiny hole and not resurface in your presence. If you're the gambling type, you might bet you saw a mouse. It wouldn't be a bad guess, but you would be wrong. For this animal is a little rodent, and like mice, it does have a tail, round ears, and a snout. On proper inspection however, you would notice there's something that sets it apart – the fur. It has red, brown, and grey patches. Hairdressers and victims of hair-dyeing disasters don't despair, this look suits them. These furry little creatures are called bank voles. They are very common and live all over the island. They are also extremely elusive, only coming out of hiding when they think you're not around.

Right now, it is very quiet in the woods, so a few are out in the open. One is hovering by a hole in the ground, looking at another of his kind. She's the bank vole he's bred with and the hole in the ground is her burrow. She's cleaning around it and chatting away, unaware he isn't listening. He wants to, but he's busy thinking about his upcoming therapy session. That's right, in these woods with the narrow river, there's a doctor who helps if you have an injury or a disease. She's called Doctor Hedgehog. There's also a therapist, which is a role Pine Marten has taken on. He assists those who are struggling with their brains. It's a rather new position and Bank Vole is his fourth patient. So far, he's not sure what to make of it. He appreciates being able to talk confidentially about his thoughts, it feels good to be honest. What he's not so keen on, though, is hearing himself express things he didn't even know he'd felt. This can happen sometimes, and it shocks him, creating a feeling of disconnect within himself. Whether it's forgetfulness or trickery, he isn't sure, but his brain seems to operate differently in therapy. It seems very switched on. It remembers every little thing it has stored and as soon as the session commences – thud! Like a descending pinecone, it drops all the hidden thoughts and doesn't care in the slightest how much it hurts his head afterwards. Despite this, Bank Vole wants to continue. He started going not long after their last pups matured and left. If anything, it gives him something to do.

'Alright, I'd better scurry off,' he says. The other bank vole is engrossed in her own conversation, so he waves at her dramatically to make sure she knows he's leaving.

Now, it's important that you understand all the animals in the woods call themselves by what they are. All the bank voles are called Bank Vole, all the pine martens are named Pine Marten. It doesn't confuse them, but in case it confuses you, let's call the female in this instance, Myodes Glareolus, the scientific name for a bank vole. Just remember that whenever she's being spoken to or about, she's really being called Bank Vole.

As he jumps over the pile of dirt she's accumulated with the sweeping of her tail, Bank Vole realises Myodes Glareolus always starts sweeping whenever he mentions therapy. He thinks it's rather odd. She had originally said she thought it was a 'wonderful idea', so he doesn't quite understand why she immediately grabs her tail and drags it in brushing motions along the ground. To him, the suddenness of it signals a sort of awkwardness. Also, she wasn't a particularly rigorous cleaner when they were breeding, so the change in her behaviour makes him question her anti-dirt act even more.

'… and then I said to her I have too few sunrises left to have a so-called balanced diet… oh you're off!' Myodes Glareolus registers what he's said and lets go of her tail. She pauses briefly, watching him as he turns away from her. 'Have a wonderful chat!'

As soon as the words spill out of her mouth, she worries they sound facetious and inconsiderate. Truthfully, she finds it hard to know what to say. She wants therapy to help him, so she is glad he's doing it, but she's concerned he builds the notion of it into a big deal. As if his receiving it is a major life event. She herself sees it as a mere tool, a supportive aid, not a requisite for him to function. Therefore, whenever the topic is raised, she strives to emit a featheriness. A *light, comforting air* is how she thinks of it. To demonstrate that, she attempts to make herself look unfazed by sweeping. If her approach works, it may stop him from compounding his suffering by associating therapy with pain. She desperately wants him to attach it to the future him, the happy-go-lucky Bank Vole who simply takes life for what it is. To stop asking for more. He's never divulged what he says in the sessions, and neither has Pine Marten, but she can guess. Since they've stopped breeding, he's changed. He's much more serious. She suspects he's resentful because she decided to stop having pups. He had told her it suited him, but she's not sure that's true. If he was really content with it, she doesn't think he would be obsessing over evolution. Recently, he has been wanting to find ways to improve the lives of their species. He talks about it all the time. It's as if his achievements with her and the lives they've produced aren't enough. She wishes he'd concentrate less on evolution and focus more on his jokes. He usually has a fantastic sense of humour, and she misses it. She would love for therapy to restore it. *Thank goodness Pine Marten decided to take up this vocation*, she thinks. It gives her hope.

Bank Vole scuttles through the woods to meet his therapist. It's the beginning of spring and buds are beginning to grow on trees. He hears birds singing new tunes and notices that smells are changing. The musty wood and nut odours that have dominated all winter are now being eclipsed by sweet, juicy aromas.

No matter the season, though, it's not hard to find your way around the woods, even if you're a small rodent. This is because everything looks different. Nothing is identical – no two trees, two bushes, two leaves, two sticks, two animals, two flowers are the same. Reference points are easy to make. Bank Vole knows that once he gets to the imposing bumpy, brown trunk of the yew tree, with its two oval-shaped hollows that remind him of Badger's facial markings, but is, in fact, home to Doctor Hedgehog, he needs to veer left and continue until he gets to the evergreen, spiky juniper. Here, Bank Vole can't resist nibbling on a few fallen seeds or berries, and whilst doing so, he likes to breathe in the tree's refreshingly bitter fragrance. Invigorated, he turns left again and heads towards the magnificent oak, so demanding of attention with its wide crown and ostensible request to stand alone.

Pine Marten meets him at the bottom of the trunk. He is slender and covered in brown fur. Well, except for his neck and chest. That patch is a shortbread yellow. You might think he looks similar to stoats, who live in the woods opposite, across the river.

Last spring, Bank Vole had an accident that caused him to lose a claw. His physical abilities are now limited. He would struggle to climb the tree, for example, so Pine Marten gently places him in his mouth and with a semi-circle whipping motion of his neck, manages to throw him up on to his back. The momentary flying is quite enjoyable for Bank Vole, but he detests how damp and cold Pine Marten's saliva makes him.

## AN EXCEPTIONAL AURA

They climb the tree until they reach an uninhabited former squirrel's nest. It's a quiet area that seems guaranteed to harbour confidentiality. Once inside, they sit next to each other. Pine Marten demands this because he believes you're more likely to be honest about your feelings if you're staring at a tree trunk instead of another animal. This way you aren't able to interpret someone's expressions, which could affect what you say, causing you to omit, exaggerate or digress. Pine Marten also believes that for symbolic purposes, sitting this way shows the animal is beside you, supporting you. Seated in front can illustrate a blockage. It can even insinuate judgement. So, as it goes, Bank Vole always sits on the right and Pine Marten on the left.

Before they start the session, Pine Marten does one final scour out of the tree hollow, looking and sniffing in all directions to check if anybody's eavesdropping. As soon as he's satisfied that no one is, he sits, moves his tail to the left, spreads his legs and begins.

'So, Bank Vole, this is going to be our third meeting.' His deep voice speaks with a deliberate slowness. 'We last saw each other 42 sunrises ago. In that session we discussed your injury, and you told me one of your offspring was pregnant. I've seen the little rascals running around since. They are energetic, aren't they? Anyway, our breakthrough conversation was about Myodes Glareolus and your desire for bank vole evolution. It is the former that is clearly making you suffer. Now, before we analyse your brain, particularly your mind, it is imperative I ask you a few questions to assess whether Doctor Hedgehog needs to see you too. Firstly, do you have an appetite?'

As soon as Doctor Hedgehog's name is mentioned, Bank Vole darts towards the edge of the hollow and begs to be lifted down. Under no circumstances can he be made to visit her. Calmly, Pine Marten tells him to return to his seat and stop panicking. He informs him the questions are compulsory, so it's better they get them out of the way now. Displeased, Bank Vole crawls back with his head down. Sitting once more, he starts playing with his damp fur, stroking and twisting it to try and dry it.

'Yes, I have an appetite, but I don't like eating alone.' He mumbles his response so Pine Marten won't be able to hear him properly, thinking if he can't be heard, he shouldn't meet Doctor Hedgehog's assessment criteria. What he's forgotten is that Pine Marten is a brilliant listener. He's paying great attention and continues asking questions, wholly undeterred by the muffled, almost inaudible answers.

'Is the accident still causing discomfort?'

'Sometimes I get a sharp pain, but other than that, I'm ok,' Bank Vole says, this time coherently. When it comes to this part of his life, he believes he's fine and so is confident whatever he says won't lead to an appointment with the spikey torturer. 'I'm used to not using that paw much anymore. It's actually not a big hindrance. I'm slower, of course, and it does slightly restrict what I can do, but I can handle it.'

Pine Marten nods, noting his optimism. *So, some positive, buoyant iotas are still reaching Bank Vole's mind*, he thinks.

'Really glad to hear how well you are doing on that front, Bank Vole,' he says sincerely. 'You have not yielded to adversity. You're not self-pitying. Your determination to carry on as before sets a great example to us all. You should be very pleased with yourself.'

Pine Marten says this, knowing full well Bank Vole isn't. Not a lot gets past him. He knows Bank Vole wouldn't want the accident to happen again, but the injury itself, he only sees that as a minor impediment. He's more concerned with something else: his fractured mind. You see, the animals have always known they have different organs and muscles. Historically, the stomach was the most prominent. It's craving for food would cause their ancient ancestors to travel great lengths and endure bloody battles. Their stomachs effectively controlled them. This, however, is no longer the case. They now know they are governed by their mind. The mind's existence isn't a new phenomenon because post-mortem examinations are often carried out on animals. The four sections of the brain, which are the mind, the memory, the imagination, and the dream, were identified a while ago, as well as how they work. They know the mind is found at the very front of the brain and it produces thoughts. When it becomes full, they know the mind moves these thoughts downwards, into the depths of the brain, to a place called the memory. This is basically a storage box that returns thoughts to the mind whenever the mind requests it. They are cognizant of the imagination, which sits above the mind and drip-feeds it with ideas. The dream, they have been told, is located at the very top of the brain. They are aware this gets activated when they are asleep and is the only part of the brain that has unlimited access to the other three. Compared to the stomach, the mind is a very small part of every animal's anatomy, but when Doctor Hedgehog told the animals it rules them, they all accepted it as part of natural evolution and didn't ask any questions. It is quite obvious after all that they do more than eat and are often busy with thoughts. Doctor Hedgehog didn't divulge more than that at the time because she was still undertaking an intense investigation. As soon as she felt her study was complete and she had accurately uncovered the mechanics of the mind, she sat them all down to explain her findings. What she revealed then took them all by great surprise.

According to her, when a new situation presents itself to an animal, be it an event or even a simple conversation, the back of their brain receives it and forms an orb with it. Similar to a bubble, this transparent sphere travels directly up the middle ridge of the brain and stops when it gets to the mind at the front. But the mind consists of two other elements in addition to orbs. As you know, all situations have to have emotions attached to them. This means all orbs have to have iotas. Iotas are the second element. As soon as an orb is released, iotas are too. Instead of passing through the middle, these minuscule, also transparent balls travel through the crevices and fissures of either the left or right side of the brain. They are smaller than orbs, so they travel faster. As their journey is more difficult, however, they reach the mind at the exact same time as the orb. This results in a collision, which sparks a flare. This light is the third and final element of the mind. A flare is effectively a thought, and this will speak to the animal. It is an internal voice. Flares speak about everything and can become active even whilst other flares are shining. This means animals can have many thoughts occurring at the same time.

Now, what each flare says depends on which direction the iota went. Doctor Hedgehog claims that if the iota travels on the right side of the brain, which she's adamant feels smoother, the iota will produce a satisfactory emotion. This means the animal will view the orb happily, or comedically, comfortably or resiliently, with hope or positivity. If, however, the iota travels through the left side, it will create insatiable emotions. The animal may perceive the orb greedily or jealously. It could make them stressed, sad, irritable. They could feel curious, conflicted, or impatient.

In some situations, for example, a death, it's reasonable for an iota to travel left, but on the whole, most animals strive to feel satisfied and fulfilled. Doctor Hedgehog therefore advises them all to drink plenty of water. She believes the more liquid there is in your brain, the quicker the iota will be, and usually, the quickest iotas travel on the right because there are fewer crevices for them to pass through.

Since she announced her new theory, which Pine Marten vehemently supports, some of the animals have felt uncomfortable because their thoughts seem so engineered. They had always believed their thoughts were natural, that nothing could tamper with them. For others though, it has been a revelation. They now don't feel responsible for their thoughts and if they think something bad, they don't feel guilty about it. Then there were a few who found this news uplifting. They trusted that with help and guidance, they could possibly alter the way their mind produces a thought and so could potentially be happier. This is why therapy was introduced.

Bank Vole didn't even consider joining until he had to live on his own. He started feeling sad, and around the same time, he overheard Doctor Hedgehog say that the backs of some animals' brains have a wider opening on one side. Again, she's not sure why this happens, but it means more iotas naturally veer in that direction. Despite not fully understanding the whole concept, this is what Bank Vole thinks has happened to him and why therapy suddenly appealed. He believes he's developed a large hole on the back left side of his brain, and this explains why he's suddenly receiving more upset and lonely iotas. He would like to see if Pine Marten can find a way to get more of his iotas travelling right so he doesn't feel such an empty void in his life.

Now that you know the inner workings of the mind and what Bank Vole would like to get out of therapy, we can return to the session.

Having ticked off all of Doctor Hedgehog's questions, Pine Marten moves on to his own. He begins by asking his patient to share how he's feeling. Before Bank Vole responds, he takes a quick, deep breath in, then exhales slowly. He likes to imagine he's preparing himself for the new orb that will develop from Bank Vole's words.

'Well,' Bank Vole pauses, picking at knots in his fur. 'I am enjoying visiting my offspring's pups. They're so happy and innocent. My offspring, however, still claims I'm "lurking." Says it's not normal for me to still be in her life, nor her descendants.' It's not the bank vole way, she says! We don't have families. She thinks I'm being a nuisance, but I don't mean to be. I'm lonely, Pine Marten. It's all these left iotas. They're making me crave company, particularly Myodes Glareolus's. I know I'm repeating myself, but my mind is continuing to torment me. It still thinks her and I should be together. I seem to have the same flares all the time. They refuse to accept the way bank voles live. And you pine martens! With these thoughts, I find it hard to understand why we don't do what owls and pigeons do. They're never alone! They stay with each other forever. They always have someone to find food with, to eat with, and to be warm with. I always cherished those times with Myodes Glareolus, Pine Marten. Why did it have to end? Why do I have to be on my own because it's typical for my species? It doesn't *feel* right. When we were breeding, we were always together, and it was marvellous. Every time I woke from a nap, she was there. We shared everything. We became so close. What we had, it felt exclusive and precious. An experience only for her and I, and one only we would hold dear. We all know what it's like to be hungry, to feel tired, but I felt like I entered the realm of something entirely new and imitable. Now…'

Bank Vole stops picking at his fur. Sitting very still, staring at the trunk opposite, he says, 'Now I feel incomplete, as if a part of me is gone. It's worse than my accident. I'm still trying to work it all out, but I think I'm like an evergreen leaf, Pine Marten. They don't change colour depending on where the sun is in the sky and neither do my feelings. I'm constant. My feelings for Myodes Glareolus haven't changed now we've stopped breeding, now we're older. I'm at a loss. My mind is making me miss her. It's terrible because you know as well as I do that I have nowhere to go with these thoughts, these feelings. If I ever told her I feel this way, she'd have the same stance as the rest. It's not what we do! She wouldn't want to deviate and become an outsider. She would hate being a woodlands conversation topic. But my mind wants to be with her. It wants to have a family. What can I do?'

Pine Marten hasn't told Bank Vole this, but unlike his patient, he doesn't think he's developed a wider opening on one side of his brain. No, he thinks the flares Bank Vole produced about Myodes Glareolus are stubborn. He assumes Bank Vole developed these feelings for her a long time ago. They're now so used to being in his mind they're refusing to move into his memory. He's heard it happen before; it's one of the ways obsessions can form. The fact the flares about her aren't budging means they're taking up so much of Bank Vole's mind. They are dominating it. That was fine when they were breeding, but the flares don't make sense in his current life. They're making him think he misses her and should be with her. It's wrong. The flares about Myodes Glareolus should have left his mind when their last pups departed. If that had happened, he'd no doubt be fine living life on his own. It's as if Bank Vole's mind planted a figurative seed about Myodes Glareolus a while back and he's unknowingly been watering it. He's been letting the roots stretch out, letting the trunk grow tall, allowing the branches to extend and the leaves to flourish. Now the flares have effectively connected, they've become a tree and all other thoughts in Bank's Vole mind are malnourished, unattended to, shrinking and shrivelling in the shade.

Truth be told, Pine Marten reckons this may be something that needs Doctor Hedgehog's operative attention, but knowing how afraid Bank Vole is of seeing her, he's going to try and help him as much as he can. If he can somehow force strong iotas through, preferably right ones, then they might push the flares about Myodes Glareolus into Bank Vole's memory, where they now belong. He just needs an incredible situation to arise that could make that happen, something that will startle Bank Vole's brain so it's knocked back into functioning as it should. He goes to answer Bank Vole's question, but his patient continues talking, words flowing out of his mouth like the river he sleeps next to.

'I was like one of the pups when I was breeding with her. Uncomplicatedly happy. Sometimes I'm still that way, but then I remember I've got to go back to my own burrow and the sadness returns. You know, I watch her in a different way to how I watch others. I notice things, little things. The way her ears prick slightly forward when she's astonished or sympathetic. How they lean away from each other when she's relaxed. It's marginal, but I see it!'

## AN EXCEPTIONAL AURA

He starts laughing. 'I've never known anybody to wave their body around as much as she does when she talks. She flings it and hurls it like she's avoiding some invisible swinging acorn.' His voice changes, becoming quiet and serious. 'She's kind to me. I feel attached to her kindness. You know, I've been thinking about life. Bank voles have approximately 730 sunrises... I'm not sure how many I have left, just less than half, I think. Anyway, it's finite. If what you believe is true and we've naturally evolved to have dominant minds, then I've got to try and continue to change. Why stop? I want to find other ways for my species to evolve. I want us to become something better. Pine Marten, we all think that being inconspicuous is the best thing we can do to ensure our species' survival. But what's the point in reproducing if other bank voles end up feeling the way I do? I want to change the future of my species, mould it into something more fulfilling. I want to improve my species' lives. That's my mission! Clearly my mind thinks I should do it by forming a life-long partnership, but if you have other suggestions, I would be willing to hear them.'

Having dropped the proverbial pinecone into the room, Bank Vole proceeds to play with his fur again. He always notices how dirty it is whilst in therapy. He promises to spend more time cleaning it but never gets round to it unless something is really bothersome and itchy. He wonders if his fur being wet brings the dirt to the surface. Oh, how he wishes he could climb up the tree himself and avoid Pine Marten's mouth!

Hoisting himself up so he's sitting taller, Pine Marten rests his paws over his mid-riff. Although Bank Vole's words are worrying, he's comforted by the fact he still has hope and determination.

## MIND IN A MUDDLE

'Thank you for being so open with me, Bank Vole. I think it's admirable you want to improve the life of your species, but it's plain cruel that your mind is convincing you to want something you're not conditioned to have. I want you to know you have my utmost sympathies.' His low voice becomes higher and more excitable. 'I've got to tell you, I'm glad my mind isn't doing the same to me. I thoroughly enjoy meeting new females when the sun gets warmer, and I really like flaunting myself. The whole process makes me feel fantastic. In my opinion, we are smarter than owls, pigeons, and all the other animals that have one partner because we realise there are myriad personalities and looks out there. Why stick with one? Having different partners, well, it fills your mind with a wide range of orbs and provides your brain with different memories. All in all, it makes life feel full! How can you be sad when you know there are always more females to get to know and show off to? It's also fascinating being able to produce such different offspring each time. I'm telling you, this lifestyle shuns stagnancy. Perhaps things seem painful for you now because you've allowed your life to become stale. You stuck with Myodes Glareolus, but she doesn't represent every type of bank vole out there. You can have constant company if you keep breeding with other bank voles, perhaps that'll cure you. If that idea doesn't appeal, then I think you need to purposefully get new orbs forming that have nothing to do with her. In other words, you need to distract yourself. I will try to help.

'Yes, let's get you immersed in new situations, find you a new focus and try to manipulate your iotas to travel right so you're satisfied with your existence. There are plenty of ways we can try to make this happen in the woods. The obvious solution is to frequent the Thicket more. I know it can be overcrowded with badgers, but you'll hardly ever be alone there. Lots of conversations that you can get involved in. Also, I've seen you laugh there. Laughter is always a result of iotas travelling right.

'Oh, you could also join the choir with Muntjac Deer? They're looking for new sounds and I don't think they have a squealer. You know it's not strictly about singing, it's about making our natural noises to songs. They've opened it up to everyone. Apparently Robin's a great conductor. I don't think they're quite melodious yet, but they're making real progress! That's something totally new for you to experience, and it will definitely shake your brain up a bit. It's rather revolutionary, no? Animals making noises together at the same time?'

While Bank Vole considers the vapid options, Pine Marten takes the opportunity to stress something he thinks is very important.

'If you keep yourself busy and resist visiting Myodes Glareolus, all the feelings you had for her when you were breeding might move over to your memory. It means the emotions you have for her now will fade. You must not see her. Do you hear me, Bank Vole? Let other things take over. I know our mind is very powerful, but we must try to get it to behave the way we want it to. It cannot control everything. Otherwise, who knows? Maybe we'll lose organs because it will convince us we don't need them. Wouldn't it be dreadful if our stomachs became inactive? I love eating!'

There's silence. He doesn't need to look at Bank Vole to gauge how he's feeling; his dejection is palpable. Pine Marten sighs. This is the best advice he has for now. There isn't really any other choice. Bank Vole doesn't want to tell Myodes Glareolus how he feels. If he does and it makes her uncomfortable, she could demand he leave their woods. That frequently happens when bank voles are no longer mating; the females order the males to live elsewhere. Bank Vole would be bereft. They must try to change his mind.

They close the session and plan to meet again once Bank Vole has shown he's tried to distract himself and sought other company. He doesn't see what's revolutionary or inspirational about making noises he already makes to bird music, so he pledges to visit the Thicket more. The Thicket is a dense group of trees and bushes in the middle of the woods where animals congregate to chat. Bank Vole usually meets the Copse Council there, and between the eight of them, Rabbit, Squirrel, Owl, Muntjac Deer, Badger, Mole, Pine Marten, and himself, they discuss a plethora of subjects, but if they were honest, the conversation usually revolves around descendancy, fur, food, and the relay race (we'll get to that later). This is unless Pigeon, an honorary member, joins them. She is one of the only animals who regularly spends time outside the woods, so when she returns, they're always keen to hear what news she has from beyond the trees.

Technically, the council's job is to make sure all the animals in the woods, regardless of their species, live a comfortable life, one that offers the chance to breed and live for as long as your species is meant to. A former council, their predecessor, created this fair and harmonious environment many sunrises ago. It is instilled in the animals that whatever your size or status, whether you're as small as a bank vole or as big as a badger, you are free to roam as a family or on your own. All the current council have to do now is maintain this way of woodland living. The animals are generally obedient, so it doesn't require much work, which is why they can spend their time debating who would fly the fastest if they had wings and whose style of eating nuts is the best. Pine Marten's plan could work. Spending more time in the Thicket might help Bank Vole. The trivial conversations he has in there often provide light relief for his troubled mind. But is it enough of a distraction?

~ CHAPTER TWO ~

# The Beast

Pine Marten climbs down the tree with Bank Vole in his mouth. His fur didn't really dry in the damp oak hollow, so after another episode lathered in Pine Marten's saliva, he is soaked. He's thankful it's now spring, so he should dry quicker than last season when it was much colder. By the time he'd returned home then, ice had formed on his fur!

He thanks Pine Marten, and they go their separate ways, with Bank Vole travelling back the same route as before. He thinks about his friend as he walks. In his opinion, pine martens are the most remarkable woodland animal. Almost everybody is in awe of how agile and elusive they are. They're barely ever seen by moving sticks, so much so that he's wondered if moving sticks remember they exist. Moving sticks are the species they all try to stay away from. They don't live in the woods but sometimes visit, usually during sun-sky. Stories about them have been passed down from all their ancestors. Apparently, they used to live here, many sunrises ago. Back then they were called hapo simneos, or something similar to that. The animals don't call them that name anymore because they've morphed into something so different; hapo simneos and moving sticks almost seem unrelated. Hapo simneos used to be able to read the woods like the other animals, they used to be able to speak their language. Moving sticks can't do either of these. The animals think it's evident they're unfamiliar with

## AN EXCEPTIONAL AURA

the place because sometimes when they visit, they just walk round and round the same area and then leave. All the woodland inhabitants find them very strange. Some think the circular trail is a ritual, some think there's no reason behind it, and they're just odd. Others think they may get an instinctive calling to come back, but their minds struggle to work out why. They believe moving sticks have changed their way of life so much it's likely they have no idea they used to live here. That's why they're called moving sticks, because they never stay, and sticks are the closest woodland entity they now resemble.

Their temper snaps like sticks too, apparently. The animals have heard they can appear calm, but their demeanour can change in an instant. Out of nowhere, they can turn violent. None of them have witnessed this themselves because they stay out of their way as much as they can. It's a woodland way of life. Ever since Bank Vole can remember, they all run and hide as soon as a moving stick is smelt, heard or seen. The only ones who don't always do this are birds. Pigeon says the answer to ensuring your species' survival (against moving sticks in particular) is to not be inconspicuous but to be omnipresent. She says when there are so many of you, moving sticks aren't interested. She believes they are amused by things seldom seen and therefore hiding is effectively more dangerous. Bank Vole enjoys listening to Pigeon and all her tales and observations from outside the woods. Once, all the animals got themselves into a frenzy because Pigeon, who claims she has taught herself the moving stick language, said she heard one say to another, "it will all blow over." The animals believed this meant a harsh wind was coming and the trees would fall down. They buried themselves underground – they were so squashed and hot – but nothing happened. For ten sunrises, they worried their homes would be destroyed and the trees would be dead. They waited and waited for the imminent, dreaded gale, but it appears Pigeon either misheard or doesn't really understand the language. The latter is the most popular belief.

Bank Vole actually knows more about moving sticks than most, as one took him out of the woods after his accident. He knows how they feel (slippery) and what they smell like (a hot river). There's something else he's learnt about them too: they're confusing. Bizarrely, the moving stick who removed him also seems to have helped him – it managed to stop his bleeding. He can't make sense of this because they're not meant to be kind or caring. He's never delved into his experience in therapy, even though Pine Marten has tried to coax him. He deliberately avoids it, thinking it's too risky. He's worried he'll reveal his new-found ambivalence, and Pine Marten would not approve.

He passes the juniper and stops to chew on seeds again. *Moving sticks are so complicated*, he thinks, more complicated than his own mind even. As he continues wandering through the woods and observing the uniqueness of it all, he recollects something else Pigeon told him about them. She said that where they live now, in the Grey, lots of things look exactly the same. She said moving sticks have made many things, some big, some small and some completely identical. Bank Vole can't imagine what it's like to see two things that are indistinguishable. Pigeon says it's both remarkable and detrimental. If moving sticks are often exposed to things that look exactly alike, she thinks they might find it hard to value and appreciate any variances. This could mean they'll end up rejecting nature even more because nature is non-uniform and inconsistent. She worries about moving sticks and has a different view on them to everyone else. She still sees them as animals. She's adamant life in the Grey is unhealthy for them and thinks it could be making them sick. She's very vocal about her mission to help them return to the woods.

In case you haven't realised, a moving stick is you.

Bank Vole has reached the yew tree and is about to turn right to go home when a hoof appears above his head. Squealing sharply, he dives left and narrowly avoids it. Muntjac Deer is dashing past so quickly he almost tramples on his friend.

'I'm so sorry, Bank Vole, I didn't see you! I was too busy concentrating on my escape!' he says. His teeth are chattering and he's visibly shaking. 'Thank goodness you're alive! Living so close to the river I worried you'd been gobbled up by the beast! Did it throw you in the water? Is that why you're drenched?'

Bank Vole shakes his head and tells him he's just been with Pine Marten. Without wanting to be quizzed any further, he asks Muntjac Deer to describe the so-called beast.

Although he's still panic-stricken, Muntjac Deer's eyes are now sparkling. He has gossip to share and it's huge! This is his favourite past-time. He begins trotting around in a circle, a preparatory performance he undergoes when he knows he's delivering exclusive news. When the 360-degree movement is completed, he bends down and whispers rapidly. 'An animal has arrived in the river on a log of wood. No one I've spoken to recognises it. It's brown with enormous orange teeth that look like they'd rip us all apart! Squirrel said he saw it fighting a tree using them! I knew something bad was going to happen to our woods. Ever since your accident I've been wondering what was going to be next. The moving stick who took you probably cursed us!

## THE BEAST

We have to meet the rest of the council in the Thicket at sunset to work out how to beat this beast. In the meantime, I'm hiding!'

Lifting one leg up, he gets ready to run but waits in case Bank Vole has any questions. With so many flares talking to him at once, Bank Vole doesn't speak. His mind is struggling to digest how there could be a beast in the woods. They know everything and everyone here, even the animals who only visit occasionally, like geese, who stop by when it's cold, and Choir Robin, who flies in from the opposite woods to teach singing. Something new none of them have ever seen before, that's too bewildering to comprehend. He assumes Muntjac Deer is exaggerating and spreading rumours, as usual. When his flares start to quieten, he tells him he'll attend the council meeting. Before that though, he wants to take a peek at the beast. Muntjac Deer doesn't think this a good idea and tries to deter him. When he's serious, the black lines that furrow above his eyes seem more pronounced, making him appear authoritative. The look doesn't get Bank Vole to concede. He's intrigued. Plus, he needs to check that Myodes Glareolus is safe, as well as his offspring and her pups. They all sleep right where the so-called beast apparently is.

Scurrying towards the river as fast as he can with his injured paw, Bank Vole halts suddenly when he hears singing. Well, singing is generous; a rather discordant, loud wailing describes it more accurately. Having never heard this noise before, he gathers it must be coming from the strange animal. It's a rather upbeat sound, not sombre or menacing like one would expect from a terrifying beast. Eager to see it as soon as possible, he jumps into the nearest bush and runs towards the bank. Upon reaching the edge, he peeps through a gap in the foliage. His eyes follow the unpleasant racket and when he catches sight of it, he gasps! For once, Muntjac Deer wasn't being over-dramatic. Bank Vole has never seen anything like this animal before. He studies it meticulously, taking in its stockiness, its dense brown fur, its tiny eyes, and bulbous black nose. He notices its feet are webbed like ducks with claws that look like moving stick fingers. He sees it has small, spindly front-paws which don't seem in proportion to the rest of its body. It has a long, black and extremely unusual flat tail too. The shape of this is so peculiar to Bank Vole; he's convinced it's not meant to be like that and assumes it has been squashed. The beast is chomping on sticks, squatting on their side of the river. It's howling in between bites, so Bank Vole is getting a good view inside its mouth as well. Again, Muntjac Deer wasn't exaggerating. Its teeth really are orange and they do look extraordinarily sharp. The singing continues as the beast discards the stick, throwing it to the side while it wades into the water. Bank Vole is amazed at how elegantly it glides. To him, the singing and swimming styles do not match one another. He's never encountered a rowdy and graceful animal. Normally you're one or the other. The beast's floating skills make Bank Vole question how likely it is to settle. *Clearly it's a swimmer, so it could easily be a travelling river monster,* he thinks. He's not sure if these exist, but if they do, he imagines they keep moving. His thumping heart quietens at the comforting thought. The beast may leave. Just because it's here now doesn't mean it'll be here forever. A bird flits past, obscuring his view. His attention turns towards the sun, which is now positioned low between the trees. He must go. He darts quickly to the bank vole burrows to make sure everyone is ok, and then he heads to the Thicket.

## THE BEAST

Crawling over and under brambles, Bank Vole reaches a wide circular clearing, which is the centre of their meeting place. It's teeming with animals from all over the woods. The beast has clearly caused quite a stir. He makes his way to the council's usual spot and finds them all huddled together. He realises he's the last to arrive and because the news is so pressing, they've started without him.

Badger, striking a defiant pose, is claiming that unless the beast is banished immediately, they'll all be left homeless. 'The way it went to war with that tree, destroying it senselessly... It's going to take them all down, I can see it.' He sounds even gruffer than normal. 'This was the "blow over" Pigeon heard the moving sticks talking about! We cannot let it ravage our homes; this is our land! We must devise a plan to make sure it leaves and never returns,' he bellows.

His speech is met with a chorus of agreement. Rabbit, ears pricked and heavily pregnant, chimes in. 'It's not just the fact it is trying to eradicate our woods, it's how obnoxious it is! Why is it constantly shouting? It's revolting.'

Despite missing the beginning of the meeting, it hasn't taken Bank Vole long to gather the consensus. The beast's arrival has shocked everyone; no one knows what it is, and no one wants it here.

Stamping on a hind leg, which is council etiquette to show you have something to say, Squirrel brings up the beast's impact on their favourite spring activity. 'How can we do our relay race with the animals across the river if the beast is there blocking it?' he whimpers. The question makes the animals shriek in unison.

Now is the time to describe the relay race. One sunrise every spring, the woodland animals on one side of the river compete with the woodland animals on the

## AN EXCEPTIONAL AURA

adjacent side to see who can put a chain of leaves on a crown the quickest.

The race begins when birds from each team make a crown with sticks. When they complete their crown, they fly it over to the opposite side of the riverbank and place it securely at the bottom of the hill. As soon as that's done, they gather in a line and fly past the ash trees which feature on both sides of the woods at an equivalent distance to the river. This signals that it's the next animal's turn to race. In this woods, it's Squirrel. He must climb one of the ash trees and start collecting eight leaves from whichever part of the tree he chooses. When they're picked, he has to use his nails to pierce a hole into each one and then tie them together to make a robust chain. The moment this is achieved, he needs to run back down the tree and put the chain on top of Muntjac Deer's head, looping it around his antlers. As steadily as he can, Muntjac Deer has to gallop over to Pine Marten, who is waiting at the entrance of a fallen, hollow tree trunk. Continuing to keep his balance, he needs to carefully bend down so the chain slides off his head and into Pine Marten's paws. If this is done successfully, Pine Marten enters the trunk on all fours and must drag the leaf chain along with him until he reaches the other side. When he is able to poke his head out of the hollow, he throws the chain in the air for Owl to catch in his mouth. Resisting the urge to clamp down and accidentally break the chain, Owl has to fly for 50 flaps in the direction of the river and drop the chain. Having practised and practised, Mole should be waiting at the exact place it'll land. Scooping it up, Mole needs to dig a fresh tunnel and crawl underground for 40 breaths. It's Rabbit's turn next. Listening out for Mole's movements, she waits at the place she thinks she'll emerge. Almost always right, as soon as Mole appears, Rabbit seizes the leaf chain and hops it over to Badger, who is waiting by a strip of bluebells. Holding on to it tightly, Badger needs to run as fast as he can through the flowers and not stop until he's down the hill and by the riverbank. Here, he has to pass the leaf chain to Bank Vole, who needs to have already worked out a way of getting across the water. If he has and his strategy works, he can climb up the crown that's sitting on the opposite bank and rest their leaf chain over it. The winner is the team who manages to keep the leaf chain intact and attach it to their crown first.

As you can imagine, the course on both sides of the river isn't identical, and neither are the animals who take part, but the pigeons who monitor and commentate on the race try to make sure it's as fair as possible. Although taken very seriously and with fierce competitiveness, it is ultimately just great fun. The race has only ever been completed once and that was by the opposing team. That's absolutely no deterrent, though. Perseverance runs deep in the woods. But it is clear the beast's presence makes even trying to reach the finishing line an impossibility.

'We have to make sure it's gone before the relay, Squirrel. We must! However, I think before we force it to move, we should try to find out more about it,' proposes Mole, awkwardly scratching her protruding pink nose with her extra-long claws. 'I know we're currently hiding from it, but I think it's better to know what it is and why it's here. There could be more coming. I think one of us should be conspicuous for a little while and ask it a few questions. It will help us be better prepared in the future.'

Everyone ponders over Mole's suggestion. It's an astute idea, which is typical for Mole, but would any of them survive to relay the beast's answers, or would their necks be broken, heavily indented with four teeth marks?

# AN EXCEPTIONAL AURA

'I definitely want to know what it is,' responds Muntjac Deer. 'But I can't speak to it. It would see me approaching and become defensive because of my size. It wouldn't be relaxed and open to talking to me. It needs to be handled by someone smaller.'

Frightened Muntjac Deer manages to twist the fact he's bigger than the beast to his advantage. Confrontational and brave Rabbit says ordinarily she would, but it's too risky in her pregnant state. She suggests someone with less to lose should do it. Mole said she came up with the idea, so someone else should execute it. Plus, it's an effort for her because she's usually underground. Even though Badger had begun the meeting sounding combative and commanding, he chooses to agree with Mole. He isn't as strong in his older age and wouldn't want to be shown up in a potential fight. He recommends someone living near the river do it, as that's more convenient. Owl, as ever, stays silent, glaring at everyone with his black, beady eyes. The animals have only heard Owl speak twice. The first time was when he joined and introduced himself, and the second was to pay his respects to a former neighbour of theirs. Clearly, he's not going to volunteer himself, and given how mute he is, it seems stupid to put him forward. Squirrel shakes his head frantically when the animals look at him. He thinks he could do the job well but is convinced his species is the beast's favourite food, so he says it's best he stays away.

Bank Vole isn't listening. He's looking around the Thicket and counting all the badgers. *Pine Marten's right*, he thinks, *there are a lot of them*. Suddenly, his therapist's claw points down at him. He yelps. What's going on? Surely Pine Marten isn't suggesting he speaks to the beast?

'No way,' Bank Vole says unequivocally when he realises that is exactly what's happening. 'I'm quite possibly the smallest one here *and* I have an injured paw. I'm sure it'll be gone by sunrise anyway; I doubt it's staying. Why don't we leave it be? Or why don't we all go and speak to it together?'

The animals unanimously agree the beast needs to be spoken to urgently, and that it's likely to be more receptive if only one animal approaches it.

'Consider it company,' Pine Marten says. 'I would do it myself, but I think you would be better. Come on, you're good at talking and you wouldn't be considered a threat. The rest of us would look like we're wanting to fight. You would look like you're merely enquiring. Plus, you've spent time with moving sticks! If you survived that, you'll survive this! Also, you live right by the river. There are so many reasons why it should be you. All you have to do is poke your head out of a bush, ask it a couple of questions and then you can dart off before it even knows what's what.'

Seeing he's not managed to convince Bank Vole, who is repeatedly shaking his head, Pine Marten, wholly unprofessionally, decides to bring up his patient's plight.

'It will be exhilarating and will expose your mind to *other things*. Give you a new focus. This is exactly what you need,' he says.

All the animals silently stare at Bank Vole, not quite sure what is going on. He, on the other paw, is stunned. He had zoned out because he didn't think anyone would consider him a potential candidate. Pine Marten, however, seems serious. Not wanting to disclose their private therapy discussions, Bank Vole answers Pine Marten as discreetly as he can. 'I have a mission… you know. Not this. I don't want to die yet,' he says.

Pine Marten now has a loud flare that is desperate for Bank Vole to seek this remedy. It's telling him this new and uncharted situation with the beast will reset his patient's brain. He doesn't give in. Wanting to maintain some professional credibility, he moves to stand next to Bank Vole so what he says can't be overheard.

He leans down towards him and whispers, 'The best thing you can do is throw yourself into something else. Form an orb that startles your brain, knocking all its parts into the right positions again. Getting it to function properly. You must take this shining opportunity. It is truly for your own good. You know, your mind will be better at working out ways to improve your species' lives once those flares to do with you-know-who have moved into your memory. A bond with her isn't the answer. Maybe beast interaction will help you think of another way to evolve. It could lead to something great! It could put you on course to changing the lives of future bank voles.'

Bank Vole closes his eyes to think over what Pine Marten is saying. He really tries, but all his thoughts focus on is Myodes Glareolus. He wonders if there's any way his talking to the beast could lead to a partnership with her. He thinks about how scared she was when he'd told her about its existence and wonders if valiantly confronting it will impress her. The whole ordeal might make her realise she doesn't want to live solitarily, that she should live forever with the brave Bank Vole. With that thought, his lined mouth curves upwards. It could work! It's plausible. The beast could help him get everything he wishes. He imagines waking up with Myodes Glareolus and going to search for fruit. Pine Marten is right; he has to take this shining opportunity. He has to try!

'Ok, yes,' he says hastily, standing on his two hind legs. 'My whole brain may be playing awful tricks, but it's convinced me to do it. I put myself forward. I will speak to the beast.'

# ~ CHAPTER THREE ~

# Reality Exposed

When you want to stop thinking about something, what do you do? Bank Vole eats. It's a great distraction for him. It's a time when his brain and stomach organs fight for power, and temporarily, his stomach wins. He savours every mouthful. It makes him rather envious of his forebearers and their dominant stomachs because if he didn't get full, he would eat non-stop and never have a worry in his life.

After the meeting in the Thicket, Bank Vole stuffed his cheeks with masses of moss so he didn't have to think about the nerve-racking task he's taken on. It was a good idea because not only did the scoffing divert his attention, it also resulted in him having a restful sleep tucked in his burrow by the river.

He wakes up now as the sun turns his home from black to brown. After stretching and shaking his body, he begins making plans. He's feeling energetic so chooses to visit the sprightly pups. Climbing out of his burrow, he runs over to theirs, which is five holes across. Just as he approaches the entrance of their home, however, the awful singing resumes.

'Oh no!' he mouths, slapping a paw over his eyes. Bank Vole scolds himself for momentarily forgetting about the beast. He scurries to the nearest bush once more, this time for safety as well as to peep. Pushing his paw down on a leaf, he manages to create a spyhole. He sees the beast

## REALITY EXPOSED

sitting on the bank. Luckily, it's facing the water, so it shouldn't have seen him running around in the open. He breathes a big sigh of relief.

The beast turns slightly to the left and begins whacking its tail up and down in an unrhythmic beat. The movement is impressive and strange simultaneously. It dawns on Bank Vole that the beast could be so different, what with its tail movements and loudness, that it might not even speak their woodland language. Its singing so far has never contained words, only 'oohs', 'aahs' and 'dees.' If this is the case and he can't talk to it, what's he meant to do? Shoo it away? He giggles, imagining the ridiculous scene. Comfortable in his covert spot, Bank Vole allows himself to be amused by the beast. Whatever it is, it's unusual and certainly unlike any other animal in the woods. Not believing he's in any imminent danger, he lets his intrigue set in. While the beast continues munching, thumping, and chanting, he ponders over how scary it actually is. Looks can be deceiving, after all. Muntjac Deer could look intimidating if you didn't know him when, really, he's the most easily frightened. Owl has definitely sent shivers through him with his unrivalled, ravenous stare, but he's surprisingly rather docile. He nods. Yes, there is a chance the beast will be approachable, and everything will work out how he wants it to. Excited by the prospect, Bank Vole takes it to the next level and starts imagining them becoming friends. He watches the beast drop the stick it was gnawing and waddle over to a tree. When it slides its paws up and down the trunk, Bank Vole smiles. He's seen his friend Badger do this. They're meant to be a good claw sharpener. Then it starts sniffing the trunk, so Bank Vole guesses it's trying to detect whether there are any of its kind around because this is what his friend Squirrel does. It could be checking if there are scent markings on the tree, signalling a desire to breed. There you go, he thinks, it's not that different after all! He tilts his head sympathetically. Poor beast. There's certainly no one here for it to produce offspring with. He guesses their shared loneliness will be what ends up making their friendship so special.

In an instant, Bank Vole's hopeful fantasy is throttled. The beast begins hacking at the tree with its teeth, rapidly thinning the trunk. The animals had mentioned this odd behaviour in the Thicket, but now Bank Vole is seeing it for himself. He's incredulous. He can't comprehend it. Why is the beast being so unnecessarily destructive and aggressive? He watches the bark fall like rain and his body turns cold. One bite. That's all it would need for the beast to cut him in half. Oh, how he suddenly misses only having Myodes Glareolus to think about! It's not torturous or painful pining over her. It's not heart-wrenchingly lonely. It's perfect! Warm, cosy – paradisical even! He cannot believe he's got to risk this wonderful life of his to try and talk to the raging beast. He doesn't want to die! He wants to make bank vole life more fulfilling – being prematurely eaten won't achieve that! His mind had convinced him that speaking to the beast could be a catalyst for a lifelong partnership with Myodes Glareolus. Not a chance!

Bank Vole feels awfully duped. The beast, meanwhile, steps back from the trunk to check its progress. Evidently pleased, it starts clapping its paws together triumphantly. It scuffles back into the water, but this time, it doesn't glide. Clearly wanting to be as disruptive as possible, it starts splashing, hitting the water with its paws repeatedly. Although this bizarre behaviour captivates Bank Vole, it doesn't stop him noticing something else: the unmistakable whiff of moving sticks. Their smell invades his nose, and he instinctively crouches down despite already being hidden. The beast, however, seems oblivious. It's apparently so consumed with its own rowdy antics it fails to notice moving sticks are in the vicinity. When they get to the riverbank, they shrill, shriek, and jump, pointing directly at it. To Bank Vole's astonishment, their presence doesn't make the beast swim hurriedly away. No, it stays put. In fact, it starts interacting with them!

The beast lies on its back and paddles in circles, churring and showing off its teeth. It then swims over to the opposite bank, sits on the mud, positions its tail between its legs and stares at them. More and more moving sticks arrive. A large group forms; they click and produce small lightning flashes, yet the beast remains seated motionlessly out in the open. Bank Vole has no idea what is going on.

The reciprocal gawking continues for a long time. When the moving sticks eventually leave, it's star-sky. The beast, having exhausted itself, curls up and promptly falls asleep. Bank Vole, meanwhile, hasn't eaten since he awoke from his nap, too transfixed by the commotion to think about his stomach. He scampers out of the bush to forage for some fallen seeds and bumps into Rabbit. She tells him they're holding an emergency council meeting and she's on her way to the Thicket now. Unable to leisurely look for the food he fancies, Bank Vole grabs what's closest to him. Repeating the manner of his previous meal, he shoves as many leaves as he can into his mouth. What he just saw was shocking, but he feels rather soothed. If everyone else just witnessed what he did – the belligerent, unruly behaviour and the casual attitude towards moving sticks – then he's guessing his task will be cancelled. Nobody will expect him to speak to the beast now. He tells himself he'll just have to find another way to form a life bond with Myodes Glareolus.

The Thicket is heaving. Bank Vole thinks it may be the busiest he's ever seen it. He struggles to make his way through the crowd until Badger fortunately appears behind him. Using his thunderous voice, he orders everyone to move so they can pass through.

The Copse Council are bunched closely together, and Bank Vole senses an uncomfortable tension when he joins them. Rabbit asks if she can lead the meeting and nobody objects. Owl uses his beak to snap some twigs off a shrub and quickly builds her a makeshift podium. Rabbit hops onto it, and as she turns to face the council, it's clear she's distressed. She's shaking and her normally pointed ears are flat against her head.

She begins by telling them she was able to see everything that transpired because she'd been thirsty and was standing on top of the hill by the riverbank, trying to work out how she could discreetly get water without the beast seeing her when she smelt moving sticks. She had darted into a bush and so was able to watch the event as it unfolded. Her voice starts quivering. She tells them she's frightened, especially for her unborn kittens. She says she wants them to be able to enjoy the harmonious woodlands that they've worked hard to preserve. She's scared they're not going to have the chance to produce babies of their own.

Rabbit normally speaks fast, but her agitation accelerates her speech, so much so the animals have to concentrate hard to hear what she's saying. 'This beast, if allowed to remain on our premises, will irrefutably destroy us. I counted 83 moving sticks in our woods during sun-sky and every single one came to watch the beast. How many usually come? No more than ten between sunrise and sunset. We've never had so many of them on our land, it is *extremely* alarming. If our woods become too popular, we'll struggle to remain inconspicuous. They will inevitably find us all, and our peaceful home will change forever. "If they catch us in plain sight, we will face a mortal blight," remember our motto? They threaten our existence. They don't understand us. They left our home more sunrises ago than any of us could fathom when they decided there was more to life than nature. All communication we had with them is gone. Sure, they returned Bank Vole to us, and it looked like they worshipped the beast, but we've recently heard they've devastated some badger clans. I know we haven't seen this with our own eyes, but we can trust our sources. Our exchange with them is volatile, it's too unpredictable to trust. If they don't kill us, they might destroy our woods and force us to live separately in the Grey. We would all hate it.'

Rabbit takes a well-earned breath. She scans the council, keen to make sure she has everyone's utmost attention. 'The beast is dangerous, yes, but we've all been raised to believe moving sticks are the most powerful and erratic species that live on top of Earth. We are tolerant; we let them walk in circles around our woods, but that's all we can allow them to do. We cannot let them encroach any further. We have to do all we can to prevent them from coming in troves to our precious land, and that means we have to get rid of the beast who is attracting them here. I have no doubt it splashed in the water and hacked at the tree to call them over.'

She looks directly at Bank Vole and replaces her combative, emotional tone with one that is slower, softer, and more agreeable. 'I still think we stick to the plan we created in our last meeting. Bank Vole, you must demand it leave before the next sun-sky. You have nothing to worry about. You're so small and harmless. You're not a threat like the rest of us. I guarantee it will be impressed by your courage; it will grant your wish and move on. We believe you can do this. We think you're the saviour this horror needs. Please, Bank Vole, please do this for all of us.'

With her eyes revealing harsh desperation, she cradles her bump. In this regard, Bank Vole can't deny he's in a better position. His pups have all grown up and can look after themselves. Most have moved on to other woods, seeking partners elsewhere. Only one from his last batch has remained, and even her pups may now be agile enough to outrun a moving stick. His lineage is secure. Each sunrise, Rabbit is getting heavier, drowsier and increasingly vulnerable. It is of critical importance they all breed to help sustain their species. Rabbit doesn't want to fail. But Bank Vole doesn't want to speak to the beast anymore. It frightens him.

'I've been told the beast destroyed the last woods it lived in, so it's inevitable it'll eventually do the same here if we let it stay any longer. I support Rabbit's request for urgency,' Muntjac Deer says, unintentionally compounding Bank Vole's fears.

'Now, now,' Badger says, trying to quell Bank Vole's obvious trepidation. 'We'll be there to protect and defend you, Bank Vole, if the beast dares attack. Let us know when you plan on speaking to it and we'll make sure we're close by. Mind you, we can't be too close in case the beast sniffs us out. Ok, so we'll be stationed a distance away, but near enough to see what's going on...'

## REALITY EXPOSED

Bank Vole shudders. He's effectively going to be alone with the beast, the ruinous, unorthodox, terrifying beast. Him, a little rodent, an animal with a missing claw, is going to have to confront an animal that can shred a tree trunk as easily as Owl can fly. He completely resents the position he's been put in. He knows they all have good reasons not to speak to the beast, but he does too. Yes, his lineage is secure, but he has other pursuits. It's fundamental he finds a way to improve bank vole lives. That's his real purpose, not this.

He's not speaking, so the animals start to talk amongst themselves while they wait for his response. He listens to their voices and wonders if each of them really think he's the best candidate for the job or if they're just putting him forward because they think his life is worth less than theirs. After all, Rabbit had said, 'someone with less to lose should do it.' Perhaps, he wonders, they're wanting him to do it *because* he's missing a claw. They think he's going to slow them down in the relay and want the beast to get rid of him. He looks at the ground and tries hard not to let out a sorrowful squeak. The council start to lean over him. They're growing impatient, but their encircling is only adding to his feeling of entrapment.

Bank Vole's never doubted their affection for him before, always seen himself as an integral part of the gang. He knows his strength doesn't equal Badger's, he's not as elusive as Pine Marten, and he'll never be as astute as Mole, but he didn't think those things mattered because he's Bank Vole. He has good knowledge of the river and all the animals who live by it. He's nimble, he's chatty. Usually, he can tell jokes to alleviate tense situations. Listing out his skills helps him see that he does potentially have successful beast-probing and beast-banishment qualities. But he just wishes he *knew* they were all being sincere, that they genuinely believe he is the best animal for this endeavour. Then he would feel more inclined to do it. If they really do believe he can achieve it, then he most likely can.

'Are you going to say anything, Bank Vole? You did put yourself forward, remember?' Rabbit asks.

That's right; he had the opportunity to refuse Pine Marten's proposal, but he didn't. Bank Vole remembers that his mind told him to agree to it because it convinced him it could lead to a life partnership with Myodes Glareolus. That's what this was all about for him. He thought he could improve the lives of bank voles by starting an eternal bond with her. The most recent event shows that outcome to be impossible. The beast clearly isn't to be reckoned with, and Myodes Glareolus will think he's mad, not brave. Overcome with a strong wind of regret and frustration towards his troublesome mind, he remains looking down. Rabbit, now restless, takes his silence as approval of the plan.

'Right, let's proceed then,' she says. 'We have to endure this beast for one more sunrise and then Bank Vole will come to our rescue, ordering it to leave so we can live happily again with only those of us who belong here.'

## ~ CHAPTER FOUR ~

# A Genius New Plan

Drifting aimlessly through the woods, Bank Vole is unsure what to do with himself. He left the council meeting at the earliest opportunity, desperate to get away from talk of the beast. He misses the pups and wishes to stop by their burrow, but he doesn't want them to pick up on how miserable he is. He thinks they're too young to be bogged down by fear or angst, so vows to visit them when he's feeling jollier.

'Psst!'

Bank Vole looks around, unsure where the noise is coming from and who is making it.

'Over here, to the right, in the strawberry bush!'

Ahh. Now he knows exactly who is talking to him. Myodes Glareolus adores berries, so much so that she struggled when winter arrived because she hated only having nuts and leaves to eat. The problem is, when berries were around last spring and summer, that is *all* she ate and every so often she became ill, queasy from an overdose of sweetness. Extraordinarily, it didn't put her off. She enjoys them that much. Smiling at her obsession, Bank Vole pretends he's forgotten about Pine Marten's instruction to avoid her and enters the bush, finding her in the shadowed section with strawberry juice down her front. The sight cheers him up immensely.

## AN EXCEPTIONAL AURA

'The berries are returning – quite early I believe, must be the recent heat the sun gave us! How marvellous! But look at your chest. Do you not hate how sticky you get with it on your fur?'

She rebukes him for asking such a ridiculous question. The smell of lingering juice sometimes makes her dream of berries, which are, of course, her favourite dreams. She thought he'd remember. Bank Vole does, but he likes to hear her re-tell these kinds of stories. They capture the little quirks he treasures.

The green, tiny, unripe strawberries surrounding them don't look very appetising to him, but he asks if he can join her because he would rather eat with her than eat alone. She sighs dramatically, telling him that although she believes she should have exclusive rights to the berries, she doesn't, so he can go ahead. They smile at one another as she helps him tug a low-hanging strawberry off a stem. He takes a bite and understands instantly how Myodes Glareolus is making such a mess. The hard-looking strawberry is surprisingly juicy inside.

Mid-slurp, Myodes Glareolus tells him she's heard about his mission with the beast by the river. Bank Vole's mood had changed so quickly upon seeing her he'd forgotten how sad and worried he was. The moment he'd heard her voice, he'd been like a white dandelion wisp, floating joyfully in the air. But now, with the mention of the beast, it feels like the wisp has plummeted to the ground, and someone has mercilessly trodden on it.

He picks at the outer layer of the strawberry before responding. He thinks he needs to be strategic. Previously, he would have been honest no matter what, but now he wants her as his life partner he feels the need to impress her. He opts to sound undaunted, as if approaching a monster and issuing it marching orders is something he's used to doing.

Myodes Glareolus frowns at him while he speaks. She doesn't buy it. The Bank Vole she knows would be terrified. She doesn't question him but tactfully tries to put him off. She believes the task is too dangerous and doesn't want him to get hurt. 'Nobody will think any less of you if you decide against it. You don't have to prove anything to anybody, you know. If you're trying to because of what happened with your claw, it was an accident and could have happened to any of us. We all commend how well you're coping; you don't need to show you're tough or brave. We already know you're those things. At least I do,' she says.

She shrugs at him, not sure if her words will have any effect. They do. Bank Vole is so comforted by them he drops the cool façade and confides in her. 'I don't want to do it! I'd originally agreed to it, but this beast… it seems so unapproachable, so untameable. How can someone like me talk to it?'

'You shouldn't! No one should. It's a stupid thing to do,' Myodes Glareolus says emphatically, pleased he's dumped the tough act. 'Why would anyone reveal itself to a beast? We hide from moving sticks because we've heard they can be violent, but we've never actually experienced it. We've physically seen the beast display aggressive behaviour, yet you're being asked to go over to it! I don't understand! It goes against our beliefs. We want to preserve everything we've built: our home, our lives, our lineage. It could destroy all of that if you confront it.'

At her use of the words 'we've' and 'our,' Bank Vole's chest pangs. To him, it sounds like she's speaking of them as bound beings, connected together for eternity. Does this mean she feels the same way? Is this her admitting to

## AN EXCEPTIONAL AURA

having romantic feelings? He studies her to find out. Having said her piece, Myodes Glareolus moves to lie down, releasing a big exhale when she gets into a comfortable position. She has remnants of strawberry on her cheek and speckles of mud on her head. She feels him looking at her, so she manoeuvres her body in case there's something else he wants to say. She looks at him sweetly, but something about her face, the way her features have positioned themselves, tells Bank Vole it's not in a loving way. She's merely worried about him. Concerned for his welfare, like any kind bank vole would be. It's a look of platonic endearment. He turns away and focuses on an incoming fruit fly, hoping concentration will mask his disappointment.

Noticing he's deliberately averted his gaze, Myodes Glareolus assumes he wants to stop talking about the onerous task. She changes the subject slightly and asks if he has seen any animals from the opposite side of the river recently. Bank Vole, thankful for the digression, says he hasn't. She tells him Muntjac Deer told her they're all in hiding, trying to avoid the beast. Usually, they live out in the open because moving sticks rarely visit their woods. They both express their sympathies, aware it wouldn't be an easy transition. Their conversation naturally drifts to other neighbour news, as well as the lack of such from Pigeon, who has been gone a long time now. Speaking of Pigeon gives Bank Vole an idea.

'Pigeon, she's lived such a full and eventful life already, don't you think? I wish our species were able to do some of the things hers can.'

At this comment, Myodes Glareolus lets out a forced yawn, tipping her head back so the mud resting on it slides off. Bank Vole watches each fragment crumble into minute pieces on the ground, quickly becoming one with the soil.

Then, he looks at her. She has risen and is preparing to leave. She doesn't think she should entertain these types of conversations. As far as she's concerned, evolutionary talk or anything pertaining to it won't bring the funny Bank Vole back. Besides, she knows what he's hinting at, and of course, given the choice, she's sure most flightless animals would evolve to have wings. She tells Bank Vole she's going because she wants to nap before the sun rises. Generally, bank voles are cathemeral, happy to sleep whenever they feel like it, and be active whenever they want too. This is something Bank Vole would not change about his species. It pleases him they can respond to their bodies' needs in the moment. He accompanies her back to the riverbank, hoping he's given her something to think about while she's lying in her burrow. He doesn't think he was subtle there at all. To him, it's quite clear he was referring to the fact that pigeons are able to create life-long bonds and bank voles aren't.

Now that he's on his own, Bank Vole can't escape his monstrous plight. His mind won't settle and it's preventing him from sleeping. He crawls out of his home and observes the beast from the same bush as before, the one nearest his burrow. If he familiarises himself with it, the animal might feel less intimidating when he goes to approach it. That's his plan, anyway. It's sunrise, and the council had agreed he was to talk to the beast by the time it's sun-sky. This is when the sun is at its highest position, furthest away from them. Birds are busy chirping in the trees and ducks have left their feeding spots to roam the river. He doesn't have long. He sits with his paw resting on his cheek, frustrated, and discouraged. The beast is snoring away, so he becomes entranced by the hypnotic flow of the water that's in view behind it. The rhythmic movement allows his mind to wander, and he begins to think about the relay. His memory connects with his mind and brings forward all the options he'd tried to get across the river. You see, the animal who has to traverse the water must be one that can't competently swim. This is the rule for both teams. The animals who set up the race many sunrises ago figured it would be too easy otherwise. The opposing team were able to get across once because they found a long, thick material on their riverbank. It looked like a lengthy, blue tail but it hadn't belonged to any animal. Anyway, they were able to throw one end all the way over the water and keep the other end in their woods. Dormouse, a racer at the time, pulled herself along it and successfully tied the leaf chain onto their crown. They tried to keep the prop afterwards, thinking they had secured a tactic that guaranteed them future wins, but a moving stick came to retrieve it. After some investigating, Pigeon learned it was called a rope and the moving stick had needed it for the floating structure it was balancing itself on.

Bank Vole lists all the ideas he'd had last spring. It was his first relay, and he had thought the most obvious thing to do was ask to sit on Mallard Duck's back. How naïve he'd been! Clearly that had been tried and tested before, but his team were willing to give it another go. Mallard Duck was very enthusiastic, and Bank Vole gave him numerous chances, but each time he'd head in the wrong direction, paddling downstream instead of westwards. Eventually he gave in and turned to Carp, who promised she'd swim shallowly so Bank Vole could remain above water. Unfortunately, she struggled to remember this pledge and dragged Bank Vole under as soon as they got going. Luckily Badger saved him before he drowned. After that, he'd become desperate and had asked the copse council to blow him across while he held on to a stick. That was a debacle but not quite as disastrous as his last method. He had thought it was brilliant. He had asked Spider to build a web for him that stretched from one tree on his side of the woods all the way over to a tree in the opposing team's woods. Spider was eager to help, she spent ages creating her web, she even spun clusters into it so it became thick and sturdy. When it was deemed ready, Bank Vole had to make his way across the web vertically, holding on with four paws. He had known it was risky, he had worried about getting a paw stuck and becoming tangled. He certainly didn't anticipate what ended up happening. That's because the relay makes you hopeful, excitable, almost invincible.

The first time he practiced, it had worked. He'd got to the other side, loosened himself from the web, gripped onto the tree, climbed down it with a leaf chain and positioned himself on the ground where the crown would be. Everyone had been so impressed.

The second time he rehearsed, however, there was a different outcome. He was just over halfway across when the weather started to change. Heavy winds began to blow, causing the web to sway back and forth. Bank Vole tried to cling on as much as he could without breaking the silk, but with each swing, he could feel the web was hanging looser. Knowing he must quickly get to the other side, he dropped the leaf chain and used all four paws to hurry himself along. When he was almost within touching distance of the tree, though, it started to pour. Heavy rain thrashed onto Bank Vole, and his fur became too cumbersome. Suffice to say, the increased weight made the web snap.

He felt the air pushing against him, tearing at his body as he fell. He screamed and screamed until he smacked the ground, his chest crushing his paw. Pigeon had been so close to catching him, but the wind had thrown her backwards. When she was able to be by his side, she curled her claws around his wounded body and carried him back to their side of the river. Laying him on the bank, she helped the council dab leaves on his body to soak up his blood. They did this not only so Doctor Hedgehog could assess his injury but also because Owl could smell it. Believing he was dying, Owl was desperate to devour him. His desire was so extreme Badger had to push him back and physically block him from getting access to their injured friend. This may sound barbaric, but it had always been normal for animals to concentrate primarily on their stomach. You must remember that their advanced mind is a recent development, and sometimes, albeit rarely, they revert to how they once were. Also, if Doctor Hedgehog had concluded that Bank Vole's injuries were fatal, Owl would have been allowed to eat him. No assessments were able to be made though. While Pigeon had gone to fetch the doctor, Rabbit had detected moving sticks. In a scramble, all the council animals raced to hide. Mole had kindly tried to scoop Bank Vole up and take him underground with her, but her nails were too sharp for his injured body. He had squealed in agony and begged her to leave him.

Well, it didn't take long for a moving stick to spot the little rodent lying out in the open. Bank Vole remembers being cupped into its hands as it lifted him. He vaguely recollects being close to the moving stick's face and feeling its hot breath scold him. His memory doesn't let him know much more. Most things remain unclear. For example, he thinks he saw a small, bright sun that wasn't in the sky, but his mind may have imagined this. He must have visited the Grey too but can't be certain.

The second time he was enclosed in their hands, though, that is very lucid. He was bouncing around in the

## A GENIUS NEW PLAN

dark, desperately trying to grab onto some moving stick skin, but couldn't because it was too slippery. Oh and their stench! It was so overpowering, he doesn't think he'll ever forget it. As mentioned before, it reminded him of the smell the river makes when the sun is really hot. He'd started to feel ill and thought he might pass out when, to his surprise, the moving stick opened its hands and gently lowered him to the ground. He'd hobbled to the nearest hiding place as soon as his paws touched the soil. Safe inside a shrub, he was immediately hit with a flurry of familiar odours. The musky smell of badgers, the musty smell of squirrels. He couldn't believe it. He'd been brought home.

  At first, he'd thought it such strange behaviour on the moving stick's behalf. Why take him away to bring him back? Then he'd looked down at his body and saw his paw was no longer covered in blood. He had lost a claw, but he wasn't in unbearable pain. Before he had time to think whether the violent, cruel, moving stick had helped him, he was surrounded by all his neighbours, who were delighted he had returned. They doted on him, and that sunset held a big celebration in the Thicket. Collectively, they gathered the juiciest fruits, the softest leaves, and the biggest nuts and threw them onto one big pile so they could all feast together. It had been sensational. That was the only good thing to have come out of the disaster. The accident, the danger he'd put himself in, the sheer horror of it… that had all been traumatic. The thought of anything like it potentially happening at the next relay makes him feel terribly agitated. Even worse than having to take part in the race, though, would be to not. He would be mortified if the Copse Council asked him not to compete because of his condition.

  Now that Bank Vole's really given the relay some thought, he realises just how much he doesn't want it to go ahead. It almost seems counter-productive. Practice takes up so much of his time and he'd rather put his energy into other things. His ideal scenario, in fact, would be that it got cancelled. But how can it not happen? He stops looking at the water and starts pacing back and forth in the bush. What could call the race off? He tries to think amidst the beast's belting, irritating noise. It's woken up now and sure is letting everyone know. He wishes it would shut up so he could concentrate. Hang on! He's got it! What he's thought of is genius and he curls his tail up to give himself a congratulatory pat on the back. The last time he did this was when a succulent leaf fell directly onto his paws just as he'd decided he was hungry. He hadn't made it happen, but he'd felt impressed he was involved in something so spectacular. This pat feels extra special because he's conjured it up himself. He's decided the beast has to stay. With it there, the relay *cannot* happen. The council had said it themselves in the Thicket. The magnificent creature makes it impossible! He strokes his ear as he plots. The best story he can come up with is to tell everyone he did speak to the beast and the beast said that it categorically wasn't going to move.

'That's that! There's nothing we can do, I'm afraid.' He practices what he'll say to the animals after giving them the news. He thinks it's realistic, he thinks he sounds confident. It's a shame, even he doesn't actually want the beast to stay, but this way, Bank Vole still gets to be seen as brave; he's still, as far as the animals are concerned, kept his word. They will think he's honourable.

'The beast was adamant that no one is to cross its river.' He adds this to prevent any loophole attempts. 'It doesn't want anyone to speak to it either, and said if anyone tries, it'll bring more moving sticks here.' He says this line emphatically. He's got to make it sound threatening.

## A GENIUS NEW PLAN

He does feel guilty, he'd rather not lie, but his life is on the line here! The relay going ahead is just too stressful and dangerous for him. Hurting himself again will not help bank voles evolve. Plus, Myodes Glareolus said she thought speaking to the beast was stupid. Now that he knows it wouldn't impress her, he's lost all motivation for that too. His plan means he gets to avoid the race and the beast and continue on his bank vole evolutionary mission.

Wholly satisfied, he decides to try napping again. He should be able to now he doesn't have to go through with either of the frightening ordeals. Feeling too lazy to go back to his burrow, he begins clearing a smooth surface for himself in the bush. He's hidden well here, and the soil is soft. He lies down, wriggles himself into a snug dip and closes his eyes. All he has to do now is bring on his perfect dream. He pictures himself lying on a pile of leaves with Myodes Glareolus by his side. All the woodland animals are there too. They're standing in front of them, listening to him tell joke after joke. In the dream, they're always hailing him as the funniest animal and are throwing hazelnuts and berries at him and Myodes Glareolus to say thank you for making them laugh so much. The food lands right in their mouths every time. He giggles, enjoying the scene he's managing to re-create. He feels his eyes get heavier as he starts to drift off, but as he's mid-mouthful, nibbling an imaginary nut, he hears scuffling behind him. Knocked out of his reverie, his eyes shoot open. The rustling gets closer. To his horror, a round silhouette is descending over him, shrouding the light.

'What's so funny?' it asks.

## ~ CHAPTER FIVE ~

# Thwack

Bank Vole squeezes his eyes shut and holds his breath. He remains lying down and tries not to move a muscle, hoping the beast can't see him through the thick bush leaves.

'Hello, hello, can you hear me in there? I heard some laughing and thought, finally another animal I can chat with!'

The beast pauses to see if the tiny creature will speak. When Bank Vole doesn't stir, it carries on.

'You see, I've been here a fair few sunrises and haven't met anyone. Actually, no, that's not true. I've seen some unfriendly, judgemental birds. As soon as I look at them, they fly off without uttering a single word to me! Rude, eh? I was sure I was smelling other animals, but then I would doubt myself because no one was appearing. I even went for a wander in both woods, but nothing! Anyway, no point talking to you if you have your back to me and are possibly dead. Or are you shy, is that it, eh?' The beast's voice is low and gravelly, but its tone is surprisingly tender. 'If you can hear me, I would like to talk to you please. I'm keen to know more about this area and who lives here. Hello?'

Bank Vole senses a pressure coming in his direction. It's the beast's claw poking him in the back. He makes use of the push by flinging himself towards the nearest stick. He picks it up, ready to defend himself. He waves the weapon at the beast like you might imagine a witch would wave her wand. At this, the beast lets out a hollow laugh, one that comes from its mouth and not deep within.

'We can make it a fun game, sure. I keep trying to poke you, you keep trying to knock my claw away with your little twig. But I was thinking we could talk first. Perhaps we can enjoy a little fun later. So, can we talk?'

Bank Vole can see through a space in the bush leaves that the beast is holding both its paws up to prove the poking will stop. He chucks the stick down. Whether the beast is telling the truth or not doesn't matter. It's pointless holding it. The beast could, of course, just flick it out of his grip. He should've tried to run away before it properly saw him. *That would have been a much better idea,* he thinks. How he regrets his giggling! He curses himself for trying to summon his perfect dream, it's created the reverse in real life!

'Are you going to say anything?' the beast asks, one eye now fixed on Bank Vole through the foliage.

Bank Vole takes a step back. He definitely preferred it when he was the one doing the peeping. He strokes the fur on his chest for comfort while he works out what to do. Here he is, face to eye with the beast he'd agreed to question and force out. He's trembling with fear, and he has to take several deep breaths to try and calm himself. *Clearly, the beast is getting a good look and smell of me,* he thinks. If he scarpers and doesn't speak, it will probably just hunt him down until he does. The ingenious plan he'd created where he would pretend that they'd spoken has to be aborted. As far as he's concerned, he doesn't really have a choice. He's got to be the brave Bank Vole.

With a quiet, quivering voice he says, 'Hi, I'm B-B-Bank Vole and I live in these woods. Can I pl-pl-please ask what you are? My friends and I have never seen anything like you before.'

When Bank Vole starts introducing himself, the beast breaks into a smile. When it hears his question however, its expression becomes more contemplative, as if it's not sure what to answer. It stops looking at Bank Vole and turns its attention towards the ground. Then its eye flicks back up to the opening in the bush, and it says, 'Pleasure to meet you, buddy. You can call me... Thwack because I can slap the water with my tail, or Natter because I talk a lot, or Chomper because I take big bites out of my food. Those are just my suggestions, but you can call me whatever ya like. Do you and your friends have a name for me already?'

Bank Vole vigorously shakes his head. Imagine telling the beast they call it beast? He might as well run directly into its mouth and ask to experience the chomping for himself.

'B- b- but you must have an actual name,' he says courageously, confused by the beast's response. 'You know, one you share with all your species, one that defines you and makes you... you?'

Again, the beast takes its time to answer. Bank Vole doesn't understand. It's not difficult! He can't think of any other animal who doesn't know what its species is called.

'Oh, that's boring,' replies the beast nonchalantly. It picks up some mud and sprinkles it onto its other paw. When its first paw becomes empty, it stretches the other, widening the space between its claws so the collected mud filters through them and scatters back where it belongs. It repeats this process while it talks.

'Do you know moose? They're huge, long-nosed beings with antlers. They live in the place I lived in before I came here. Anyway, when their youngsters are born, they have a selection of five names to choose from. Let's see, they can call it Meklorya, Mityloa, Merugloia, Motloya or Mahjoya. All very different. I like the idea, but I've added my own twist to it. I'm happy to be called multiple things, as long as they're distinctly about me.'

It ends the mud fun it had been having and shakes the excess off its paws. 'Oh, there are two things I should mention before you make your decision. I do not want the name to be derivative of my being female. A name like Femaley is stupid. And please, do not come up with a name that has any association with my soft fur.'

These are not the exceptions Bank Vole was anticipating, especially the second one. In their woods, having smooth fur is a blessing and the council regularly debate whose is the softest. Badger resentfully admits his is too coarse to be a contender. Owl obviously doesn't have any. The rest, however, are adamant theirs should win.

He tells the beast he's never heard of animals being called anything other than their species, but he will call her Thwack because of the unique tail slapping. Privately, he thinks designated names for each individual sounds fantastic, albeit a lot for memories to store. He notes it as a possible option for bank vole evolution.

With that settled, Thwack resumes talking about the impolite birds. She rambles on and explains each occasion in detail despite them all following the exact same pattern. Thwack would notice a bird sitting on a branch, staring at her. She'd call out to it, but it would fly off. The only difference with each story is the bird's species, so a flare of Bank Vole's starts to speak over her. It is shocked Thwack isn't revealing her species and lists possible reasons why she could be doing this. It puts forward that her species might

## AN EXCEPTIONAL AURA

have treated her badly, so she ran away and now finds talking about them too painful. It suggests they might've done something embarrassing, and she doesn't want to be associated with them. Or alternatively, and terrifyingly, it proposes that maybe she's been banished and is evading them. Not stating what she is will help conceal her. A shiver runs from Bank Vole's head all the way down to his tail. He really could be in the company of a fugitive, and what Muntjac Deer said about her destroying her old woods could be true. He discreetly begins digging himself a hole to escape into but then hears snippets of her sixth bird encounter, this time with Crow, and stops. She's really bothered about the unwelcoming birds. If she only came here to pulverise the place, he doubts she'd care how they treated her.

While he ponders over Thwack's motives, he notices the sun is now higher up in the sky. As Thwack is out in the open, moving sticks might see her and if they do, they could find Bank Vole too. He hasn't completed his task; they have to continue talking. This can only mean one thing. They're going to have to hide somewhere together.

'What is it, bud? Why do you look so worried?' Thwack asks, confused. Nothing about her story was scary. Bank Vole tells her they need to be inconspicuous. As soon as he says it, he regrets it. He's just suggested to a beast they take cover together! He feels like he's gone from brave to plain foolish. *The council had better appreciate this,* he thinks.

'Well, tell me where we should go, littl'un. I won't fit in that small little space with you that's for sure. Look at your frightened face! Is it me? Look, I ain't gonna hurt ya. It's purely information I seek, buddy.'

Thwack throws her paws in the air again. Last time she did that, she said the poking would cease and it did, but Bank Vole still doesn't feel very reassured. He apprehensively and shakily emerges from the bush and points towards the direction they need to head in. He knows an area close by with dense vegetation. If they both climb inside the shrubs there, they won't be seen. Thwack jumps back into the water and drifts beside him. Bank Vole scuttles along the bank and makes sure to keep a safe distance from the river so he can't be pulled in. If he's going to be this daring, he must keep his wits about him. Before they reach the secluded place, Thwack asks why they need to move.

'Moving sticks visit here,' Bank Vole explains meekly. 'They live outside the woods but come here to walk around. It's hard to describe what they look like. They're sort of stretched and they don't have fur. Anyway, they're unpredictable and potentially very dangerous, so we always make ourselves as inconspicuous as possible when they're around, otherwise they might kill us and cause our species to become extinct.'

Thwack shakes her head in the water. 'So that's whatcha call them here?' she asks rhetorically. 'Where I just came from, they called them furless. Weird to think they call themselves humans, isn't it? A name that means connection with Earth, apparently. The irony! They are ugly things, aren't they, eh? There's nothing I hate more…' Thwack stops, not finishing her sentence. Her tone, hyper and zestful, suddenly becomes slower, more composed. 'So, you hide from them here, do you?'

'Yes, we have this saying, "if they catch us in plain sight, we will face a mortal blight." So as soon as we sense they're coming, we dash to the nearest bush, hedge, burrow, hole, water, tree. We try to never let them see us.'

Bank Vole glances over and sees Thwack's tilting her head and gliding quietly so he can speak. Realising he's got the big beast's attention spurs him on to divulge more.

'Obviously, they have seen us on occasion, and I think they actually quite like some of us, but it doesn't matter. We have a duty to look after each other, and therefore we cannot openly display ourselves in front of them. For us to live harmoniously together, we must follow this woodland way of life.'

Thwack, fascinated, says she likes the sound of 'one force working together.'

The thick greenery is now in view. Bank Vole bolts into it first and hides behind a mound of soil in case Thwack enters and charges at him. He's still very wary of her. Thankfully, all is fine. Thwack takes her time to come ashore. In fact, when she waddles in to join him, it's her that's attacked. Bank Vole has underestimated her height. The protruding sharp twigs are jabbing her from all angles and she's struggling to avoid them. She doesn't make a fuss though and sits herself down. As soon as she's seated, Bank Vole cautiously reappears and positions himself opposite her – an arrangement he thinks Pine Marten would agree with. He slowly looks up at the furry, round animal in front of him and is taken aback by how her face makes him feel. He's in a bush with a beast. Someone who has bone-snapping teeth. Yet now that he can study her close up, he doesn't feel half as intimidated as he expected to. Something feels oddly familiar about her. She looks a little rugged and withered but wise and determined too. His jitters begin to subside. Thwack has resumed her bird story; she's now telling him about Magpie. He listens properly this time, stretching himself out to get comfortable. It's all going well until Thwack's wet fur forms a huge puddle that eagerly rushes to greet him. Unable to avoid it, he recoils into a ball and accepts that he'll be having this conversation the same way he does therapy: cold and wet. He tries to ignore his discomfort and focus on his task. He apologises on behalf of his winged neighbours, keen to wrap the story up. Then, he brings up moving sticks again. He had forgotten that Thwack interacted with them. Now that he's remembered, he wants to find out why. He tries to ask her cooly, casually, with just a hint of judgement.

Although sat down, Thwack is still having to crane her neck. She starts pulling at the sticks above to make some room for her head and answers Bank Vole at the same time.

'Oh, you saw that? Yes, I didn't shy away. What's the point? If they're going to kill me, they'll find me and kill me. I refuse to cower from them and be afraid.'

Bank Vole is astounded. Thwack can't fly away like birds can, so he can't believe she's so brash. He's desperate to know more, and his avidity overtakes his original hesitancy. Questions start spilling out his mouth. First, he asks her if other animals would hide from moving sticks in the place she used to live. Immediately afterwards, he asks exactly where that place was.

Thwack only answers his first question, and her response is abrupt. 'Some hid, some didn't.'

It's a strange role reversal. All of a sudden, she's the less chatty one. The erratic change in her behaviour reminds Bank Vole of the arbitrary tree hacking. The qualms quickly return, and he feels a fluttering of nerves. He cannot afford to upset her, she's too unpredictable. He shouldn't have allowed himself to be so talkative. Looking for another potential escape route amidst the deluge, he vows to stay quiet until spoken to. To his surprise, however, she asks if he has any more questions. Pulling on his whiskers, something he often does when he feels awkward, Bank Vole knows he has to keep going. She may not be very forthcoming, but he has to continue trying to get the information he was tasked with. He bravely asks why she's ended up in their woods and if any more of her species are coming.

Thwack starts picking stick-dirt out of her claws and mumbles, 'I don't mean to frustrate you, but I can't really answer that.'

It doesn't just frustrate Bank Vole, it pains him. Thwack isn't giving him anything, not even her species name. He doesn't understand it. He also doesn't get why she asked if he had any more questions if she's not going to answer them.

'Ok, my turn to interrogate you now!' In the blink of an eye, Thwack's whole demeanour reverts back to how it was when they first started talking. She's lively and talkative again. The speed of change causes Bank Vole's head to spin, and he has to hold on to it to curb the dizziness.

She asks him what other animals live in the woods. Openly and obediently, Bank Vole lists them. She tells him she knows what each of them are. She then asks if anyone is in charge of their woods. Bank Vole describes the council and explains that within the group, they're all equal. She claps her paws together at this response.

'And you're telling me that no one has seen anything like me before?'

When Bank Vole nods, she says, 'Right… last question for now, have you encountered any other new species recently?'

To this, Bank Vole shakes his head. 'You're the first unusual and unrecognisable animal to enter our woodlands.'

He immediately worries about the consequences of his honesty. His answer has made her face tighten, she looks forlorn. He takes a step to the left, ready to flee in case her sorrow turns to anger.

# THWACK

'Want to play a game?'

Thwack passes him a leaf. Taken aback once more, he gingerly sits down and holds it.

'Let's see who can eat their food the fastest. You bite that leaf and I'll chew this stick! Ready… go!' she says.

Bank Vole chomps away, gnawing as quickly as he can. He finds all food games fun, especially when others take them so seriously. He watches Thwack frantically try to devour a gigantic piece of wood. Her face, having lost its former sadness, is now creating all kinds of wild, crazy expressions that only competition can produce. He wishes he didn't have to ruin the moment by forcing her to leave. Given that she's not actually been hostile, it almost seems undeserving. He must do it, though. Nobody wants her here and he's not been able to achieve any other part of his task thus far. This is the last and most important thing he has to do.

After purposefully letting her win, he says, 'Well, Thwack, it's been nice getting to know you. When are you leaving here?' He tries to pose the question as if it's an inevitability. It's not offensive or unacceptable to ask because she is obviously going to go. They'd all be daft to have thought anything else. He hopes this strategy works.

She doesn't respond straight away, so he considers the pros and cons of her leaving while he waits. A positive is that, of course, it will mean their woods will be peaceful again, without many moving sticks and without Thwack's singing. Nobody will need to be scared of the beast by the river. The cons are, well, her leaving will mean there's nothing stopping the relay race from going ahead and that could result in him getting another injury. If this happens, he'll be unable to concentrate on forming a partnership with Myodes Glareolus or finding another alternative for bank vole evolution. He'll probably abandon therapy because he'll have to focus on his physical recovery.

Another negative is that it'll mean they never really got to know her. In his experience, she's not the beast they all thought she was. She's more pensive than aggressive. More inquisitive than destructive. In time, there's a chance she could actually become a friend.

'I'm not going anywhere,' Thwack says firmly with her head held high. The sticks above rustle and snap as she forces her posture upright.

She's staying! She's really staying! An excitable heat swarms through Bank Vole's body as he processes that the race is going to be cancelled. The courageous, daring Bank Vole confronted the beast and look what's happened. He's been rewarded for his valour!

'Won't you miss where you came from, your home and the rest of your species?' he asks. Now she's said she's going to be a permanent neighbour, he's hoping she'll open up more.

'This is my home now. I fit in here.' Her response is brusque, stern and matter-of-fact. It's also, according to pretty much all the other animals, incorrect. They're going to be appalled she's staying, and they certainly do not feel she belongs. He wonders what's given her the impression she does.

Without getting into it, he simply tells her he'll speak to the council and inform them about her decision. Despite him saying it cheerfully, she inches closer to him and gruffly asks if he's having to seek their permission. Bank Vole, a little uneasy, scuttles backwards and tries to reassure her. 'I'm sure it'll all be fine… it's just polite…this is their woods…'

## THWACK

Thwack lets out a groan, which causes her whole body to sink. Her head now hangs and her tummy swells. For the second time since laying eyes on Thwack, Bank Vole feels sorry for her. He can identify with that stance. It's one of defeat, of desolation. He thinks he knows why she's adamant she has to live here. She, like him, is lonely. She wants to stay here so she can be amongst others. That's why she kept trying to talk to the birds and why she sought him out. She wants company, she wants friends.

He decides he'll try to convince them she should stay. He knows that's going to be difficult, especially as he can barely tell them anything about her, but he's got to help the lonely.

He's going to get such a hounding, though! This might not be quite the distraction Pine Marten had envisioned. At this rate, it's only going to add to Bank Vole's troubles. *It's probably because of the hole at the back of my brain,* he thinks. *No matter the situation, all my iotas go left.* He decides he needs to lie down and momentarily bury the burden. He promises Thwack he'll meet her in the same place the following sunrise with an update. Then, he heads straight for his burrow and digs himself an even deeper hole. For now, he wants to temporarily shut out all life above Earth.

# ~ CHAPTER SIX ~

# Six Rules

Bank Vole wakes up hungry. Almost instantly, he knows where he's going to get his food. There's a place in the woods that can offer the most delicious meal and at the same time keep him away from the council. They're going to be aching to confront him, he's sure of it. The beast is still on their premises and that is not what was agreed. But this place, the place he's going to head to, should delay the litany of complaints for a little longer, and it should treat him with a beautiful, well-deserved moment of tranquillity.

It's windy when he sets off and he's getting battered by all sorts of woodland matter. Normally this would put him off and he'd resort to nearby leaves and seeds, but he perseveres keen to avoid the inevitable outrage for a little longer.

He'll be able to handle it at some point. Yes, later, he'll be running into the Thicket, keen to brief everyone. Not now, though. Now, he must head to his favourite place. When the next leaf smacks him, he catches it and runs with it beside his body. With it there, he can be protected from other forest furies and be obscured too.

As soon as he arrives at his destination, the helpful leaf shield is meaninglessly cast away. He's come to the hazelnut tree, the only one of its kind in the woods. It's quiet, as Bank Vole had hoped it would be. If it was autumn, it would be a different story. That's when the tree produces nuts, so the whole area surrounding it is mayhem. Its rarity and popularity, particularly with nocturnal animals, is pretty stupendous. The nuts often get demolished before they're even ripe. Now, as it's spring, the tree is bearing catkins and these yellow cylindrical flower clusters are much less in demand. Bank Vole enjoys them, though. Not as much as hazelnuts, of course; they're his absolute favourite, but he still finds them tasty. Also, while he's there, he often rummages around to see if there are any little fragments of a nut left. He was lucky once and found a chip of a shell. He spent the whole star-sky licking it, revelling in the faint taste of sweet soil-like delight.

He's had a debate with Myodes Glareolus before about what food is better: the hazelnut or the blackberry. He thinks the hazelnut is the winner because it has more texture and doesn't provide you with only one flavour. She, as expected, vehemently disagrees, arguing the sweetness of blackberries provides abundant energy. She also claims they should win because they can be a drink substitution, so they are multi-purposeful.

Bank Vole heads inwards, ready to inspect what's on offer. He picks up a bright, slim catkin and thanks the tree while he nibbles on it. Although he is tiny, Bank Vole can see that in relation to other trees, the hazelnut tree is small too.

'You and I, we are the same old friend,' he tells it, displaying a broad smile. 'Small but wonderful.' He chuckles, finding his self-praise amusing.

Then something causes him to drop his food and take a big, worried gulp. While he was giggling, someone else was too. He heard it, he heard a snigger. Someone else is

## AN EXCEPTIONAL AURA

here – someone is watching him! He hasn't steered clear of everyone after all!

'Who's there? Make yourself known,' he demands.

Almost instantly a little, fluffy bank vole scuttles out from behind the trunk. It's one of his offspring's pups.

'You're funny, Bank Vole,' she says in her high, squeaky voice. 'You think you look like this tree, but you don't!' Laughter overtakes her, and she turns on her back, kicking her legs in the air.

Relieved, to say the least, Bank Vole feeds off her joy. He doesn't correct her and explain what he was really saying to the tree. Instead, he grabs some leaves from the ground and puts them on top of his head. 'What do you mean? I look exactly like this tree. Don't you see the resemblance?'

Thinking he's being serious, Pup knocks her head back and squeals with glee. She tries to say something, but her words are incoherent. Bank Vole realises instantly he should have continued to visit the pups. Their innocence is the greatest solace.

He puts his paw back down on the catkin and resumes eating. When Pup has finally calmed down, he offers some of it to her. She shakes her head, claiming she's already eaten too much.

'Wait! It's just dawned on me that you are out alone. Are you allowed to do that, or did you sneak off?' Bank Vole asks.

Proudly, she tells him she knows how to be inconspicuous, so she can do as she pleases as long as she regularly visits the burrow and continues to sleep there. 'I was able to hide from you, wasn't I?' she asks rhetorically.

Bank Vole is surprised. Myodes Glareolus didn't have the same approach with their pups. She always kept them close and would never let them roam on their own until they were of age to leave. It's interesting that their offspring is doing things differently. He likes to see others break from tradition – he connects it all to evolution. He's sure, however, his offspring would claim she isn't straying, that she's as conventional as can be.

After Bank Vole's finished eating, the two rodents leave the hazelnut tree together. Both are keen to nap and hope doing so will aid their bursting bellies. Bank Vole passes Pup's burrow before reaching his own, so quickly pops in to say hello to everyone else.

He sees his offspring first. She's sitting on the ground, cleaning her tail. His emergence makes her eyes roll.

'I wondered when you would be making an appearance; you haven't lurked around in a while.'

Bank Vole is used to her inhospitable manner. He waves at her from the edge of the burrow. He always positions himself here. Even when the pups grab his paw and try to pull him in, he remains on the periphery. His offspring has never invited him in, and he wouldn't dare ask her to.

'Bank Vole, look what I can do with my tail!' says the same pup he'd met at the hazelnut tree. She curls her tail up so it becomes a tiny round swirl.

'That's impressive,' Bank Vole responds enthusiastically. 'How did you learn to do that?'

'I practiced! I roll my tail up with my paws and then clench my body so it stays in this position,' she says, delighted with herself. 'I prefer it like this. What I really wish, though, is that we didn't have a tail at all. Then other animals wouldn't call us Rat.'

Now it's Bank Vole's turn to roll his eyes. He remembers being called this when he was a pup too. It's meant to be an insult. He used to get riled up and find it derogatory, but it doesn't have the same effect on him now. Rats are smart and develop a close family bond. Now he's older, he envies them. Rabbit, on the other paw, still detests being called Hare. 'I do not have those ghastly ears!' she screeches.

Bank Vole tells Pup not to be offended by it, but instead of listening, she messes up the fur on top of her head, pushing it forward so it looks like she's been struck by lightning. Bank Vole, confused, asks what she's doing. She informs him that before the beast arrived, she had been playing with Duckling by the river when Duckling accidentally splashed her. To get her fur to dry quicker, she messed it up.

'I saw my reflection in the water afterwards and thought this looks so much better,' she says. 'If we permanently looked like this, everyone would know straight away that we're bank voles, not any other vole, not mice and certainly not rats!'

Bank Vole's ears start to ring. Pup wants the same thing as him – she wants to better their species by making them feel unique and special! Now that her intentions are clear, she has his utmost support. He tells her she looks fantastic and applauds her for being a young pioneer. Overhearing this, his offspring immediately intervenes. She tells him to stop encouraging her, not to pay attention to her silliness. 'She's deviant, that one. I know I let her out to roam, but she still needs some coaching.'

Then, in her normal blasé tone, she asks Bank Vole what's been keeping him busy. 'Oh, just therapy and the Thicket,' he responds casually.

He tries not to share anything that will provoke criticism because he knows he's going to get plenty of that from the council. So he deliberately omits his conversations with Thwack and Myodes Glareolus because he knows his offspring will denounce those. Perhaps he'd be more open if he knew why she often condemns his actions. It's because she cares about him and thinks he self-sabotages. Yes, she cares about him. She just thinks she should be doing so from a distance. The kind where you bump into someone once in a while, always stop to have pleasant chats and then when someone tells you they've died, you feel sad. Not achingly so, but the kind of sad where you say, 'Ahh, that's sad.'

Despite her concern, she doesn't wish bank voles had similar relationships to badgers, who still live together and show each other affection. She doesn't yearn for this at all. Bank Vole, of course, does. If therapy works, though, the gap at the back of his brain will close, and this should no longer be the case. He'll be the same as the rest of his species. He'll no longer love, and so can focus on a different way for them to evolve, one that's less frowned upon and more appealing.

That is unless something else happens. Bank Vole believes there's a chance Pine Marten will tell him his brain is healthy. He'll say there aren't any holes and that he's meant to pursue Myodes Glareolus and be a father to his offspring because, after assessing it, he's decided his mind is radical and progressive. Secretly, he knows which outcome he prefers.

His offspring catches him off guard and brings up the beast. She tells him she's instructed her pups to stay away from the river and has told them they're only allowed to leave the burrow when the beast is looking away. Unaware Bank Vole's spoken to it, she fills him in on the latest gossip.

## AN EXCEPTIONAL AURA

'The beast has eaten all fish, and its fur has turned from brown to a bloody red. Apparently it now plans to remove the hill by the riverbank, chop down the trees and create a flood so everyone drowns... so Muntjac Deer says.'

Bank Vole had been reticent about discussing Thwack, but these ridiculous scare-mongering rumours make him feel surprisingly defensive. He blurts out that he's actually had a chat with the beast so can affirmatively quash the reckless rumours.

His offspring, agape, drops her tail. She runs over to Bank Vole, who is still standing by the entrance of the burrow and looks up at him, clutching her chest. 'You're telling me you spoke to the blood-thirsty beast? Have you be-friended it? What is going on?'

Bank Vole nods, touches his nose and holds his paw out to her, palm upwards, to denote his sincerity. Instead of putting her paw on top, with her palm also facing the sky – woodland etiquette to signal that you believe or support someone – she starts clapping.

'This is extraordinary,' she exclaims. 'A bank vole has tamed a beast! Please elaborate!'

Excited by her enthusiasm, which Bank Vole rarely gets to experience, he relays his conversation about names with Thwack, explaining that she doesn't want to be called after her species. To his surprise, his offspring doesn't think the notion as revolutionary as he had.

'Whenever I introduce myself to other animals, I always call myself Bank Voole,' she admits. 'I elongate the "o." Think it's got an air of sophistication about it that way. It expresses who I am a bit more, you know?'

Bank Vole is stunned. She's meant to be rigid, traditional; she's meant to be someone who wants to conform. How can she freely change her name and effectively break away from the rest of her species yet still not consider herself a maverick? How can she blast his beliefs and do something like this? Her actions don't add up. Both irked and hurt by what he feels is blatant hypocrisy, he makes an excuse to leave. He would like to sulk at home but knows the time has come. He can't put it off any longer or he'll be in real trouble. He has to go to the Thicket.

This time it's Bank Vole leading the meeting. Unfortunately he can't use a nest podium like Rabbit. As they're built in haste, they are never compact enough for him. He's tried to stand on them but he always ends up slipping through the interlocking twigs. Pine Marten holds him in his paw instead, making sure it's raised so Bank Vole is at eye level with some of the council members. He wishes he could be carried up to therapy like this too but Pine Marten needs to use all of his paws to climb.

Rabbit, Badger, Mole, and Pine Marten were already waiting in the Thicket when Bank Vole arrived. He didn't get snubbed or chastised when he joined them. This didn't offer him any comfort though. It just convinced him they're saving their scolding for when the meeting begins.

The remaining council members were sent for. The meeting started later than it should have because Squirrel was busy teasing a whooshy who had entered the woods with moving sticks. Mocking whooshies is one of Squirrel's favourite pastimes and it's difficult to stop him once he gets going. Whooshies used to be called wolves, but they've changed too much to have that name. Wolves were refined and majestic. Whooshies stick their tongue out and dribble and seem unable to control their tails. They're always swinging them up and down and round and round, hence their new name, "whooshy" – it's the sound their tail makes when it's swishing around. Whooshies scarcely understand the woodland language because they've lived in the Grey for so long. Their hunting abilities have pretty much diminished too for the same reason. It's these two things that Squirrel takes advantage of. He enjoys goading them. He likes to get close to a whooshy, say something offensive and run off as soon as the confused creature tries to catch him. It's simply all a game for him. Not for the whooshies though, it leaves them terribly frustrated.

Despite Squirrel's mocking, Pigeon thinks that on the whole, whooshies are happy. She's observed them in the Grey and studied their behaviour. She believes their brains haven't developed like the woodland animals. She's sure they're still being led by their stomachs and rely on moving sticks to regularly feed them. She says they've got a strange dependency relationship of some sort. This belief makes sense to the others, they can see it. The whooshy who was just in the woods, for example, got separated from moving sticks when it was looking for Squirrel. It was frantically running around trying to find them, and moving sticks whistled and shouted continuously until they were reunited.

It's now very dark, it has turned to star-sky and the diurnal animals are very tired. This ironically includes Squirrel, who is desperate for the meeting to start so he can soon go to sleep.

Pine Marten signals for everyone to be quiet by stamping one paw on the ground. Immediately, conversations cease, and all eyes lay upon Bank Vole. Surprisingly, he finds their gaze fuels him. It stirs up a concoction of nerves and excitement. He has their attention, he has the control, the knowledge. He knows more about Thwack than anyone else in the council. Inhaling their sudden silence, he relishes this moment of power. His exhale is slow and drawn out as he stands up, steadies himself on Pine Marten's paw and draws his shoulders back.

'Everyone, as promised, I spoke to Thwa... the beast at sunrise. I charged over to it, asked it everything we wanted to find out. When I'd had enough of its blathering, I ordered it to leave. I was forceful, insisting it obeys my command! By the time I had finished talking, it was cowering into the water, and I could only see its eyes upwards. Must have been terrified.'

Bank Vole catches himself. Oops, he realises he got a bit carried away. One flare tells him to stop, another tells him to continue. The latter convinces him he's enjoying it and that the story is a *tiny* bit plausible. It's this one that wins.

'I let it know all about us and how we must behave inconspicuously around moving sticks. Where she's from they call them furless, and—'

Bank Vole jumps. Badger's roaring voice puts an immediate end to his storytelling.

'Enough!' he shouts. 'You spoke to it, that's great, that's what you put yourself forward to do. But spare us the details. It's still here, Bank Vole. What is it, where has it come from and why hasn't it gone yet?'

Well, the power he thought he had drains away like rain falling on dry ground. Badger has brought Bank Vole back to reality. He had a task to do, and they need answers. He places his paw over his mouth, tapping it while he figures out what to say. His memory replays his conversation with Thwack, focusing mainly on his perceived sadness and her desire to have friends. How can he spin this so they will want Thwack to stay? How can he make them like her when he doesn't have any of the facts they were after? Unable to think of anything, he regrets not rehearsing before-paw. It's what he usually does. Should he resort to telling a joke?

'Come on, answer!' demands Squirrel, yearning to shut his eyes and enter dream-woods.

Panicking, Bank Vole confesses that he doesn't know. The animals, frowning, ask what he means.

'I don't know what it is,' he murmurs.

The telling-off he expected commences.

'I did ask, but you see, we don't need to know because she has a different view on names!' he cries frantically. 'Where she's come from there's this animal, it sounded like mouse, but I think it was meese. She said they have five different names they can choose for their young and it wants to copy that. She came up with some names for herself, like Chump and Nutty, but I'm calling her Thwack because I'm not sure if you've seen, she can slap her tail up and down in the water.'

Again, Bank Vole is interrupted. This time, it's Rabbit. 'Fine, you don't know what it is. It's probably a cat or something Pigeon's mentioned to us before. Actually, come to think of it, I reckon it's a guinea pig. Didn't she say they had four sharp teeth? She definitely said they were covered in fur. Or maybe it is just simply a beast. That might be an actual species. There must be a reason we've heard the word. Anyway, Bank Vole, do you know if she has come from the Grey? I bet more will follow if she has.'

Bank Vole doesn't want to say the same three words he said before, so this time he answers by shrugging. He's met with a band of grunts and headshakes.

'I did ask where she's come from!' he squeals. 'She didn't say but she speaks the same language as us which is a bonus! She also knows what we all are, so I don't think she was previously living in the Grey. I think she's come from somewhere like here. She's friendly and chatty and interested in getting to know everyone. These are all good signs if you ask me.'

Not convinced, Rabbit places two paws above her enormous swollen belly. She stands opposite Bank Vole and looks directly into his eyes.

'When is it leaving?' She asks the question aggressively, accusatorily, as if she already knows she won't like the answer.

The silence is deafening. Bank Vole's mind can't think how to get around this. He wants to help Thwack, but other than listing a few good qualities, he doesn't know what else to say. He looks down and whispers, 'It's... it's not.'

The council start yelling and gesturing wildly. Pine Marten curls his paw to safeguard him from the vitriol. Bank Vole uses the space in between his friend's claws to see if anyone looks remotely sympathetic. He could do with an ally. The only animal he manages to spot a hint of compassion from is Muntjac Deer, but he also knows he's terrified and wants Thwack to leave, so he doesn't think he can offer much support. He turns to look up at Pine Marten and thinks his face looks more concerned than annoyed. He scratches the surface of Pine Marten's palm to get his attention. Pine Marten looks down and tries to hear what Bank Vole has to say but struggles amidst the racket. He lifts his paw up so Bank Vole can speak to the side of his face instead. Bank Vole stretches upwards and leans into Pine Marten's ear. To his disgust, he's met with a block of yellow wax. Pretty sure he doesn't flaunt that to the females, he steps back, deciding to shout up at the ear rather than into it.

'I think we're going to be ok. I think there could be a place for Thwack here.'

# AN EXCEPTIONAL AURA

Having heard him, Pine Marten promptly lowers his paw from his face and holds it towards the council as he had before. He stamps his back paw again and bellows, 'Quiet! You all sound so outraged at Bank Vole. It's not fair. He spoke to the beast. We asked him to do it and he did. He may not have come back with all the answers, but he tried. He can't be held accountable for the beast's reticence. Now listen, Bank Vole has more to say, and we must let him finish! Harmonise!'

The animals instantly shut their mouths but remain glaring at the raised rodent.

'Thanks, Pine Marten. Now listen here, everyone,' Bank Vole says coolly, trying to ignore the scowls. 'Thwack wasn't a beast. I barely felt scared or intimidated by her. I admit she wasn't very forthcoming about her past, but I think she will open up eventually. We chatted for a while you know, we even hid together. She could easily have hurt me, but she didn't try to once. The main takeaway I got from the interaction is that she wants to stay. And I... I think we should give her a chance.'

The animals are aghast.

'Have that tree-killing, attention-seeking monster stay in our blissful woods? Not an option!' Squirrel exclaims.

Again, the animals descend into disarray, objecting as loudly as they can. Pine Marten senses Bank Vole's distress. He thinks about how lonely he is and how much his mind needs to be distracted from Myodes Glareolus. The beast really could be what helps cure him. It's different, it's compelling. Bank Vole already seems to have formed an affinity with it. He decides to stand by his patient, his fellow animal, his friend.

'I will consider it,' he howls, shouting over the rest. 'I will consider it if she starts behaving like us. I think we need to impose rules that this beast, this Thwack, must obey. Otherwise, she cannot stay.'

Badger, appalled, accuses both Pine Marten and Bank Vole of being disloyal. The simple fact is the beast attracts moving sticks and moving sticks sometimes kill badgers.

'I understand, Badger, and your concern is valid,' Pine Marten says, attempting to console him. 'I still want to be the most elusive woodland animal. *I* do not want a lot of moving sticks here. That is why I'm suggesting Thwack abides by our rules. One of them must be that she does not court their attention. She has to live inconspicuously, amongst us, as well as with moving sticks. Why don't we collaboratively establish these rules, then afterwards we can hold a vote to decide if we're going to communicate them? If we decide not to, well, we'll force her to leave before the sun rises.'

Considering it a reasonable and democratic approach, Badger relents. It doesn't take long for them to all agree on six rules, which Pine Marten recapitulates to the group:

1. 'Live inconspicuously – hide immediately if moving sticks are in the vicinity.'
2. 'Stay by the river. We do not want you entering our woods unless we say you can.'
3. 'Stop hacking trees. They're our homes.'
4. 'At no point can you see us as food unless we are in a critical condition – we are your neighbours, be civilised.'
5. 'Be quieter – we like singing, but you do not need to belt out a song all the time. Try lullabies, stay away from ballads.'

> 6. 'Do not at any point interfere with the relay race, this is another opportunity for you to be inconspicuous. Stay away from all practices too.'

Nodding at one another, the Copse Council think they've covered everything they need to. They've tried to be extra careful. Even if what Bank Vole tells them is true and Thwack only really eats sticks, they don't want to take the risk. They also kept the sixth rule in, despite Bank Vole being adamant it wasn't necessary. Frustratingly, he wasn't able to convince them Thwack hates games. So, six rules it is.

The animals proceed to hold a vote: let Thwack stay, living within the rules, which Bank Vole must reveal to it, or force it to move, which will require another meeting to plan. Pine Marten and Bank Vole are in favour of Thwack staying. Surprisingly, taciturn Owl is too. Rabbit, Squirrel and Muntjac Deer are certain it doesn't belong and therefore it shouldn't be allowed to stay, even with the imposition of rules. Mole and Badger are unsure. They don't like the beast, especially how she interacts with moving sticks, but are aware she'd be different if she had to follow rules. They go off to chat privately and after a long deliberation, they decide she can stay. They stipulate, however, that Bank Vole must still socialise with it so he can continue trying to get answers to the questions they originally sought. They need to find out exactly who she is. Until then, even if she's behaving accordingly, no one else should approach her.

Their decision means Thwack can remain. Bank Vole is only half pleased. He's glad she can stay but has no idea how she's going to react to such stringent rules. Luckily, that's not something he has to worry about for now because

## SIX RULES

Muntjac Deer suggests they go in search of some spring shoots. He lets his stomach take over.

## ~ CHAPTER SEVEN ~

# *An Epiphany*

Before Bank Vole goes to meet Thwack, he sits in his burrow and tries to work out how to communicate the rules to her. He wants to have a plan prepared so he can avoid the disaster he had last star-sky in the Thicket. He can't be fumbling over his words.

Truth be told, he's dreading telling her. Now he's allowed himself to think about it, he doesn't think she'll respond well. She won't like being told what she can and can't do. She strikes him as the independent type, someone averse to commands. He's going to have to impose rules on someone who's travelled to the woods on her own, someone who so far has acted however she pleases. The rules are demanding she change, forcing her to assimilate.

What concerns him the most, really, is having to take the brunt of her resentment. As the messenger, he's bound to be in the firing line. He doesn't want this; he wants to help her. To prevent it, he's come up with an idea. He's going to try and assuage her frustration by downplaying the rules. He wants to make them appear minor and immaterial compared to the other news he has, which is confirmation she can stay. He relates the situation to times he's been really hungry, started chewing on a leaf and, mid-mouthful, tasted urine. It's not pleasant knowing another has peed on your food, but he continues eating it because it's the leaf he

# AN EPIPHANY

wanted, and he's got it. So, he thinks if he keeps reinforcing that she can remain (despite her being adamant she was going to anyway), she should focus more on that rather than the conditions which come alongside it. Basically, he wants her to focus on the bigger picture.

Another tactic he's thought of is to refer to the rules as "customary behaviours." This way, he thinks they seem softer, less rigorous, less draconian.

By the time he arrives at their discreet spot on the riverbank, he's feeling more confident than he'd anticipated. Not devoid of apprehension, but prepared and determined. Unfortunately, he's unable to get right to it. Thwack is singing so loudly, lying on her back in the water with her eyes closed that she fails to notice Bank Vole. He yells her name, but she doesn't respond. He starts yelling different names in case she's forgotten she's called Thwack. No luck. The singing continues. He even resorts to throwing stones (albeit very small ones) at her, but she doesn't flinch. It's futile.

'This is a task alright,' he mutters to himself. The arrogance of her disruptive behaviour irritates him, and he starts to question whether he's been foolish wanting her to stay. Getting her to fit in isn't going to be easy, and helping her defeat her loneliness might be more effort than it's worth. He thinks the only way her ear-splitting performance should be allowed is if she was either living in her own woods or if all the animals around were deaf.

He moves to sit inside the bush they'd last chatted in. Cupping his paws over his ears, he tries to drown out some of the noise while he waits. He waits some more… And some more. It isn't till the sun is high up in the sky, radiating an oppressive heat, that Thwack finally stops singing and opens her eyes. She rolls on to her front to get a drink and as she dips her tongue into the water, Bank Vole emerges and stands in front of her.

'Oh, hi! Good to see you, buddy!'

Her warm greeting doesn't pacify him. He's fed up and reaching his limit.

'Thwack, I was here before sunrise ready to speak to you like we'd arranged! I've been waving myself around, trying all sorts to get your attention, but nothing, and I mean *nothing*, can be louder than your jarring screeching!'

Thwack screws up her nose and shrugs, evidently unaffected by his words. 'Old habit of mine, I guess. I've spent so much time on my own now, my voice is my friend. The louder I sing, the more company I feel I have. It's a way of letting others know I'm here too…'

'Oh, we all know you're here alright! You're going to be banished from these woods if you carry on acting like this.'

Now, she's not so apathetic. Bank Vole's remark shocks Thwack. It's as if the possibility of being forced out never really occurred to her. Bank Vole registers her dismay and is encouraged by it. It incentivises him to say more. He disregards that he's less than an eighth of Thwack's size. All his pent-up stress pours out of him and he speaks with unrestrained candour.

'Thwack, I had a meeting with my friends – the members of the council – and I don't think you quite realise the upset you're causing! Your incessant wailing, your massacring of trees – our homes might I add! Not to mention socialising with moving sticks… you haven't given a hoot about the animals who live here. You've terrified pregnant Rabbit, who's worried her young will be taken; you've scared Badger, who thinks he will be murdered. Poor Muntjac Deer has barely slept since you arrived…!'

## AN EPIPHANY

Bank Vole takes a breath and whilst doing so, realises just how exasperated he sounds. He must be mad! You don't speak like this to an animal you barely know, especially not one who is much bigger than you! He pulls on his whiskers and stretches his back legs. The movements help calm him, and he concentrates solely on what he needs to convey.

'Look, even after all that, we've decided you can stay,' he says softly. 'You wanted that, didn't you? You are allowed to continue living here!'

He jumps in the air and gives her his biggest smile. He needs to highlight this good news, accentuate it to the nth degree. Thwack doesn't react. Bank Vole had envisioned her splashing exuberantly, or at the least, clapping her paws. He hopes her lack of celebration isn't because of his outburst. He hadn't wanted to upset her. *Perhaps she's just too hot to bother,* he thinks, comforting himself. He decides to carry on with his plan. He's passed her the leaf. It's time to sprinkle the urine on it.

'So, as you're going to be living here, there are a few, uh, customary behaviours you've got to agree to. If you can follow these, then I really think we could all end up becoming friends. That's what we're both hoping for, right?'

That's the impression he got when they last spoke, anyway. She'd been so chirpy and inquisitive. This time, however, Thwack is different. She's silent and sombre. She's turned herself away from Bank Vole and is looking at the ducks floating by. Again, he opts to continue talking, assuming she's still listening.

'The customary behaviours have been created by those of us in the council. As we're from here, we know what is acceptable and what isn't. They shouldn't be difficult to abide by. Before long, I bet you'll be feeling like one of us!'

Thwack sniggers and shakes her head. Bank Vole wonders what she's thinking. Had she believed she was fitting in, even though he's the only one who's spoken to her? He doesn't enquire, believing it's best not to delve deeper. He doubts she'll be honest about her feelings anyway. Instead, he tells her they should move inside the shrubbery so they can be hidden from the heat and moving sticks. Thwack ignores him.

'Right, well, if we're going to be in the open, we need to be careful. I'm going to get right to it— '

'Not now, Bank Vole.' She dramatically drops a paw into the water and leans on it to roll over and face him. 'I need to swim and use up some energy. Perhaps you can come back before I go to sleep and tell me about the customary behaviours then?'

She sounds quiet and croaky. Her tone makes it plain to Bank Vole that his previous convictions were correct. This is someone who is dreadfully lonely. She's seeking camaraderie and is sad she has to work to get it. This, in turn, upsets him and reinforces his desire to help her. He agrees to delay their conversation.

She turns back around in the water to leave and as she does so, Bank Vole's body stiffens instantly. Something really startles him. He can't be certain, but he thinks he sees her melancholic expression flip to one of anger. For a very brief moment, she looks incandescent. Her eyes resemble scary, dark holes that could suck you in and trap you eternally in a torrent of hatred. Very bravely, he calls after her to see if he's right. He isn't. The animal who stares back is biting down on her lip, resisting the urge to whine and wail. She's undoubtedly sad. Only sad.

## AN EPIPHANY

Bank Vole doesn't know what to do with himself while he waits. He's not tired enough to nap and not hungry enough to forage. He sits in his cool burrow and listens to what's going on around him. He hears someone air sniffing, someone else scuffling through foliage. There are definitely a few mouths munching on food. Many birds are flitting from one tree to the other.

He pokes his head out of his home to see if any of these animals are close enough to talk to. At the exact same time, ants march past. He places his paw down in front of them so they crawl on top. Bank voles are encouraged to eat insects. Doctor Hedgehog says they provide nutrients other food can't. Unfortunately, they're not the tastiest, so Bank Vole doesn't seek them out. If they're passing by though and are an easy catch, like these ants right now, he makes sure to eat one or two. Myodes Glareolous doesn't do the same. Every time an insect passes, and he suggests she has some, she makes out she can't see what he's on about. She looks everywhere but the area she knows they're in, which Bank Vole finds very amusing.

He picks up another ant, places it on his tongue and swallows it immediately. That's two ants. That's enough. Now what? He doesn't want to go to the Thicket until he can say he's told Thwack the rules. He could peer into Myodes Glareolus' burrow and see if she's around. Yes, he thinks that sounds like a good idea. He grips onto the surface and heaves himself out of his home. Scuttling over to hers, he realises something is niggling in his mind. It's as if he's created a thought, but the flare hasn't quite reached him yet.

Oh! It comes to him. He's not meant to visit Myodes Glareolus. He told Pine Marten he wouldn't and he's broken the pledge once already. He hovers outside her home while despair boils up inside. It doesn't seem fair. If he wants to see the animal he loves, he should be able to. It shouldn't be forbidden. He lets out a big, disheartened sigh. *When is this all going to be resolved?* He wonders when life is going to make sense to him again.

Oblivious to his quandary, Willow Warbler chirps hello to him from the air. Bank Vole tilts his head upwards to say hello back. As he looks at her gentle eyes and happy yellow chest, he's reminded of Thwack's bird story. He's never found any of them unfriendly and thinks it's a shame she does. Alone, with nothing to do, Bank Vole walks back to his burrow and reflects on his time with her so far. He realises she's actually taught him a lot. He now knows other animals call moving sticks "furless" and that they call themselves humans. He's learnt there are animals called meese and that you can have your own name.

Suddenly his paws shoot up to grip his head. Then he starts pulling on his whiskers. It's not quite sunset yet, but he decides to sprint down the hill. He's got to see Thwack. His pricked ears have informed him she's not singing, and panic has quickly set in. He's worried she didn't want to hear the customary behaviours, so has left.

Thinking about Thwack has caused Bank Vole to have an epiphany. It's dawned on him that it might not be his bravery against her that leads to a life bond with Myodes Glareolus. It could be their friendship. Through Thwack's knowledge and experiences, there's a chance she could help him be with her. It could be Thwack who puts an end to his misery. His heart starts to thump in his chest and his breathing intensifies.

'Please still be here,' he whispers. 'Please.'

## AN EPIPHANY

He needs her to stay. Not just because he wants to help her escape her loneliness, but because, for the first time, he can see that she really could help him escape his too.

## ~ CHAPTER EIGHT ~

# Short-Lived Fun

She's not there. Ducks are gliding in the glistening water, birds are dipping in and out, but a round, brown animal with orange teeth isn't paddling beside them. Bank Vole feels an uncomfortable bubble rise up in his throat. He needs her. They need each other. He lifts his nose in the air and tries to detect her odour. Thwack's scent has a muddy sweetness to it, like a hollow nut that's had a little fruit dripped into it. As the wind blows, he thinks he can get a faint whiff of it downriver. He crouches down low to follow the smell. It gets stronger and stronger and takes him to a secluded reedy spot.

As he forces his way through the sucking, squelching soil, he hopes his nose is right. Thwack had better be here because it's going to take a long time for him to get all this dirt off. Fortunately, the mess is worth it. He finds Thwack lying stomach first in the water with her paws resting on the bank's surface. Even though this isn't where they'd agreed to meet, Bank Vole lifts his own heavy, mud-laden paws and goes to join her. When he reaches the river's edge, he dangles his mucky tail into the water and sees the dirt that had temporarily lived upon him swirl away in search of its next home.

'You're early! Happy to see ya, pal! About before, I just had so much energy to expel, you know. Now where were we… ahh yes, the customary behaviours!'

Despite Thwack's chirpy disposition, Bank Vole thinks she looks exhausted. Her eyes are even smaller than their usual dots. Considering she clearly needs a good sleep, he's thankful she's now willing to hear the rules.

He tries to mirror her upbeat greeting to show he doesn't mind they were previously delayed. 'Absolutely delighted to see you too, friend!'

Oh dear. That, he believes, was over-zealous and cringey. Embarrassed, he starts coughing to take the attention away from it. When he thinks he's spluttered for long enough and his dramatic address has become a thing of the past, he swishes his tail and regains composure. The next time he speaks, he makes sure to sound calm and natural.

'Ok, Thwack, I'm pretty sure none of these *customary behaviours* are going to come as a surprise given that I revealed a lot in my outburst earlier, which, by the way, I would like to apologise for. Although everything I said was in fact true, I know I shouldn't have spoken to you the way I did. We're generally a harmonious bunch here and my shouting wasn't quite representative of that.'

'Yes, you were rude, bud. It's ok though. You can make it up to me at some point. This woodland way of life, it does sound very sweet…'

'It really is wonderful here, Thwack,' Bank Vole says seriously. 'I would like you to fit in as much as possible. And you know what? I don't think it'll take you long. I noticed you weren't singing loudly during sun-sky, so you're already on your way to becoming more like us. Alright, without further ado, these are the customary behaviours.'

## AN EXCEPTIONAL AURA

By now, Bank Vole has accepted his surroundings. He stands up and lets his paws sink deep into the mud.

'Number one: please try and follow the very important woodland way of life I've mentioned to you before. You must be inconspicuous whenever moving sticks are around. It is imperative we hide unless you're Pigeon or some other bird. Not letting them see us is how we preserve our species. So, if you hear or smell them near, you must quickly and quietly conceal yourself. Where we are right now, anywhere in the water here or inside the bush, is a good spot for you to dash to. Even if you go exploring up the river, you must surround yourself with safe hiding places. Any comment on that before I move on to number two?'

Thwack rests her head on her paws and lightly paddles her webbed feet in the water. Sighing heavily, she tells Bank Vole she's not afraid of moving sticks and that hiding from them would make it appear like she is.

'That doesn't matter though, does it? You've got to think about your neighbours. You've got to consider all of us. Moving sticks, well, we've been told they're dangerous.'

'Yes, fine, fine. I get it. Unless you fly, you're scared of them. I want to be everyone's friend, so I'll try and stop interacting with them. I'll try my hardest to stay away when they're around.'

'That's great, thank you. I guess we can move on to number two...' Bank Vole starts pulling on his whiskers. He's just remembered what the second rule is and feels awkward about it. He scratches his ear even though it's not itching and says quickly, 'Please stay by the river for now.'

To him, this rule illustrates very clearly that the animals don't feel the same as Thwack. They do not want her to become their friend. Not wanting her to dwell on this upsetting and uncomfortable fact, he moves swiftly on to number three.

'It's about the tree cutting you do. Must you do it? Is it essential for your species? We want to be understanding, but it's so loud and you're displacing animals. There are other reasons too...'

'Sure, I was just doing that for fun,' Thwack says cooly, interrupting him. 'I sleep in the open now anyway, so I can stop.'

Confused, Bank Vole tries to squeeze information out of her. 'Oh, so would you usually knock a hollow tree down and sleep inside it? You can do that if you like. Lots of animals sleep inside trees here. You've taken a few down now, so you can just use any of those, right?'

Thwack asks her own question instead of answering his. 'What eats you here? Do you have foxes, otters, wolves?'

'We have foxes and otters; they don't permanently reside in the woods though. Neither do wolves; well, they're not really wolves, they're whooshies.'

'Whooshies?'

'You know, the animals you sometimes see with moving sticks. They run around on four legs. Some make the woods slippery with their drool. They like to stick their pink tongues out and their tail seems to have a twitching problem.'

'Ahh, waggy!' Thwack responds. 'I know who you mean now. Yeah, we are fascinated with their tireless tails too.'

'Waggy! That's a good name. Anyway, why do you ask about them?'

'I was just wondering what could potentially eat me.'

'You don't need to worry about that here, Thwack. You'll only get eaten when it's your time to go.'

## AN EXCEPTIONAL AURA

Bank Vole explains that an old council issued a rule many sunrises ago that stated animals, regardless of their size, can't be eaten in their prime. The only exceptions to this are insects, such as ants and houseflies, because they're in abundance. Other than those, you must only eat another animal when it needs your help getting back inside Earth's skin, so mainly when it's ill or old. This news visibly shocks Thwack. She tells Bank Vole she's surprised the animals can go against their stomachs' natural desire.

'Well, a lot of woodland animals are herbivores, you see. The ones that aren't realised that to live harmoniously, something had to change. If owls were to eat every mouse or vole they see, those rodents would end up extinct in the area. It's an effort having to constantly migrate, and the animals here know that. They believe their diets are expansive enough to wait until it's the animal's time to go. There are always leaves and insects in the meantime whilst you're waiting.'

He adds that he doesn't feel any qualms knowing it will probably be Owl who devours him. Owl has been patient and behaved accordingly, and he's part of Owl's diet. He understands everything has to return to Earth's reproductive organs and Owl can help him on his journey. Thwack is amazed. She can't believe how willing the animals are to cooperate. Their subservience astounds her.

'In case you hadn't noticed, I myself am an herbivore, so as I previously mentioned, I fit in well here,' she says cheerfully.

Now that Thwack is in a much better mood, Bank Vole tries to get to know her through the art of digression. He asks her what animal she would eat if she had to.

'Furless, I mean, moving sticks,' Thwack responds instantly.

## SHORT-LIVED FUN

It's not the speed that surprises Bank Vole but her answer. Moving sticks would never be his choice. Their smell alone is abhorrent. In fact, as far as he's aware, they've never been on any animal's menu. That's partly why they were able to expand as much as they have, why their lineage is so secure. Intrigued, he asks Thwack to explain why she'd pick them, but she starts laughing, telling him it was a joke. To be kind, Bank Vole pretends to laugh too. He wouldn't classify that as a joke though. He knows that unlike him, most animals find it hard to be funny, but Thwack's attempt was, in his opinion, particularly poor. *Maybe*, he thinks, *I can teach her how it's done.* He's told some really great ones before, which everyone in the woods enjoyed. He tries to get his memory to resurface them so he can demonstrate what a proper joke sounds like. When one pops into his mind, he starts laughing before he's even said it, just like Pup had done by the hazelnut tree.

'Ok, ok,' he says, his paw up, facing Thwack, who is blowing bubbles in the water. 'Why should badgers be called badge-ow!-ers?'

Eyes wide, he stares at Thwack to see if she can guess. She lifts her head up, spits, then shrugs unexcitedly. 'Are they aggressive here?' she asks. 'Is it because their booming voices hurt your ears?'

Bank Vole shakes his head. 'Wrong! It's because their fur is embarrassingly rough.' He knocks his head back and squeals. To him, the joke gets funnier every time he says it.

When he's finished laughing, he looks at Thwack. Judging by her breathlessness, he guesses her laughter ceased just before his. His assumption is incorrect. She looks him in the eye and states matter-of-factly that fur jokes aren't funny.

Disappointed he's not tickled her, Bank Vole tries again with a different topic. 'How about this… why do fungi grow so close to one another?'

Again, Thwack shrugs unenthusiastically.

'Because they don't think there's mush room in the woods.'

This time, he holds in his laughter so he can watch her reaction. He is thrilled when her mouth turns very slightly upright. This minor movement spurs him on. He wants to get her laughing properly.

'What's more of a moving stick than a moving stick?'

Her mouth becomes linear again. Then it gets worse. She begins frowning.

'Nothing is worse than a moving stick,' Thwack says sharply.

'That's not really what the… a stick insect is more of a moving stick.'

Even with the answer, her expression doesn't change. Bank Vole figures she must have an issue with her brain. It must be struggling to pass comedic iotas. He decides to stop there and resumes telling the rules, but as he flicks a leaf that is stuck in-between his claws, that cross expression he thought he'd seen before reappears. Out of the corner of his eye, he sees Thwack's face looking furious. His heart feels like it's enlarged instantly, banging against his body and drumming loudly against his ears. He scrambles to get away, slipping on the wet mud in his hurry.

'Fantastic jokes.'

He swivels around. Thwack is now beaming at him and softly asking if he's hurt himself. When Bank Vole shakes his head, she tells him to continue with the customary behaviours.

## SHORT-LIVED FUN

Confused, flustered and dirty, Bank Vole fumbles his words. 'Animal eats not, please. I said only for you sticks but... erm, I mean...'

'What? Animals eat snot? Gross!' Thwack exclaims, utterly disgusted.

Bank Vole takes a breath, pulls on his whiskers and calms down. As soon as he does, he relays the rule correctly. Relieved the animals aren't actually savouring their mucus, Thwack reiterates that she's an herbivore, so nobody needs to worry about her eating them.

The fifth rule, the one about not singing so loudly, also causes confusion.

'Well, if that's how they want it, fine, but it's a shame they don't appreciate a good singing voice when they hear one, eh, buddy?'

Thwack attempts to tell another joke, and Bank Vole, unable to detect her sarcasm, pulls on his whiskers again. He can't believe she's forgotten how he'd described her vocals. She absolutely does not sing well! He decides not to answer her directly and instead suggests she practices singing at different volumes so he can tell her the level that's tolerable.

'I'm not gonna sing at all if I can't do it loudly,' Thwack says, turning down his offer. 'It's not fun and enjoyable if you aren't reaching your maximum sound.'

Bank Vole wouldn't know if this statement is true or not. He's never tried it. He only ever hums and only ever does that when he's rummaging through seeds and nuts. Her decision suits him though, so he doesn't try to get her to reconsider.

The only customary behaviour left to tell Thwack is the sixth one, which focuses on the relay. Bank Vole would like to omit this. He decides to postpone it for now and asks

Thwack about her sleeping pattern instead. He wants to know if she's like bank voles who don't particularly have one.

'I've started sleeping when the sun sets, which I never did before. That used to be when I woke up,' she says.

His next question, naturally, is to ask why she's suddenly become diurnal. She doesn't respond. This behaviour reminds Bank Vole of snails. They have a habit of slithering over with interesting news, but as soon as they've said it, they recoil back into their shell and refuse to reappear. All questions remain unanswered and everybody finds them most frustrating.

'Are there more customary behaviours, pal, or are you just gonna start interrogating me again?'

Bank Vole gulps. The sleeping questions didn't veer Thwack off course. She's still thinking about the rules.

'There's one more,' he says reluctantly. 'But this is going to take longer to explain as I need to give you a bit of background first.'

Bank Vole explains the relay race to Thwack, highlighting how much everyone enjoys it and how seriously they all take it. Thwack listens intently and before he's even finished, she says, 'So tell me how I can participate!'

Bank Vole starts making random shapes in the mud with his paw, not sure what else to do.

'Oh… I get it. That doesn't seem fair. I would like to be part of the relay race. I'm going to try to follow these strict rules, which, let's face it, is exactly what they are. You can call them customary behaviours, but they are strict regulations I have to follow. They're rules. But why should I go out of my way and stick to them if I'm not going to be seen as part of the woods, just like y'all?' Thwack asks. 'Look, I did some thinking when we left each other earlier. I can see I haven't been behaving the way I should have. I went about it all the wrong way. I want to be liked by everyone. I want to start again. I think I have a lot to offer. I have knowledge you may not have, ideas I can share, plans we can action. I would like to join the Copse Council and be part of the relay race.'

Bank Vole didn't expect this candour from Thwack. He also didn't expect her to want to fit in this much. It confirms what he suspected. She's lonely and wants friends. Although she has his sympathies, he tells her honestly that council membership is exclusive. It just isn't possible for lots of animals to be in it and this in turn affects who can take part in the relay. He also adds that additional animals have ruined the race. Thwack doesn't relent. She says she'd like her species to be represented, and the only way for that to happen is for her to join the council.

'Well, may I remind you that you haven't actually revealed what your species is. For us to even consider you, we'd have to know exactly what you are. Now, tell me, are you a guinea pig?'

Bank Vole hopes Thwack's desire to be included will outweigh her reticence. It doesn't. Thwack offers a proposition instead.

'No I'm not a guinea pig. I don't even know what that is! Look, if I correct my conduct and adhere to your rules can you at least promise to think about it? We can devise a plan later down the line.'

Bank Vole willingly makes this pledge. He thought she'd push him a lot more, so happily says yes just so the conversation can end. With her pleading over, it means he can dwell on the exciting admission she made. She said she has extra knowledge! He instantly feels one step closer to a life bond with Myodes Glareolus.

# AN EXCEPTIONAL AURA

Oblivious that her words have caused such elation, Thwack playfully pushes herself away from the bank. 'Now that we've got all of that out of the way, how about you and I have some fun?' she says.

Remaining on her front, Thwack instructs Bank Vole to scurry backwards so he can run and leap onto her back. Bank Vole doesn't want to go anywhere near the water, so he refuses. Thwack insists, promising he won't fall in.

'The only way I'll even consider doing it is if you touch your nose and then hold your paw out in front of you, with your palm facing the sky,' he says. 'This gesture is taken extremely seriously in the woods because it either means you're really thankful or that you are telling the truth and being genuine. You simply can't do it if you're not.'

'You're going to enjoy yourself, bud!' Thwacks responds, hitting her nose and extending a paw dramatically.

Bank Vole hesitates. This is a massive risk, but she has now sworn her sincerity. He has to believe her. Clenching his eyes shut, he jumps off the bank and onto Thwack's back. The landing is surprisingly very smooth, and he discovers Thwack is blessed with the softest fur. Holding on to it tightly, he surveys all that's around him while Thwack paddles downriver. He's never properly looked at the woods from this view. It all looks so different. The bank vole burrows seem like tiny little holes on the riverbank hill. And the trees, there are so many of them! They appear so much bigger from the water too. The whole experience is filling him with adrenaline. The buzz encourages him to share things with Thwack, things he normally only tells Pine Marten in therapy. He reveals his feelings towards Myodes Glareolus, his offspring and her pups. He explains what he's hoping to achieve and how he wants to improve his species' lives. He even shares the reasons he's scared of Doctor

## SHORT-LIVED FUN

Hedgehog. Thwack's silent throughout, but Bank Vole isn't disheartened. He's sure she's simply concentrating on swimming and will reveal how she can help when they're back on dry land. After his ramblings stop, however, he tries to get her to talk.

'So, how did you get here, Thwack?'

Thwack tersely says she crossed a big river.

'Wow! Why did you leave your home? Did you swim all the way across? Were you alone? Did you deliberately plan to arrive here?'

The moment the questions escape Bank Vole's excited mouth, he knows he's made a mistake. Thwack's never going to answer all of them. He wishes he'd been more strategic and asked one at a time. He waits patiently to see if she's going to answer any. Eventually, she says she had heard of these woods and was hoping to end up here. Bank Vole knows this woods is better than the one he was born in, but to hear Thwack say she travelled a long distance to try and get here... well, it confirms just how wonderful his home is. He finds this news so spectacularly rewarding, it quietens him.

At the same time, the river starts to widen, so Thwack turns around to swim back.

'Have you had any of your own experiences with moving sticks?'

Lost in his own thoughts, Thwack's voice makes Bank Vole jump. He tightens his grip around her fur to steady himself and then describes how a moving stick helped him after his accident. Brazenly, he tells her he thinks it was kind they brought him back to the exact spot they found him.

'I do wonder if they're changing, or if maybe the rumours about them are wrong,' he confesses.

'Or, maybe after inspecting you, they realised you didn't have anything they wanted,' Thwack snaps.

She quickly changes the subject, telling Bank Vole she has another fun idea. He asks what it is, but instead of explaining, she starts rolling around in the water, so her front and back alternate in the river. Bank Vole, on top of her, panics. Had Thwack lied – is she now trying to drown him? He's unable to hold on to her so to avoid falling into the water, he starts running on the same spot of her body. It helps him stay afloat, so he keeps going. Thwack doesn't change or add anything so evidently this is it; this is the fun. He relaxes a little and tries to follow her rolling rhythm. Thwack is seemingly in her element. She's laughing and shrieking every time her face emerges from underneath the water. Now that he knows what he's doing, Bank Vole gets the giggles too. Running and laughing however eventually causes him to get out of breath. He takes a big inhale and… oh no! His nose isn't just filled with timber and fish. He also smells moving sticks! He yelps and Thwack instantly stops rolling around. Turning their heads to the right, they both see three vertical figures walking towards the riverbank. Apart from after his accident, Bank Vole's never been out in the open around them. He quickly realises he's gone against his own rule, and they don't have anywhere to hide. He coils into a foetal position on Thwack's stomach and begs her to swim away as quickly as she can. He closes his eyes and tries to imagine he's safe in the strawberry bush with Myodes Glareolus. Unfortunately, it doesn't work. He's unable to pretend he's anywhere else as the sickly moving stick smell becomes overpowering. He pleads again for Thwack to move.

'I'll swim away if whilst doing so, we interact with them. I won't leave otherwise,' Thwack threatens. 'Go on, stand up and do a little dance.'

Bank Vole can't believe what she's saying. Despite her sharp, instructive order, he outright refuses. He cannot communicate with them! So, Thwack, true to her word, stays where she is. Bank Vole realises he's trapped and defenceless and that he'll have to yield to her command if he wants to get away. Shaking, he stands up, shuts his eyes, and starts tapping his paws. His legs wobble as Thwack moves too. Whack! Whack! Whack! He hears a clapping sound. Forcing one eye open, he rotates his neck and sees she's hitting her tail up and down. He needs her to swim away, not frolic around! He looks at her, ready to rage at how merry she is. Surprisingly, she's frowning, focused, as if she's determined to get her performance right.

Feeling Bank Vole's eyes on her, she says, 'They can't do anything to you here; we're in the water and I can protect you. Please keep dancing.'

Bank Vole detects a desperation in her voice. He's completely puzzled. If she's not having a good time, why are they doing this? He shuts his eyes again and tries hard to ignore the moving stick shrieks. He focuses on tapping his paws until a wave causes him to fall onto Thwack's front. Gripping onto her fur once more, Bank Vole bravely looks around. To his relief, he discovers they are now at the secluded area he'd taken Thwack to the first time they spoke. He jumps onto the bank immediately.

'Thwack, you played a horrible trick on me!' he yells. 'I thought you were going to avoid them from now on. I thought you wanted to fit in with all of us?'

Thwack, indignant, responds, 'Don't give me that, buddy! We both didn't see them until it was too late. I thought we might as well show ourselves off. I can't have them think I'm afraid of them, I've told you this. Besides, I said I would protect you and I did, didn't I, eh? Oh, they were pathetic, weren't they? Did you hear the sounds they were making? They were fawning over us!'

Bank Vole is dizzy with worry. If any of the animals saw that, they'd think he deliberately went against them. They'll think he's now influenced by Thwack, that he's willing to put them all in danger. He can't believe what's happened. He'd been really enjoying himself! Now he feels like a big stone has rolled over and flattened him and all he can do is lie there and accept the pain. Whether he intended to or not, he's disrespected everyone. They might both be banished from the woods for this.

Thwack places her paws on the bank and tells Bank Vole he's got to stop all this worrying nonsense. 'They should be lenient as I'm still learning. Hard to break a habit right away! Don't be upset, buddy. What happened was a good thing, you'll see. Everything will work out as it should, pal. I can assure you of that.'

Bank Vole doesn't know what Thwack means but is too distressed to enquire. He crawls into a shrub and opts to take the concealed route back home.

# ~ CHAPTER NINE ~

# Reciprocal Relationships

'I never took you for a traitor, Bank Vole. Passionate, definitely. Irrational, possibly. But a traitor, no! I, I just...' Mole places her paw on her forehead and looks up at the sky, too upset to speak.

'It's ok, Mole, we all feel the same,' assures Badger, patting her on the back. 'We're all in shock. How can someone in such a prestigious and sought-after position like the council do this? Someone we consider our friend. How could he dance for animals that murder us?'

He tuts and shakes his head. 'Don't you dare try to deny it, Bank Vole. You can't. Many of us saw what you did. We watched your act of treachery. What do you have to say?'

Bank Vole looks at the feet of the seven animals surrounding his burrow. He can't bring himself to look at their faces. He had wanted to be alone, to lay underground in his dark home and forget about what just happened, but they got to his burrow before he did. When he initially spotted them, he considered running away. He turned to go back into the shrubbery, but mid-spin, saw Rabbit stick her nose in the air. This meant she'd already smelt him. Knowing he couldn't outrun her and that trying to would compound everything, he reluctantly stayed.

He dares to flick his eyes up. In the very brief moment, he sees furrowed eyebrows, folded limbs, head shakes and pursed lips. It's clear they only want him to speak, so they have something to argue about. They're not looking for an explanation, he thinks. Their minds are certain they know what happened. Their flares have presented them with one conclusion, and they can't imagine an alternative. Their minds aren't letting them think of one. He purposely betrayed them and that's that. Nevertheless, Bank Vole feels compelled to speak and prove his innocence.

'Everyone—'

'Wait!' Pine Marten, who is chairing the meeting, interrupts. He asks them to climb up the hill, away from the riverbank, so Thwack can't swim by and hear them. They all do as he says. 'Now, can we all please sit so Bank Vole can see us better?'

Although considerate of Pine Marten, Bank Vole would rather they didn't get comfortable. He wants this to be over quickly so he can be on his own. He starts rubbing the space where his claw used to be, finding strength and comfort in the fact he's faced adversity before and got through it. He can do this.

He builds up the courage while the animals shuffle, wriggle, and writhe to find their desired seating positions. 'I'm sorry. Very, very sorry. I know you're all extremely disappointed in me, and I would be too if I saw what happened. But please, remember your eyes can't tell you everything. It may have looked like Thwack and I started dancing for the hell of it, but that simply isn't true. What happened was... well we had a conversation and decided it was the best thing to do. Please, let me explain, and

## RECIPROCAL RELATIONSHIPS

hopefully, you'll realise we're not the traitors we appear to be.'

Truthfully, Bank Vole hasn't quite been able to figure out what happened and finds it unsettling his mind is going to be processing it at the same time as the others. To give his brain more time to make sense of things, he begins at the reedy, muddy spot.

'So, I found Thwack and told her the rules. All six of them. She only eats sticks and leaves. She doesn't see us as food. She's going to stop cutting down trees. She's not going to sing. Oh, and I can explain why she's been singing. Basically, she's been on her own for a long time and she's become lonely. Some of you may not understand this, as you always have your family or partner around, but loneliness… it's quite crushing. To deal with it and suppress it, some animals develop habits. It's your mind trying to help you cope, right, Pine Marten? This is why Thwack sings loudly, very loudly. Hearing her own voice, well it makes her feel like someone is beside her. Nonsensical to some of you, I am sure. But if you don't get it, it's probably because you're not lonely. Everything can seem odd if you're not experiencing it yourself. Anyway, like I said, she's going to be quieter now, and I am going to try and be her company instead.'

Bank Vole's voice is noticeably unsteady. If you were only able to hear him and not see him, you might think he was sliding down a jagged tree trunk, not standing still on a flat bit of soil.

The animals let him talk and listen as he recounts the fun they were having on the river. It's here that everything luckily starts to add up for Bank Vole. He now realises why Thwack acted the way she did.

'You see, Thwack was scared,' he tells them, sounding much more confident. 'Moving sticks wanted her to perform again. She didn't want to, but she worried that if she didn't, there would be repercussions. She was concerned they'd get angry and take it out on the woods. So, for all of our sakes, she gave them what they wanted, and I unfortunately had to join in. But it was a one-off, never to be repeated. I promise. She really is keen to fit in here.'

His speech leaves him with a terribly dry mouth. To close, he manages to croak, 'Please don't exile us. I hated the experience and was dreadfully afraid!'

Slapping his paw over his eyes, he waits for the shouting to commence. It's Badger's thunderous roar he's scared of the most. He tries to stiffen his body to prevent the booming sound from knocking him over.

'There, there, Bank Vole.'

He jumps as someone is touching the top of his head. It's Mole. She's dabbing him lightly with her snout.

'We're not going to force you to leave. It was reckless to have allowed Thwack to take you somewhere without securing a nearby hiding place, but luckily nobody was hurt.'

Others chime in, agreeing.

'I don't think I completely believe Thwack's story, though,' she continues. 'It seemed like she deliberately called moving sticks over last time. How do we know she didn't do that again? She could be in cahoots with them. They could be sending signals that we're completely in the dark about. I mean, why did she interact with them in the first place? You know, I wouldn't put it past moving sticks to have invented her so they can spy on us. That's why she can't reveal her species name because it doesn't exist.'

## RECIPROCAL RELATIONSHIPS

The whole situation is reminding Bank Vole of fog on a wintery sun-sky. When the fog impacts his vision, he takes tiny steps to avoid sharp debris. He does the same now, believing the less he says, the better. Although he's mightily thankful they're being forgiving, he treads carefully, merely telling them Thwack doesn't want moving sticks to believe she's afraid.

Picking up on Bank Vole's emotional exhaustion, Pine Marten abruptly declares the meeting over. Unhappy, Rabbit lets out a loud groan. She's disappointed their conversation is being wrapped up already. As far as she's concerned, Thwack has been allowed to behave inappropriately again. She wants answers or punishment and tells the council this. 'Are we not even going to explore Mole's suspicions?' she asks indignantly.

'We will know all about Thwack soon, Rabbit,' Pine Marten responds assertively. 'If she follows the rules and continues to stay, then who she is will seep out. Bank Vole asked us to give her a chance, and that's what we're doing. This particular meeting was about the dance for moving sticks. Bank Vole has told us what happened, so I think we can agree that the meeting is over.'

'But Thwack broke the rule that Bank Vole had *just* told her about. How many chances are we going to give her?'

'Rabbit, you said it yourself. Bank Vole had *just* told her. The rules wouldn't have even moved into her memory yet. If this behaviour is repeated, then it'll be a different story. She'll have shown she can't follow our rules and so will certainly be made to leave.'

It is customary for the chair to have the last word so the animals disperse as requested. Before departing, Pine Marten ushers Bank Vole forward.

'How about you and I have another therapy session soon? A lot is going on. It will be good to address how you're feeling,' he whispers. His concern isn't hidden. Neither is his suspicion. 'Remember, whatever you say is confidential. It can be barmy, it can extreme, as long as it's the truth.'

Bank Vole pulls on his whiskers. What's Pine Marten insinuating? He had been completely honest. He'd relayed exactly what had happened. Hadn't he?

Last summer, a younger bank vole entered the woods. Her fur was silky smooth, and her eyes were sparkly like the stars. She looked delicate and pure, as if she should be walking on flower petals instead of mud. At the time of her arrival, Bank Vole and Myodes Glareolus's second round of pups were on their way, and poor Myodes Glareolus was suffering. She was exhausted. On top of that, as the sun was intensely hot, she was unable to leave her cool, dark burrow. Bank Vole was kindly making sure she had everything she needed. It was after dropping off a blackberry to her that he encountered his new neighbour. She was digging herself a hole next to his. The scorching weather meant she too was struggling, so Bank Vole offered to help. This pretty new arrival was chatty and amiable and openly looking to breed. Bank Vole had assured her it shouldn't take her long to find someone. Pleased, she settled into the woods quickly and the two of them became friends.

Things still weren't great for Myodes Glareolus though. After giving birth, her suffering worsened. Being pregnant again had taken its toll. Despite having only lived around 250 sunrises, she was feeling old. She wasn't sure how many more times she could do it. As their species normally has around six to eight litters in a lifetime, she suggested Bank Vole start breeding with the newcomer. She'd heard they were becoming close, and she didn't want him to miss out on having a large and stable lineage. Her suggestion devastated him and made him realise his true feelings. He only wanted her warmth, her affection, and her offspring. It was also around this time that his brain shifted and widened on the back left. At least, that's what he thinks.

To get out of breeding with another, he told her he felt the same. He said he too was tired and could only cope with one more litter. But of course, even after their third and final set were born, his attachment to her didn't dissipate. Each sunrise it kept growing.

As for the other bank vole, Pigeon found her a suitable partner in the woods further down the river, so she left to breed with him. By this point, Bank Vole was glad to see her go. He had sensed she was getting impatient with his lack of courtship, and he'd felt more and more awkward ignoring her obvious hints.

Bank Vole remembers all of this as he approaches Myodes Glareolus's burrow. He knows he shouldn't be going to see her. Pine Marten strictly told him not to, but after all the recent drama, he wants to be with the one animal that always makes him feel better.

He steps into her home to see if she's there. She's lying on her back with her mouth open, napping. As you should never wake a sleeping rodent, he retracts his steps, crawling backwards to leave.

Thud! Unfortunately, just as he reaches the entrance, he slips and crashes, narrowly avoiding her. She wakes up immediately.

'I didn't want to disturb you! I had tried to go quietly, but your burrow is too smooth, it must be because of all your sweeping. It's actually quite dangerous!' Bank Vole sulks, massaging his back.

Myodes Glareolus stretches and waits for her brain to leave dream-woods. When it does, she ignores his silly excuse and studies the bank vole in front of her. He hasn't been sitting in her home like this for a long time, and she notices a stark contrast between the face she used to see here and the one she's looking at now. Gone are the plump, soft cheeks and the smooth mane of fur. Everything now looks sunken, lined, and frayed. *It must be his antics with moving sticks that's caused this,* she thinks. Muntjac Deer told her all about it.

'Do you fancy going to the hazelnut tree?' she asks.

Bank Vole places his paw on top of the catkin he likes the look of and takes a bite. With each subsequent chomp, he feels more relaxed. He thanks Myodes Glareolus for accompanying him to his favourite tree. What a good idea! She, on the other paw, wishes he would stop showing his gratitude. Each time he says thanks and looks at her, she's having to eat and feign enjoyment. She had been sleeping off an earlier over-indulgence and is now far too full to even eat a crumb! She's relieved when Bank Vole finishes and she's able to throw hers away.

Aware she's only taken him to the tree to be kind, Bank Vole gestures for them to start heading back but Myodes Glareolus has another idea. She pulls lightly on his tail and says she'd like to talk to him about something.

You see, since they've stopped breeding, she feels he has forgotten about her. He doesn't remember her good qualities or the little things she'd tell him about herself. For some reason, this bothers her, and she'd like to, in some way, change this.

## RECIPROCAL RELATIONSHIPS

'Bank Vole, I know you have Pine Marten to open up to now, and as I said before, I think you going to therapy is wonderful... I just wanted to say that I am an attentive listener too. You might have forgotten. Anyway, it was nice when you confided in me about your scary task. I'm here if you ever want to talk about the beast or anything like that again.'

Bank Vole is full and tired. He would much rather just amble back with her by his side, but he can see Myodes Glareolus would like a conversation. He's sure she wants a few of his jokes plonked in as well. Always wanting to please her, he tells her the latest news about Thwack and explains that although she's still somewhat of a mystery, he'd like her to be accepted because he thinks she's lonely.

'If she follows the rules, won't she be accepted then?' Myodes Glareolus asks.

'Who told you about the rules?'

'Muntjac Deer.'

'Of course he did,' Bank Vole mutters. Unless it's classified as confidential, Muntjac Deer eagerly tells everyone everything. 'No, I am not sure she'll be accepted, even if she follows the rules. So many council members are adamant she doesn't belong here. It may look like they're giving her an opportunity to redeem herself, but I don't think many of them are willing to really give her a chance. I think a lot of it has to do with her being private. She's not giving away much. I think it's unfair to disregard her on those grounds though. For all we know, Thwack might have felt judged in her last home, which is why she left. Now, she's protecting herself.'

Myodes Glareolus moves to sit on top of a brown, shrivelled leaf. Ants are marching past, and she doesn't want to be coerced into having any. To keep Bank Vole's attention on her and not the revolting insect, she hits the leaf a few times with her tail.

'You might be right, Bank Vole,' she responds at the same time. 'But you should be careful letting your mind speculate like this. It's filling in gaps it doesn't have the answers to. You're not receiving these thoughts from your memory. If she hasn't told you, you shouldn't really assume.

'I understand the council's concern. However, there are assumptions at play there too. I mean, can we really say we know everyone in our woodlands, or do we just assume we do because they have always lived here? For example, your friend Squirrel seems tough and proud, but I can't tell you much else about him. Badger only ever talks to me about his cubs. I couldn't tell you about his ancestors or his favourite story. And Owl, does he speak at all? In fact, what does anyone really know about any of the owls? We don't ever really question those among us because we're not looking for answers. They're one of us and that's that. If we were to speculate though, I bet there would be a few surprises.'

Bank Vole scratches his chest. Myodes Glareolus is right. The animals are only comfortable with what they're familiar with, even if they don't really know who or what that is.

'If you want to get her accepted and don't think her following the rules will do it, then may I please suggest something? To me, the best relationships are the reciprocal ones. When both parties give and take, and both expect something from each other. When it's not just one way. I believe Thwack is effectively being asked to shut up and pretend she doesn't exist here. That can't make her feel good, and the animals will never see her value. They'll never view her as one of us.

## RECIPROCAL RELATIONSHIPS

'Think about what we all bring to the woodlands, the parts we all play. I help keep it clean; you help keep it harmonious. We all contribute to each other's wellness. We all have these unspoken reciprocal relationships. So, I think if you really want to help your friend, we should think of something she can do for us. Something she can contribute that will enrich our lives and make us all happier. Then, in return, she should be welcomed inland, even if just once, so she can appreciate what we're all doing to make the woods she's living in the wonderful place it is. I bet if she were to really see it, it'll encourage her to want to behave. She'll want to belong. She might think she does now, but because she's physically removed, her mind inevitably will be too.'

Offering advice pleases Myodes Glareolus immensely. She imagines a bright bee entering her body, and as it flies round and round, it's sprinkling her insides with dust pollen from its wings and reigniting the light inside of her, which has dimmed considerably. She feels the warmth radiate externally from her restored glow. She feels revived.

Bank Vole wiggles his nose as he takes in everything she's just said. It seems to make sense, but he can't think how Thwack could make them all happier. Also, she's already being asked to change her behaviour and follow the rules. It almost seems unfair to want more, but he understands that the rules only make her compliant; they don't make her appealing.

'Well, she does have a lot of knowledge and experience. My first thought is that she could teach animals to swim, but I asked one of the visiting geese to do this before and no one turned up for the lesson.'

If he's going to focus on evolution, Myodes Glareolus thinks they're going to be here forever. She tells

## AN EXCEPTIONAL AURA

him to concentrate on what he likes about Thwack and if there's anything she's done that's made him feel good.

Bank Vole's nose twitching stops. He jumps over the catkins and runs circles around her. 'I've got it! I've got it! Those who saw us interacting with moving sticks would have also seen how easily Thwack was able to transport me across the water. She's the missing piece to the relay! How had I not thought of this before? She'll make it safe for me, and we all know how competitive the council are, we'll go to great lengths to win that race. If they say yes, then it's going to be clear what value Thwack brings. It might make them accept her. And she, well, she was desperate to take part... now she can!'

This is why Bank Vole loves Myodes Glareolus. Somehow, she always takes his troubles away, always mends his misery.

Elated, he lets words spill out of his mouth that he usually wouldn't. 'When you were talking about relationships earlier, it made me think about what you give me. Kindness. I can't thank you enough for it, and I hope I bring you something good in return.'

She smiles, straightens the fur on her front and gets something microscopic, nigh-on non-existent, out of her eye.

'Well, I'm glad I've helped you,' she says softly. 'Um, I think we should head back now.'

Bank Vole can tell she's deliberately not looking at him and feels terrible for making her uncomfortable. He should have just thanked her with a joke. She's overdue some anyway. He swallows the ball of pain that's now scorching his throat and curses life for being one big relay race. Just as you combat one struggle, you're simply passed another.

# RECIPROCAL RELATIONSHIPS

'Bank Vole, I've been waiting for you for *ages*! Have you been confusing yourself with a hazelnut tree again?'

Bank Vole is tired, but he humours Pup, telling her he was indeed at the hazelnut tree but had momentarily forgotten because looking at the tree was like looking at his reflection in the river water. 'You must see how similar we look!' he exclaims.

His reply makes Pup laugh uncontrollably. She holds on to her stomach as her whole body reverberates. The fur around her face has been made to stand up again and it manages to remain in place as she giggles away. It reminds Bank Vole of Doctor Hedgehog's spikes. Nevertheless, he seats himself on the opposite side of her, by the entrance of his burrow.

'Good to see you, Pup,' he says whilst picking up a small leaf and blowing it playfully at her. 'How come you've been waiting for me?'

Pup takes a moment to get her breath back. When she does, she sits up, places her paws on each side of her mouth and leans towards him. 'I have a secret. I can only tell you, but you must not tell anyone else,' she whispers.

Bank Vole screws his face up. It wouldn't feel right knowing something his offspring doesn't.

'Come on,' Pup pleads. 'Only you'll understand!'

If this is the case, Bank Vole believes it must be about evolution. Wanting to encourage any thoughts and ideas on the subject, he allows her to tell him.

'I've been hearing about your chats with the beast and how you both escaped moving sticks by dancing for them. I thought it was really cool… so I went to see her myself!'

## AN EXCEPTIONAL AURA

Pup's eyes sparkle with wild excitement. Bank Vole is totally taken aback. His jaw locks in a position that feels very close to the ground. He didn't think anybody was going to talk to Thwack until she'd proven herself. Plus, his offspring had said she's banned her pups from going to the river.

'Pup, I'm not sure you're ready to be mixing with animals like Thwack,' he says protectively. 'Moving sticks could have turned up and Thwack hasn't shown she can hide from them yet.'

Pup dismisses his concern. 'Oh, I'll be safe with her. She's so nice! And I really like that she has her own name. I told her I want to do that, and she said, "Do it then!" Just like that! I came up with some ideas… Notrat, Ratno and Ratyuck, but she said if I'm going to make it clear I'm not a rat, I might as well stick with my impending name Bank Vole. In the end we decided my new name is going to be Tripper! Thwack thought of it. She said the name means you travel. I didn't quite get it at first because I've never been out of our woods, I've not even been across the river, but I think I know why she chose that name now. I travelled to see her, and apart from you, I'm the only other animal who has done that. I dared to go out in the open to the water. So, that's me. I'm Tripper!'

Bank Vole strokes his head repeatedly. He knows he should be telling her not to visit Thwack. He knows that's what he should be focusing on, but his pride and pleasure don't let him. They dominate everything else. This descendant of his with her messy fur, her swirly tail, her new name, she's clearly on the same quest as him! Whether her new name catches on doesn't matter. She wants to help their species progress!

## RECIPROCAL RELATIONSHIPS

He shimmies over to sit next to her and says, 'I'm getting old now. I've lived many sunrises and sunsets, and with that, I've witnessed a lot in these woodlands. But do you want to know what my proudest moment is? Right now.'

He points downwards, touching the soil. 'Tripper is a wonderful name for a bank vole who wants to travel beyond the realms of what we're "meant" to do and who we're "meant" to be.'

Pleased, Tripper nestles her body into his. Feeling her little head rest against him forces Bank Vole to not get carried away. She's still so small, he must be sensible about her safety.

'And look, I like Thwack too, Tripper. But next time you want to visit her, please let me go with you.'

Tripper massages his chest with a head nod. 'Ok, I will. So, are you going to change your name as well?' she asks, her voice muffled against his fur.

'Maybe, if I can think of a good name.'

Tripper's head jerks up. 'I have an idea,' she chuckles. 'Hazelnut!'

Her answer brings her such hilarity that she rolls back and forth and ends up slipping into the burrow. After a brief yelp, her laughter continues, echoing beautifully through Bank Vole's home.

*We may not get to be a family, but we sure are alike,* he thinks as he goes to help her, his face beaming with joy.

Just before Bank Vole settles in for a long, well-deserved sleep, he pokes his head out of his home to look for Thwack. He wants to see if she's following the rules. Spotting her isn't easy at first. She's further away than usual, sitting in front of a conical alder tree on the bank of the adjacent woods. Her rotund body is wider than the tree's trunk. It wouldn't be a good hiding place, not that this is what she's trying to do. She's actually talking to some animals. Bank Vole can definitely see Roe Deer and Shrew. He thinks it could be Stoat by the fallen branch. They keep looking up, so someone else must be talking from a tree hollow. Regardless of who it is, it appears Thwack is making friends! Even though their rules don't apply to the animals opposite, Bank Vole reckons their enforcement has helped make her more tolerable. He hopes that, in time, this will transcend to his side of the river, too. With the plan he's devised, thanks to Myodes Glareolus, he's not sure how it can't.

This may become a relay race he would like to take part in after all.

## ~ CHAPTER TEN ~

# The Return of Pigeon

Pigeon doesn't live her life hiding from moving sticks. In fact, she does the opposite. Very often she flies to the Grey, where moving sticks live. The other animals can't understand it. The Grey sounds awful. Pigeon's told them there are things that can move without using wings or legs. She's said these things are fast, and if an animal gets hit by one, it can kill them (she, of course, excuses moving sticks, believing the fatality unintentional). She also says they've cut down trees and replaced them with things that aren't sentient. She said some places don't have any trees at all.

Although the animals aren't sure what the whole of Earth looks like, they know its reproductive organs live beneath them and that all the other parts of its anatomy exist on top. Rivers, for example are Earth's veins. Flowers are Earth's eyes. Animals make up Earth's appendix and trees are, formidably, Earth's lungs. Blowing in and out of tree trunks, Earth inhales and exhales its own air. So, for moving sticks to have removed trees, they are effectively messing with Earth's respiratory system. All the animals, bar Pigeon, believe moving sticks are up to something sinister. They think they might slowly be trying to suffocate Earth.

But that's not even the worst of it. Pigeon said sometimes when you look down, you can't even see Earth's skin, mud, you just see grey. The animals didn't even know

## AN EXCEPTIONAL AURA

this was possible. They think it's egregious. Every living thing is meant to show its respect to Earth by returning back inside its reproductive organs when it dies. It's an honour to. You've lived upon what Earth's created and now you must give back your nutrients – your body, brain, and soul – so it can create more. The only parts of you that remain above Earth's skin are your descendants and your aura.

Your soul and aura are part of the same essence. Your soul is the energy you create through your thoughts and diet. It circulates around your body, enabling your blood and bones to move. Your aura is dependent on the state of your soul. It feeds off it and creates an intangible and invisible air that you emit and gift unknowingly throughout your life. You bestow it upon others. Every time you have a profound, meaningful effect on someone, be it through kindness, patience, or compassion, a little bit of your aura leaves you and lingers above them. The last of it gets released just before you die, hovering above those who will miss you the most. It remains unseen, but animals know of its existence because even though you're gone, they'll still feel you near. After they perish, your aura unifies and elevates, rising high until it reaches the sky. Here, it crystalises and becomes Earth's bones. Stars.

You can see that, according to the animals, everything is connected. Breaking this cycle, this order, seems most unnatural and they can't fathom what would motivate moving sticks to do it or how Pigeon can bear to be around them. Her stories merely stimulate them to hide in the darkest and deepest corners of the woods. They never, ever want to be found.

It's been many sunrises and sunsets before Pigeon returns to the woods. Her appearance has altered, particularly her purple chest. It is noticeably less vibrant now, almost matching the colour of her grey head and wings. It's as if she's taken on moving stick's landscape, stamping it onto her body in an attempt to understand it better.

Settling herself on a branch overlooking the river, she watches the strange beast as it sleeps in the open on the bank and admires its rich, silky brown fur and strange black oval tail. Annoyingly, she can't see its face. It is out of view, being covered by its paws. To amuse herself, she guesses what it looks like. She suspects it has big, dark eyes like Muntjac Deer, a small but powerful nose like Rabbit and a line-mouth similar to that of Pine Marten's.

She cannot believe a new animal has arrived during her absence. Usually, she's the one with extraordinary news and anecdotes to share. It does peeve her a little. She knows she's being ridiculous and tells her flare to stop acting like a young squab. The thought persists, nevertheless.

While she contemplates what kind of voice the beast has – she's toying between growling or breathy – Bank Vole emerges from his burrow directly beneath her. She's been desperate for him to wake up, so she is thrilled. She watches him shake off the remaining soil that's submerged into his fur and her eyes twinkle as she imagines swooping down and startling him. She weighs up her fun against his fright and decides against it, remembering that Bank Vole had been rather sombre before she left for the Grey so thinks it's best to not shock him in case he's still feeling fragile. Besides, she wouldn't want his screaming to wake the strange beast.

She coos quietly and Bank Vole's head immediately shoots up to look for the owner of that magnificent, mellow sound. 'Pigeon! You're back! What a pleasant surprise!' he squeaks.

## AN EXCEPTIONAL AURA

She dives down to join him on the ground. 'Yes, my friend, and it appears we've got a lot of catching up to do!'

They meander around trees, holes, and mounds, briefly stopping to chat to those they pass. Everyone is delighted to see Pigeon. It's raining lightly so they are treading carefully, Bank Vole especially. He's incurred some bruising after his fall in Myodes Glareolus' burrow and does not want to add to it with another slippage.

Needless to say, Pigeon wants to hear about Thwack, so Bank Vole fills her in with what he knows. His knowledge is, of course, minimal. This means that Pigeon's inquisition – enthusiastic and excited – rapidly turns to frustration. She still feels none the wiser. She rebuffs the council's plan to avoid Thwack and asks Bank Vole to introduce her at the earliest opportunity. The strange creature must open up to somebody!

Bank Vole tries to think what else he should tell his friend, but Thwack's arrival trumps everything. All other events seem inconsequential. He's hoping Pigeon won't ask if he's still sad. She'd done just that before she left, and he wasn't able to tell her why. He believes if anyone else should know, it should be Myodes Glareolus. Obviously, Pine Marten is aware because he's a therapist and Thwack knows for information-seeking purposes. But that's it. It isn't gossip or hearsay, so it shouldn't be treated as such. Luckily, Pigeon steers the conversation in a different direction.

'Well, Bank Vole, I'm all confused about moving sticks. I used to learn a lot about them through their conversations, as you know, but they seem to be having less of them each time I visit. They're engrossed in those rectangular blocks I've told you about. You know, the ones that light up when they touch it? They're like hand extensions. I think they might have plugged their minds into them. These things now store their thoughts, and they tap on them to retrieve flares.

'Whatever they are, they certainly don't help me gain information or increase my knowledge. And the few times I am able to listen to conversations, I seem to come away flustered. I'm beginning to doubt how well I understand their language. I think I've lost confidence ever since the "blow over" comment. I mean, I heard one say it was feeling blue, but it was not what I believe that colour to be. Another said they looked like a drowned rat, but they still looked like a moving stick to me. Maybe they were muddled. I can't be sure. What I am sure of, though, is that this fixation with these rectangular blocks has to stop. Those things damage my plan! If they're not communicating with each other, then there's even less chance of them ever being able to communicate with us again. It means they won't ever return to their real home.'

A twig is blocking the path, so she bends down and uses her beak to move it. 'All is not lost, though. I still have some hope. A few sun-skies ago, there was an injured blue tit and I saw moving sticks help it, just like they did with you. Fundamentally, they're still one of us. I'm convinced! I just need to help them see it.'

Pigeon cocks her head towards Bank Vole, expecting him to ask his usual flurry of questions. Instead, to her surprise, he awards her an even greater pleasure. He tells her he's been thinking something similar recently, although he reckons only some of them hold woodland values. She bobs her neck, watching him as he speaks. He seems older, wiser, with a profundity she hasn't seen before. She wonders what life experience has caused this. *Hopefully, not one that's stopped him from telling good jokes,* she thinks. His moving stick joke about stick insects had her chest juggling for a long time.

'I must tell you the reason I came back,' she coos. 'It's rather alarming. Now, before I tell you, I have to state that I definitely did hear right, even though what the moving stick said sounds strange. So, let me set the scene properly. I was walking across some grass when two moving sticks jogged past me. As they did, I heard one say that ever since it's made its "fort tune," whatever that is, old flames have been coming out of the woodwork. Intrigued and concerned, I flew over to a bench. Can you remember what a bench is? I pretended I was looking for crumbs while they passed me again. This time, I heard the other moving stick say the situation was awful. She advised her friend to be careful. So, I rushed back to see if it was happening here too. Have the trees been on fire?'

Bank Vole shakes his head vigorously. He's finding this a very unsettling conversation.

'Ok good, what a relief! It must be happening to another woods. Hopefully we'll be spared.,' she says.

Bank Vole tells Pigeon they should hold an emergency meeting with the council anyway because it sounds very scary and dangerous, but she struggles to hear him amidst the rain, which has suddenly become a lot heavier. She moves to seek shelter and Bank Vole follows, keen to get away from the relentless smacking droplets. They stand underneath a poplar tree. Bank Vole looks up at the majestic plant and silently thanks its shiny, heart-shaped leaves for offering him protection. Noticing him observing it, Pigeon asks how frequent their vibrations have been recently. When trees talk to one another, the animals feel slight tremors that reverberate throughout the woods. Bank Vole tells her they've become a regular occurrence, definitely more frequent than usual. This doesn't surprise Pigeon. She thinks trees are the wisest of all above Earth. There's a lot happening in the woods and the Grey, and she knows they're bound to be talking about it. Galvanised by the fact they too could be talking about flames, she suggests they listen in.

'Am I right to assume most of you haven't been tuning in and paying attention to them?'

Bank Vole nods.

'I thought as much. You really should. Listening to them gives you a greater understanding of life above Earth. I know it's not easy, but it's worth it.'

Bank Vole knows he and the rest of the council members don't have a good excuse. They understand Tree and hear their voices but never listen hard enough to decipher their words. He ashamedly tells Pigeon he's not sure he even remembers how to.

'This is what I do', she says, elongating her neck, readying herself to teach. 'When everything is still and quiet, when there isn't even a whispering of a breeze, I close my eyes and tap into their vibrations. I identify their rhythm, tune into their voices, and eventually, hear their words. You know, when the sun rises and they wake, they speak in unison. Have you ever heard it? It's like a mantra. Let me see if I can repeat it to you.'

She closes her red eyes and starts muttering to herself. '*Reyulthasreyyi Earth lae eosor.* That's what they say. It effectively means "Wedded to Earth, we soar." They chant it to each other five times.'

'I'll try to listen to them more if you think it's helpful,' Bank Vole replies. 'But if I'm honest, the few times I've listened to them, I'm not quite sure what they mean.

## AN EXCEPTIONAL AURA

That chant, for example Pigeon, I don't know if I understand it?'

'Well, I think it means that by staying close to Earth, never leaving its side, they prosper and grow into the magnificent tall beings they are.'

Bank Vole thinks about what Pigeon's just said while he watches the tree's robust leaves be slapped by the persistent shooting water. He shifts his body and looks right to the top, where the end of the tree reaches the sky. Then he turns his head to look at the trunk. Finally, he lowers his gaze and stares down at the roots.

'It's always comforted me that these colossal beings can stand alone and be proud doing so,' he says. 'I thought they were a shining example of how to hold your own, how to be solo and brave. But I've been wrong, haven't I? They're never on their own. They, as they say, are wedded to Earth. They have formed the purest partnership with the giver of life. They have all they could ever need.'

The rain abates and becomes a soft pattering. The mist that had been obstructing their view subsides, and all that is surrounding them appears clearer with deeper colours. Pigeon, however, looks as if she's still in the midst of a downpour. It's because Bank Vole spoke of partnerships.

Around 250 sunrises ago, Pigeon was in one. She had a partner, and they were inseparable. They would always forage together, always visit the Thicket together. They would build one nest and sleep in there together. Her partner would even venture to the Grey with her on the odd occasion she went. They didn't do much apart at all.

It was truly tragic when he became ill with a disease. No one is sure what caused it. Doctor Hedgehog suspects he either drank some poisonous water or ate something that had bad bacteria in it. It made him rapidly lose weight and he became very melancholy. It was as if there had been a flash of lightning and the blaze had whipped him into a drooping, sorry state. He had never been as garrulous as Pigeon, but he'd been sociable and active. He would always stop to chat if he was passing by and was fantastic at commentating on the relay race. But that all stopped. Bank Vole remembers the stages of his deterioration; how bobbing his neck became a strain and then not long afterwards, opening his beak for water did too.

Pigeon stayed by his side in the hollow of a yew tree and did all she could to make him feel better. She would shoo away anyone who wasn't being positive about his recovery. Eventually, after examining him for the third time, Doctor Hedgehog told Pigeon that Fox had to be called into the woods. She said her partner needed to be returned into Earth. It was his time.

Pigeon was in denial. She insisted a moving stick could cure her pigeon and pleaded for him to be moved to a conspicuous place so one would notice and help. But her Pigeon, her love, with all the strength he could muster, told her Doctor Hedgehog was right. He said he must go. He was in agony.

He stood up slowly and circled her. He spread his tail, puffed his chest, and bowed to her, cooing just like he had when they first met. A dance that had created a wholehearted, deep attachment to one another. A dance of true devotion.

When he rose, they looked lovingly at each other one last time. Then he asked Pigeon to turn away. He staggered to the end of the branch. Each step was more unsteady than the last, but he was determined to keep his dignity. When he reached the edge, he kept his wings close to his body and let his claws lose grip. Fox caught him before he hit the ground.

For a long time afterwards, Pigeon was mute. It was as if her nutrients had died with him, and her body had accidentally remained above Earth.

Some of the animals hoped she would find another partner, as pigeons are allowed to do that. They thought she was missing love. Pigeon refused to even contend with the idea.

It took some persuading, but Pine Marten eventually convinced her to have therapy. Similar to his treatment for Bank Vole, he wanted to immerse her in new situations so new iotas would form. He wanted her to develop thoughts that didn't have any connection to her partner. Thoughts that weren't screaming grief.

It appears to have worked somewhat. Pigeon now dedicates so many of her sunrises to finding out about moving sticks. Her expeditions to the Grey and her faith in them returning has occupied her and ironically, her frequent leaving has enabled the animals to get her back. But, of course, no matter how you train your mind, memories prevail, and judging by Pigeon's pained expression, Bank Vole thinks by mentioning partnerships, he has moved Pigeon's partner from the bottom of her brain to the forefront. He asks if she's ok.

Startled by his voice, she shakes her body and ruffles her feathers. 'The rain has stopped Bank Vole,' she says stoically, ignoring his question. 'Let's head to the Thicket.'

Pigeon's 'old flames coming out of the woodwork' news is not taken lightly. It would have been brushed off if Thwack hadn't arrived, torn down trees and proven Pigeon's previous moving sticks report. Clearly their premonition that 'everything will blow over' was accurate.

Badger is chairing the meeting. He demands they come up with a plan as a cautionary measure in case the trees start burning. A few ideas are put forward, so a vote is cast. The first option is for them to all move towards the river. This way, they can all seek safety in the water if need be. The second option is to carry on as normal, regularly monitoring the trees to detect if they smell of smoke or feel hot. The last option is to ignore it completely and forget Pigeon ever said anything. This is what Muntjac Deer and Squirrel vote for. Muntjac Deer thinks it's better if he doesn't add to his worries. Squirrel too says he doesn't want to be worrying unnecessarily about something that may or may not happen. Plus, if it does, he thinks most will be able to run away. His assumption upsets Rabbit. She reminds him he has many vulnerable neighbours and that she is one of them. Her babies are due any sunrise now, and this news is the last thing she wants to hear. She thinks it would be prudent to move closer to the water, but she'd rather everyone else didn't do the same. She doesn't want to be raising her young in cramped conditions. It had been unbearable when they had all moved underground before, and she shudders as the memory resurfaces. At the same time, she doesn't want to be anywhere near the beast. So, she votes for the second option, and it turns out most of the council feel the same. Squirrel and Owl are asked to check the trees they live in each sunrise. As this isn't much of an effort, they both agree to do it.

With that concluded, Bank Vole forges a way to discuss Thwack's participation in the relay. He thinks there's no better segue than a joke.

## AN EXCEPTIONAL AURA

'What animal in the opposite woods always disappoints?' he squeaks.

The animals can tell just by his giddy face what is going on.

'We're not sure, Bank Vole,' Pine Marten says.

'Roe deer! See what I did? Instead of "oh dear," I said, "roe deer?" Get it?'

Aware the laughs aren't guffaws and that he hasn't quite hit the comedic mark, Bank Vole quickly says, 'Well, now we're talking about Roe Deer, we might as well talk about the relay.'

He stops to clear his throat. Now everyone's facing him his eyes start to widen and dry. Nerves are creeping in. 'Umm… uh… I think Thwack should join our team.'

As expected, he is met with a barrage of rejection. Pine Marten offers his paw so he can address everyone from a raised platform again.

'We all want to win the relay, don't we?' he asks rhetorically. 'Thwack can do that for us! I am proposing she carries me across the river. I know the recent interaction her and I had with moving sticks was atrocious, *but* did you all see how well she was able to transport me? She wouldn't be like Mallard Duck and Carp; she knows what to do. Come on, it's pretty much a guaranteed win! We'd be stupid not to let her. She's adhering to the rules now! And I know she still hasn't revealed her species, but I'll get it out of her, I promise. Also, we let Owl do the relay and he never says a thing about himself! Apologies, Owl, but it's true!'

Owl doesn't flinch. It's the usual suspects who kick up a fuss. Squirrel, Muntjac Deer and Rabbit argue that allowing Thwack to participate will only mean she'll keep expecting more from them.

'Next she's going to think we'll give up our homes for her,' exclaims Squirrel. 'Wash her fur for her, hold sticks up to her mouth for her to chew.'

'Can't you see where she is, Bank Vole? She's in the river, on the periphery of the woods, at the tip of our home. That's how I see her. On the edge, not quite here,' Rabbit adds. 'She can't be accepted because she isn't one of us. She doesn't belong here. She'll slip up with the rules and be gone soon anyway, mark my word.'

'Well, if we don't ask her, the other team might!' Bank Vole says passionately. 'I saw her making friends with them last sunrise.'

At this, Badger shuffles forward, keen to speak. This is new behaviour. Usually, he shouts over everyone, especially when he's chairing. What's even more out of the ordinary is how quiet he is. The animals have to lean forward to catch what he's saying.

'What if Thwack really can help us win?' he asks, looking awkward and embarrassed. 'The relay means so much to us. Imagine us becoming champions! I know how we feel about her, but we can't let the other team gain such an advantage. We can bend the rules we issued if it benefits us. Also, we've got to think about Bank Vole. He can't be swinging from webs again.'

Badger's support is a great confidence boost for Bank Vole. With a tough nut like him on his side, he feels even more determined to make this happen.

'What if I bring Thwack to our relay analysis meeting? Then you can form your own opinion of her. In her company, you'll see she's more like us than you think. Yes, she has flaws; yes, she isn't perfect, but she's an animal like us. She's not a beast.'

## AN EXCEPTIONAL AURA

Bank Vole is happy with the decision. He's allowed to bring Thwack to the meeting. This is absolutely not permission for her to participate in the race – far from it – but it's a step in the right direction. He travels to the riverbank with Pigeon to deliver the news and make introductions. He spots Thwack in the water straight away and motions for her to meet them at a more private area upriver. Having been rolling around, Thwack arrives soaked and out of breath. Pigeon can't help but gasp when they come face to face. The newcomer isn't what she had envisioned at all! She can't stop goggling. Thwack's teeth are dreadful. They remind her of a bright orange food she once ate in the Grey after a little moving stick had dropped it. It was disgusting. She thought it tasted like sewer water. She thinks Thwack's breath smells a bit like that too. Her spinning has got her exhaling heavily and Pigeon has to flap backwards, unable to cope. Now a good distance from the stench, Pigeon collects herself and asks Thwack questions that Bank Vole has already given her the answers to, such as what food she eats and where she sleeps. She wants to get her feeling at ease so she might reveal more. She achieves this to some degree. Except Thwack being comfortable seems to only lead her to share information about others. She tells Pigeon about grey wolves. At first, Pigeon thinks she's referring to whooshies and isn't impressed until Thwack makes it clear she is actually talking about wolves. She claims they still exist, and that they live in packs. Pigeon is captivated. She's always keen to learn. Her exuberance leads her to say that because they're talking about grey wolves, she can share what she knows about the Grey place. She explains to Thwack that she studies moving sticks. While she details their home, Thwack rises out of the water and sits on the bank with her tail between her legs, evidently intrigued. Pigeon unabashedly says she believes moving sticks will eventually return to the woods because there's a void in their lives which will only be filled if they come back.

This belief makes Thwack laugh. It's not a laugh Bank Vole's heard before. It's more of a cackle. It's condescending and engulfs the previously cordial atmosphere.

Irked by Thwack's blatant impertinence, Pigeon retorts, 'Clearly you disagree. Why? Do you know more about moving sticks than I do?'

Her beady eyes glare hypnotically at Thwack. Thwack, unfazed, matches the stare.

'They will never be amongst us. This notion of yours, birdy, is nothing short of ridiculous. They're beneath us and they're only ever going to descend further beneath us,' she says.

Bank Vole did not anticipate this! If anyone was going to be a good advocate for Thwack, he thought it was going to be Pigeon. It had all been going so well!

'Ok, so there's a difference of opinion here,' he says cooly, trying to diffuse the tension. 'Thwack, I don't think calling Pigeon "birdy" is very nice…'

Hearing her name, Thwack diverts her attention from Pigeon to him. She registers what he's said, scratches her chest and rubs her nose. 'So, that was me doing an impression of moose,' she says, sounding poised. 'They're another species I don't believe you have here. They detest moving sticks and what I just said is what they always say. But me, well… you know more about them than I do, Pigeon, and maybe you're right. Who knows what the future of the woods looks like, huh?'

It hadn't been at all obvious Thwack was parodying another animal, but Bank Vole is relieved. He hadn't wanted

## AN EXCEPTIONAL AURA

to believe she was deliberately antagonising Pigeon. Quickly changing the subject, he tells Thwack she can join the relay analysis meeting. Thwack is chuffed and says she's excited to meet everyone.

The chat abruptly ends there. Even though Pigeon hasn't found out Thwack's species, she, for the sake of her nose, insists her and Bank Vole leave. Thwack's been inching closer and closer, and there's only so long any "birdy" can close their beak.

# ~ CHAPTER ELEVEN ~

# *Under Scrutiny*

The analysis meeting that Thwack's attending is when the council members, who are of course also the relay runners, gather in the Thicket to share what they think went well in the last race and what they believe can be improved. Pigeon always leads these meetings now her partner has died. She takes it seriously, like he did, making sure everybody gets their chance to speak.

    She counts the heads as they assemble into the private corner of the Thicket. A male rabbit, the one Rabbit recently bred with, tries to sneak in, alleging Rabbit will need his support if she goes into labour. Despite Pigeon repeatedly refusing entry, he persists. Disgruntled, she flies towards him and lifts her claws, curling them so they're a wasp's length away from his face. He flees instantly. Suffice to say, Pigeon is short-tempered. She's always had her limits, as everybody does, but she's become less tolerant. Life, for her, isn't how it used to be. She doesn't have the patience for inane behaviour – not now that she doesn't have the smart brilliance of someone who would counteract it.

    She's particularly irritable now because Thwack is joining them. She doesn't want her to. She understands why Bank Vole suggested it, and she knows she shouldn't dismiss her over one encounter, but she found her enigmatic when they met, and not in a good way. Her random moose impression was peculiar, bordering on an affront, and the fact she still didn't reveal anything about herself, not even to an animal as cultivated as Pigeon, feels like a snub, and she is, quite frankly, offended.

She scrutinises the new neighbour as she enters the Thicket with Bank Vole. They're the fifth and sixth attendees to arrive. Having just given Thwack a brief tour of the woods, Bank Vole is introducing her to those who are present. Thwack greets them jovially, grinning and extending her paw. The perfunctory nods and grunts she's met with, as well as the shunning of her paw, causes Pigeon to sink her face into her neck, a move she makes when she's deeply gratified.

Not long afterwards, she flies to the roof of the Thicket, making sure to leave a big enough gap between her wings and the twigs so she doesn't injure herself. It's always good to learn from someone else's mishaps, in this case, her poor partner's. She hovers above the council, flapping slowly in the same place.

'Hello from up here! What a big moment this is! Great! Fantastic!' Her partner would speak so enthusiastically and she's endeavouring to do the same. 'Right… just counting heads… I think that's all of us apart from Badger, but he should be here shortly. Ahh, I can see him actually. He's chatting to Badger and Badger. Not really what he should be doing. Anyway, come on into the corner all of you, get closer. Remember, we do not want anyone overhearing us. We must squeeze into a tight space away from the crowds. Come, come. Huddle in. That's good. Ok, well we're ready to begin… oh no, we're still waiting for Badger, aren't we? Badger!'

She swoops over to where he's conversing with his friends and pecks him with her beak. Badger crouches down to protect himself, throwing his paws above his head for armour. He immediately shuffles over to the group, massaging his body dramatically and moaning aloud. Commiserations are absent. Everyone is focusing on the badger-biter who is now standing on a mound Mole's built for her (Owl didn't fancy constructing his traditional nest podium, not for another bird who could do it herself).

'It's that time!' Pigeon announces, her chest pumped and round. 'Earth has gifted us with bright colours galore! We have daffodils in bloom, bluebells shooting up. The sun is raising itself higher in the sky. Babies are being born all around us… your turn is imminent, Rabbit. It can't be long now!'

Rabbit cuts in, begging for it to happen soon. She's uncomfortable and desperate to give birth. The animals offer their support and sympathy until the loud, beating flap of Pigeon's wings forces them to stop. She may have initiated the topic, but she mustn't let them digress.

'The most pleasurable change is the fresh leaves growing on trees,' she continues. 'Spring is upon us, which means the next relay race is too! Now, I've spoken to the crown-making birds and they're available in eight sunsets, so we must all prepare ourselves for then. Prepare ourselves to win!'

The animals cheer enthusiastically, including Thwack, who manages to eclipse their hurrahs with a loud screeching noise. 'Oops,' she says coyly, relishing the group's bafflement. 'That's called a whistle. I do that to alert animals of danger or in times of celebration.'

Bringing a claw up to her mouth, she starts flicking her two front teeth. The animals aren't sure if this is an embarrassed reaction or if she's trying to show what else she can do. Pigeon leaves no time to find out.

# AN EXCEPTIONAL AURA

'Well, this is Thwack, everyone. She is joining us for this analysis meeting, as agreed.' She exudes displeasure. Her voice is unmistakably glacial. 'Moving on, we must all truthfully say what we think worked well in the last race and what didn't. We need lots of feedback and suggestions, so don't be shy. Now, Squirrel, as you're the first to race, please make your way to this mound and tell us what you're thinking.'

Thwack claps as Squirrel walks forward and continues doing so, even after he scowls at her. She appears unbothered by his reproach, smacking her paws even harder when he reaches the mound. This really irks Squirrel, who isn't afraid to show his disdain now he knows he's not on her menu. He expels a guttural growl, opening his mouth as wide as he can for maximum effect. Although Thwack's grin remains, the applause stops, so he flicks his tail rapidly back and forth to psych himself up to speak.

'I thought what worked well in the last race was me picking the leaves at the top of the tree rather than at the bottom. I know it meant I had to travel a longer distance, but they were far easier to pick because they'd been exposed to the sun more and so were slightly drier. They came off the branch with a light touch rather than a harsh tug. I also think I did a good job tying them all together. It was an extremely robust chain.' He pauses, then mumbles, 'What I think didn't work well was the incident with Bank Vole.'

Bank Vole knew his accident was going to be brought up, but he didn't imagine it being used against him. He thinks it's unfair.

'Can I speak next please?'

Mole has startled everyone by requesting to speak ahead of her go. With the attention now on her, Bank Vole is unable to air his grievances. To mollify himself, he vows to target Squirrel when he takes to the mound.

'Well... I guess you can.' Pigeon consents out of shock; no one has ever asked this of her.

Mole crawls up the round, heaped pile of mud she constructed, turns to face them, and enacts her habitual preparatory routine. She stretches and wiggles her claws. She breathes heavily in and out four times. Then she starts tapping her nails against each other. The length of this part varies. Sometimes it's over quickly. Other times it's painfully drawn out. This time, thankfully, it's the former. The nail hitting stops and her shrill voice speaks.

'I'm also pretty smug about my last performance. I dug my hole so quickly. The rest of it was normal, travelling underground for 40 breaths and so on, but the first bit, that was done in record speed. Isn't that right, Pigeon? Didn't you say it ended up being my fastest race?'

Pigeon nods.

'Other aspects of the race were good... but you can't really top reaching record speed.'

Her nails take centre stage again. They're now being tapped for three consecutive intervals. Tap, tap, tap. Stop. Tap, tap, tap. Stop. Bank Vole is convinced he can hear the murmurings of 'Rec-ord speed. Rec-ord Speed' and wonders if this is her intention, drumming her success deep into their brains.

'The weather really didn't help us last time,' she says matter-of-factly. 'It was far too windy. I was lucky being underground, but for those of you who weren't, I'm surprised the leaf chain didn't escape one of your grips. So, I was thinking we could wrap the leaf chain up in future. Put it in an old eggshell maybe? If we stuff it in there it'll be protected from the wind.'

## AN EXCEPTIONAL AURA

Realising this is all she has to say, Pigeon brusquely waves her off the mound. Although leaf chain storage could work, she doesn't think this idea warranted her disrupting their usual sequencing. She beckons Muntjac Deer forward, keen to get back to the correct order of things.

'If Mole gets to push in front just to brag and put forward a suggestion, then I think I should be able to speak next because I'm heavily pregnant. I'd like to get my bit over and done with.'

Pigeon looks at Muntjac Deer, who shrugs at her. He's not bothered if he has to wait. Pigeon is. She wishes she'd been more authoritative. Giving into whims won't lead to a fair experience for everyone, something her partner was vehement about. She resentfully opens her right wing and points it towards the stage. Rabbit hops up with surprising ease, given her excess weight.

'Thank you, Pigeon. What did I want to say? Oh, yes. I'm so glad to have you back, Bank Vole. I don't think your temporary replacement – your offspring – helped us much at all. It was kind of her to step in, but her efforts were lacklustre. It was obvious she didn't really have a proper plan. When Badger passed her the chain, she looked lost, totally out of her depth. I thought the rest of us were real troopers, though. We kept going even after Bank Vole's terrible accident. We were without a key player, and we carried on, so bravo to us.' She jumps down, kicking the mud that trails after her back up the spoilt, flattened mound.

Pigeon has now strategically positioned herself behind Muntjac Deer so she can lightly prick him with a claw and force him forward. His moving, burly figure makes it clear Pigeon will not allow anyone else to interrupt.

After he shares his thoughts, they return to the right order. Pine Marten goes next and is followed by Owl, then

## UNDER SCRUTINY

Badger. With each speech, it becomes apparent that most think Bank Vole not taking part created a great disadvantage. Bank Vole no longer feels upset with what Squirrel said. It's clear now his friend was simply saying they needed him to have a chance at winning. It was a compliment! So, when it's his turn to climb the mound, which Owl has tried to prop up for him, he doesn't try to embarrass Squirrel. Instead, he focuses on something more impactful. He pushes once more for Thwack to help him cross the river. Her sustained smile is enough to encourage him. He's never seen her look so happy. Upon seeing her, you might assume she has a stick wedged in her mouth because her grin is so wide and fixed. Bank Vole knows it's this way because she's amongst them, where she wants to be.

'Alright, thanks, Bank Vole,' Pigeon says after he's pleaded his case and claimed for the second time that Thwack is their best chance of winning.

Pigeon's aware the council are refusing to say anything in front of Thwack because of the rules, but she fancies putting her on the spot, so she asks her to come forward and tell them about herself.

Thwack is elated. She loves public speaking, especially in front of a crowd who have all just spoken. It should highlight that she is by far the best orator.

Speaking loudly, clearly and with unquestionable ease, she says, 'Hello. For those of you who didn't get to meet me earlier, I'm Thwack. I live by the river. I'm sure y'all are aware. I'm getting the sense y'all want to know more about me... well, it's your lucky sunrise! Let me tell you a bit about myself or better yet, let me tell you what other animals say about me. That's bound to be more accurate, right? So, it's well-known I'm great at leading. That I'm decisive, strong. The best at remembering. That memory of mine

## AN EXCEPTIONAL AURA

must be huge! I'm also fantastic at giving speeches, very comfortable, undaunted. Guess y'all can pick up on that right now. Oh, I'm also good at thinking of names. If any of you would like to be called something other than your species, I can come up with a name for you. Pigeon for example, you can be called Nipper because of the way you bit Badger. Owl, you could be called Angst because your eyes are so close to one another, it's like they're terrified of being apart. Squirrel, I'd call you Bush because your tail reminds me of one. See, it doesn't take me long.'

She leans forward, veering closer to the group. Her voice becomes deeper and slower as she tries to address them earnestly. 'Now, I am very confident in my ability to swim Bank Vole from your side of the river to the other so he can place the leaf chain on the crown. It would be wonderful to take part. I look at every one of you now and can see you're all heroes. Strong in one form or another. You're a banded union and when you work together with a belief in a common goal, I believe you can achieve many things. But with me by your side, well, you become an invincible force. Indestructible and unconquerable. You don't need hope anymore. You have assurance. Do you know of any other animal that has travelled across the biggest river and survived unscathed? That's me. You will never meet another more determined and more able. I can destr– I can win anything. If this race means as much to y'all as I've heard it does, then guys, what you need to succeed is right here. Thank you for listening; it's been a pleasure having y'all meet me.'

She continues to stand on the very tip of the stage with her back hunched and neck elongated. The curved stance makes it look like she's about to topple onto everyone. Pigeon suspects it is in fact her desperately waiting for an applause. Well, she won't do that, but she'll certainly take this opportunity to ask a question.

'What we would like to know most about you Thwack, is what your species is called. Are you going to tell us?'

Thwack moves her mouth without emitting sound. When words do come out, they're uttered incoherently.

'I'm sorry, I didn't quite get that.'

'Please leave it, Pigeon. Thwack will tell me when she's ready.' Bank Vole rescues his ill-at-ease friend. He knows the situation is strange, that your species shouldn't be a secret, but he doesn't want his lonely companion to feel uncomfortable.

Pigeon thought she'd had Thwack cornered. She thought they were finally going to find out who she is. She's aware the council had awarded Bank Vole this task, but she'd thought it had made sense to enquire now. Everyone else's silence makes it clear she unfortunately has to accept Bank Vole's plea, so she drops the questioning. With nothing left to say, she wraps up the meeting. The ground feels very cold on her feet anyway, and she wants to perch on a branch as soon as possible.

She flutters upwards, curtly tells Thwack to wait for a decision, announces to everyone else that first practice will start the following sunset and, finally, wishes Rabbit luck with her imminent labour. Then, she bats her wings together in one swishing motion and declares the meeting over.

Bank Vole and Thwack walk out of the Thicket together. Pigeon decides to join the two of them, hoping she'll get to talk to her friend alone at some point. Frustratingly, they saunter slowly towards the water, during which time she has to listen to Thwack talk about her own chairing abilities. As if that wasn't bad enough, she also tells

## AN EXCEPTIONAL AURA

Pigeon she can give her commentating tips because she has 'commentated a thing or two in her life.' Now this ruffles Pigeon's feathers. Her partner taught her everything she needs to know, thank you very much. Bank Vole, ignorant to her irritation, asks Thwack what she's commentated on.

'Oh, the chipmunks challenge!' Thwack says. 'These animals, they look a bit like Squirrel but they're smaller. Anyway, they have pouches inside of their cheeks to store food so I would count how many acorns each of them was able to put in their mouth and let everybody know the winner. It was great fun! Ahh, there's the river. I'm off. I'm far too dry and need to swim.'

Learning about chipmunks was actually rather interesting for Pigeon, but she's glad she's finally got Bank Vole to herself. Now she can let rip.

'Wow, she's an unusual creature, that Thwack. Is it normal for her to be so boastful? And don't you think her flattery towards us seems forced? Also, did she get completely carried away with her speech or am I imagining things? It was as if she thought she was leading us through a real battle or something.'

She knows as soon as Bank Vole sighs that she's chosen the wrong animal to confide in. She should have kept her beak shut.

'I like her, Pigeon. Perhaps you've spent too much time with moving sticks and the cynicism you think they're plagued with is creeping into you too. She was attentive and enthusiastic in that meeting, nothing else.'

Pigeon immediately abandons all talk about Thwack. She can see the animal is a sensitive subject for Bank Vole and doesn't want to argue with him. She opts to keep their conversation light, sharing a funny story she recently heard about a confused old goose. Afterwards, she flies to an unoccupied tree. She sits in it and thinks about what Bank Vole said. Is she being unnecessarily negative about Thwack? Her thoughts on the subject become very loud. They get louder and louder until they begin to consume and exhaust her. It's not sunset yet; she shouldn't sleep, so she tries to re-energise herself by tuning into other noises around her. Indulging herself in the scuffles of wrestling badger cubs and a high-pitched cawing crow, her flares quieten. When the cubs roll further away and the crow reunites with the friend it was calling for, a quiet stillness descends upon her surroundings. She knows where to turn her attention next. Closing her eyes, she hooks her claws tight around the branch she's resting on. She hasn't been able to listen to the trees since she's returned, but she wants to know if they're worried about old flames. She connects with the tree's cavernous breath by drawing it in through the soles of her feet. It's happening. She's zoning into their rhythmic vibrations, hearing slow, vigorous whirring. Remaining completely focused, she waits patiently for their sound to morph into a noise she understands. She gathers they are speaking in unison again, chanting something. They're excited. She feels their excitement pulsate through her.

She's hearing them, their words are becoming intelligible. Whoooosh! The wind picks up, her tail feathers uncontrollably flicker, and the crow, having lost her friend again through the gust, resumes cawing. The moment is over.

The talking trees fade away from her. They become muffled, distant. Eventually, she loses them completely. What she thinks she heard them say was, '*Earth's muthserli faa dor hayrr. Al reorsyys uposmers.*' 'Earth's patience has been honoured. Life is being restored.' She's pretty certain this was it. She repeats the chant again. Yes, she thinks, it's anti-climactic, nothing to do with old flames, but it would make sense. There is abundant new life around. Colour and food are, in a way, being brought back. Yes, that must have been it. Obviously, they are celebrating spring.

While Pigeon listens to the eyes of the Earth, Bank Vole tidies around his burrow. The recent rain has littered it with leaves and debris, which keep falling into his home and waking him up. He takes a bite out of each leaf as he moves them away, attempting to achieve two things at the same time: a clear entrance and a full stomach. After all the big items are shifted, he copies Myodes Glareolus's sweeping technique. He spins round and round, tail in paw until he sees his offspring and Tripper emerge from their burrow.

'Hi!' he says, releasing his tail immediately so he can use the paw that had been holding it to wave at them.

'We're in a bit of a rush, Bank Vole,' his offspring snaps, out of breath from arguing. '*She* is going to join the choir. Robin says they have spaces available. She just needs to be kept busy. Too much fussing about her fur and her name. I've had enough. She can represent bank voles and show off her squeak.'

She marches away while Tripper, fur still pushed forward, traipses behind. Bank Vole scuttles over to her. 'I don't want to go to choir!' she wails when he reaches her side. 'I already know my sound. I'm going to hate this!'

She lowers her body and takes tiny steps, one foot barely moving in front of the other. Her petulant sulking and slow snail pace amuse Bank Vole, but he resists laughing. He wants to support his offspring, so he tells her she might actually enjoy squeaking to bird music and that Thwack will undoubtedly want to hear all about it because she loves singing. 'She could join too if the rules get lifted.'

This news makes Tripper's whole demeanour change in an instant. Her body rises and there's a revived boost in her walk. 'If Thwack joins the choir, then it'll be the coolest. I'd definitely like it then.'

'Well, why don't you and I visit Thwack soon so you can fill her in?' Bank Vole proposes, on the condition his offspring approves. Now he knows Tripper's secret isn't about evolution, he doesn't want to leave her in the dark. Tripper frowns while she contemplates the idea.

'Well, I guess she might approve of my new friendship if you're there too,' she says. 'You are older and know Thwack well. Although she does say you're a fantasist. I can't remember what she said that means, but will it stop her letting me go with you? She said you suffer because of it. What does it mean?'

Before responding, Bank Vole ponders over Tripper's words. A fantasist. Does his offspring view that as good or bad, he wonders. He's so used to only seeing the side of her that disagrees with him, the side that finds him irritating. He forgets that she can display smidgens of gaiety and interest too. She does occasionally ask him questions, has smiled at his jokes. So, she might be calling him a fantasist because of his wishes. She could think they're endearing. Or, she could label him that because she thinks he's indulgent and avoiding reality.

The complexity of her feelings makes him laugh a little, mainly because he's cognizant of his own ambivalence towards her as well. Yes, he seeks her company. He does like to know what she's up to and does find her entertaining. Her attitude, though, can be tiresome. She can be selfish and hypocritical. He often sees her fixating on her appearance, yet she's now criticising Tripper for doing the same thing.

He laughs again and shakes his head. His offspring staying in the woods has given him a tiny glimpse into family life. Her remaining has allowed him to witness the formation of her character and observe what he and Myodes Glareolus produced. He stops walking and clenches his claws into the soil; all thoughts of laughter quickly vanish. He tries to steady himself as the familiar pangs of sorrow soar through his chest and weaken his breath.

He knows all her negative attributes are forgivable. They're insignificant when he thinks about how much she means to him. Why can't he just be her dad? He yearns to do what dads do. He wants to sit inside her burrow and listen to her complain about her quarrelsome pups. He wants to make her feel better with special dad-daughter jokes. He wants to hug her when she's been brave; he wants to teach her what he's learned in life. Most of all, he wants her to want him around. The sorrow trickles down from his chest and surges deep into his bones. He has so much love to give, but nobody wants it. Nobody wants it because he shouldn't have it in the first place. Bank voles are meant to be alone.

He feels a tug on his leg.

'Bank Vole!' Tripper says gruffly. 'You're acting like I'm not here. You see me, don't you? Come on, I want you to tell me! I've been asking and asking. What is a fantasist?'

# ~ CHAPTER TWELVE ~

# An Ultimatum

There are some things that are universally felt and understood. Some things that all animals, no matter your species, can agree on. For example, sleep is better undisturbed. It's better to be near water than far from it. It's frustrating when someone has something you want. And it is darn infuriating when you think you're making progress to find out you're not.

Word has reached Bank Vole from none other than rumour-spreader Muntjac Deer that Thwack has also agreed to help the opposing team's Shrew cross the river in the race. If true, then all hope of her becoming friends with the council is lost. His efforts will have gone to waste.

He tries not to let Muntjac Deer's beaming smile bother him. He knows why his friend is happy. The council could banish Thwack on grounds of disloyalty, which Muntjac Deer would like because, unlike the others, he's still scared of her. Bank Vole feels he can't be annoyed, for that's another thing that's universal, isn't it? No one wants to be perpetually afraid.

He cradles his head in his paws. How does Muntjac Deer find out everything? In the woods where Bank Vole was born, Adder was able to shed her skin against a rock. The old skin would peel off and she'd slither away, clean and shiny. He wonders if Muntjac Deer can do something similar with his ears. If he has layers of them, he can tear one set off at a time and plant them discreetly around the woods to hear everyone's conversations.

He lets out a squeaky groan. Thwack must know she has to pick a side! How can she be able to cross the widest river and have so much animal knowledge yet not understand the fundamentals of competition? You can't be neutral and compete!

Lifting his head, he addresses the potential ear-ripper. 'I'll visit Thwack at sunset and find out what's going on. In the meantime, can you please not tell anyone? You've only heard whisperings, so let's wait to hear from her first.'

The request makes Muntjac Deer mumble something unintelligible, spin around and run off. Judging by his hasty exist, Bank Vole gathers the deed's already been done. The rumour has been spread. Well, it looks like he's got his paws full! This is certainly taking up space in his mind like Pine Marten wanted. Is it enough to move the thoughts of Myodes Glareolus into his memory, though? He knows the answer and now that he has a therapy session, soon Pine Marten will too.

It's hot, so Bank Vole walks slowly to the oak tree and tries to stay in the shade. He hopes the heat doesn't persist because he doesn't want to race in it. *Although I'd prefer this to rain*, he thinks. The thought of being soaked reminds Bank Vole that he's soon going to be shivering and uncomfortable, dripping in Pine Marten's slobbery saliva. His walk becomes even slower.

When he eventually gets to the oak's roots, Pine Marten opens his mouth wide and dips his neck, ready to collect Bank Vole in the same way he always does. Seeing

## AN ULTIMATUM

the advancing slimy, pink tongue prompts Bank Vole to take action. 'No, I can't! No!'

Pine Marten snaps his mouth shut and leans away. He sees Bank Vole's curled himself up into a ball and is hugging his body tightly. He tries to unravel him with a gentle nudge, but his patient continues to hold his body close.

'What is it? You can tell me!'

Bank Vole hesitates, then opening only one eye, says quietly, 'I hate the way we travel up the tree. I get so cold and wet. Please can you lie on the ground so I can climb on your back? Then I'll hold on to your fur tightly and stay warm.'

Relieved nothing terrible has happened, Pine Marten's shoulders drop. His jaw, however, doesn't loosen. He feels conflicted. He wants to ease Bank Vole's troubles, but there was a reason he suggested the mouth method of transportation. He despises spoiling his shiny fur. He's tempted to refuse, to tell Bank Vole it's not possible. He knows a good therapist would appease his patient though. So, he dutifully lies chest down on the ground. He senses a light dabbing as Bank Vole crawls towards his neck and waits to feel a gentle latching of claws around his nape. As soon as he does, he lifts his body and scales the tree.

Upon entering the tree hollow, Bank Vole jumps down energetically, delighted he doesn't have to wring his fur. The same cannot be said for Pine Marten. He examines his own fur meticulously, dusting off all traces of mud. What he's left with afterwards causes great anguish. The shine has disappeared. Trying hard to ignore the lack of gloss, he throws himself into therapy. Carrying out his routine inspection, he pokes his head out of the hole to double-check no one is listening in.

'It's the owls you've got to watch out for,' he whispers, rotating his head upwards to scan the canopy. 'Anything that is able to hunt mice can be as quiet as them. I don't think I can detect any… yes, it looks like we're alone. I did see Swallow talking to Blackbird a few trees over, but they flew off when they saw us ascending the oak. I think we're safe to start.'

Back inside their meeting space, he crouches down to sit on Bank Vole's left. This time, though, he stretches his legs out and slides his body downwards so he's effectively lying down, with only his neck and face upright. In this slumped position, he breathes in and out deeply and asks Bank Vole to do the same. He starts to speak slowly, deliberately elongating each word. 'I waaant usss to sychronissse ourrr breathiiing. I beeelievvve thiiisss wiiiill creeeaaate bettterr aliiiignmenttt aaaand connectiiivityyy.'

They breathe in. Pine Marten places one paw in front of Bank Vole and taps the other on his stomach five times. He exhales dramatically and gestures for Bank Vole to do the same. Bank Vole lifts a paw in Pine Marten's direction and feels his warm breath blow onto it. After seven rounds, his paw is nice and warm, and the rhythmic breathing is soothing him to sleep. His eyes are heavy, and he wonders if they could delay therapy until after he's had a snooze.

'Now, I see you are close to drifting off. You are very relaxed. This is good,' Pine Marten says, placing his paw back down beside him. 'Your mind will be slower; it will only focus on my questions. It's too tired to have its own internal conversations. Too tired…'

He continues to drag each word, speaking substantially softer at the end of each sentence. Evidently,

## AN ULTIMATUM

Pine Marten wants Bank Vole to be this sleepy. A nap is out of the question.

'Tell me truthfully, Bank Vole, have you kept yourself busy with Thwack? What are your flares saying now?'

Bank Vole is so drowsy it takes him a while to speak. Talking feels like an effort, so he uses as few words as possible. 'Yes, time with Thwack. Still want forever with Myodes Glareolus.'

Pine Marten lets out a sigh, which he swiftly pretends is a yawn. He doesn't want to startle Bank Vole, but he cannot ignore the kindling of shock and discontent that has sparked inside of him. How could his mind be unchanged? He's always found a way for his patients to move on, to cope. They haven't miraculously recovered; it's pretty impossible to when you have a memory, but he's enabled them to function without the constant torment. His patients have all managed to focus on something else and become engrossed in something new, and it's caused different iotas to pass through their brains. With these new thoughts, their memory resurfaces experiences that have produced similar feelings and removes those that are doused in misery, trauma, or pain. These end up sinking further down the brain. They become uncommon and strange. For some, they become almost inaccessible.

When Pine Marten's patients discover this healing, he likes to think they're staring at the sun and what they originally sought therapy for is now a shadow. It's there, and it will always be there, but it's behind them, no longer in their viewpoint. If asked about it, they know they could simply turn their heads and see it. Most, though, he believes, would choose not to. It's because animals are habitual. They clutch on to what's familiar. They want to remain facing forward, with light in their eyes. They don't want to go back to the darkness.

The only time therapy has been close to not working was with Pigeon. At the start of their sessions, she was in a very sad state and seemed reluctant to be anything else. Being in mourning, only thinking about her Pigeon, made her feel close to him. It took a while for Pine Marten to help her. Eventually though, she started to fixate on moving sticks and having picked up on her intrigue, Pine Marten had encouraged her to revel in it. By doing so, different iotas began to pass through. Admittedly, most of these continued to be ones that travel to the left. Moving sticks upset Pigeon, they frustrate and confuse her. This is why, at first, Pine Marten had worried it wasn't working. She didn't seem to have escaped her affliction because she wasn't producing feelings of satisfaction. Luckily, though, there was one particular left iota that kept appearing and became more and more frequent. It was an iota that trumped them all. Curiosity. This is an insatiable feeling; it's greedy and unappeasable. But it's been the key to Pigeon's survival. What she can learn about moving sticks is endless. Her mind can always be occupied with them. There's always more to discover. So, Pigeon, too, now has a shadow. But unlike Pine Marten's other patients, her shadow is a comfort. She thinks of it as her Pigeon standing behind her and that the scatterings of light that filter through the trees and into her life, he can see too. She can feel his aura and knows that until they're together, twinkling side by side in the sky, she has a mission to accomplish. She must focus on her quest to return moving sticks to the woods.

For Pine Marten, Pigeon shows how successful and adaptable his therapy is. Her case demonstrates that something or someone doesn't even have to be buried in the

## AN ULTIMATUM

depths of a brain's memory for a sufferer to feel better. They don't even have to pass right iotas. He unwittingly tuts aloud. He doesn't understand why it's not working with Bank Vole. Thwack should be a huge distraction. She's new, peculiar, hard work. Bank Vole should be reacting like Pigeon. Even if left iotas are still travelling through, they should be curious ones. It's very unsettling. He raises a claw and uses his normal tone of voice to count.

'Let's list everything we've tried so far. When you first told me your mind was getting you to feel sad, I told you to ignore it as best as you can. It persevered. In fact, you said the more you tried to ignore it, the louder the flares got, so that didn't work. That was number one.'

A second claw appears. 'Number two, I tested a new idea of mine by asking you to walk around with your head leaning to the right. You said that gave you bad neck ache and stopped after just one sun-sky. Not long after that, you revealed your feelings for Myodes Glareolus, so I unleashed the third approach. This was to follow my very successful method, one that has worked on all my previous patients. We tried to distract you. Thwack's arrival was the perfect opportunity for you to zone in on a new situation. Throw the entirety of yourself into that project. It offered you a chance to form a novel orb and build new flares to replace the ones you have permanently stored of Myodes Glareolus. But no. Futile. They're clearly stuck. So, let's go to my fourth suggestion...'

Pine Marten hasn't thought of it yet, so his voice trails off while he tries to come up with something. During the silence, Bank Vole stares at the tree trunk opposite and quietly lists all the colours he sees within the bark. Brown, red, orange, they're glaringly obvious. He keeps looking. As his gaze intensifies, he suddenly identifies distinct markings of yellow, green, even purple. He thinks this over. The other colours were always there, but it took him some time to see them. *Can the same be applied to animals*, he wonders? If properly explored, could they all have more to them? Does he even need bank voles to evolve, or do they already have a talent or skill that is waiting to be discovered? Have they already got love buried deep inside and only Bank Vole's found it?

'Before I deliver the fourth suggestion, have you heard I've got more descendants on the way?' Pine Marten disrupts Bank Vole's wild, enraptured thoughts. 'I hope this doesn't make you feel worse, but I must speak of it because you're my friend, and, well, I don't want you to hear it from anyone else. I've bred with a new pine marten. She was passing through some sunrises ago. I spotted her and naturally we started talking. Absolutely gorgeous, breathtaking fur. You know me, I didn't hesitate to show her what I've got. Stood up casually so she could see what good shape I'm in. Then dug rapidly to dazzle her with my strength and dexterity. Never fails to impress. Afterwards I circled her so she could get a good whiff of my scent. I tell you, she was looking at me with total bewilderment. I'm very good at this courting thing. There's no point being modest about it.'

Bank Vole assumes she didn't inspect his ears at any point. That wax would cause anyone to scarper. *Attractive but not observant*, he chuckles to himself.

'My fourth suggestion would be to visit Doctor Hedgehog. I so desperately wanted to help you, Bank Vole. I had hoped talking would work and had vouched for Thwack to stay purely so you could be distracted, but it's failed. I've failed. It's clear you need physical attention.'

## AN ULTIMATUM

'I'm not going to see Dr Hedgehog,' Bank Vole shrieks. His body has instantly stiffened. 'She'll bash my head open with the conkers she collects! I've heard she uses stag beetle pincers to remove iotas.' His voice breaks as he tries to gasp for air. 'After I had my accident, Muntjac Deer said she would have chopped all my paws off to give me better balance! But look at me, I'm fine! Sometimes I think it was a miracle a moving stick found me!'

'Calm down, Bank Vole,' Pine Marten says softly, pushing his body up to sit tall. 'I know her medical practices very well. She only dissects your brain if you're already dead and the animal eating you has agreed to leave that bit to her. No, I think when it comes to you, she'll likely get you to eat some special fungi or perhaps sample a minuscule piece of mandrake. Consuming one of these will reveal your inner thoughts, ones your mind harbours without you really being aware. Doctor Hedgehog calls them hidden thoughts. I've mentioned them to you before, haven't I? She's actually just found out how they work.'

He places a paw under his chin and rubs it sideways. Somehow he needs to condense Doctor Hedgehog's complex and lengthy report into something concise. 'Ok, basically, our mind is a very private place,' he says, moving his paw towards his nose and sliding it down the ridge. 'Probably the most private place on top of Earth. Minds are so private, they can even obscure or block thoughts from us. Our thoughts usually come from an orb colliding with an iota to spark a flare, right? Well, infrequently, the orb and iota latch on to one another instead and produce a slow, dim sizzle. This is less potent than a flare, so quickly gets pushed to the back of the mind, effectively becoming "hidden." However, as it's still burning, you're still thinking it, you're just not fully aware you are. Incredible, huh? She's brilliant,

Doctor Hedgehog. Now all she has left to figure out is imagination and dreams. Anyway, where was I going with this? Ahh yes, she's had previous patients of hers eat one of the foods I mentioned, the fungi or the mandrake, and they end up saying very insightful things. Well, to some it may sound like gobbledy-gook, but to Doctor Hedgehog, it often reveals a lot. In your case, you might say something that explains how your mind came to think the way it does. That in turn could help either myself or Doctor Hedgehog work out a remedy to rectify it. I really am sorry, but I think this is the route we have to take. This has gone on long enough. You must see we need to fix you.'

This therapy session has catapulted from sleepy to scary, and Bank Vole is now riddled with fear. 'But Pine Marten, if you haven't been able to help me like you have everyone else then maybe it's because I don't need anything mending,' he cries. 'Maybe I'm simply the first of my kind who realises we can love. That love is in us, and we didn't know it! It doesn't make me a medical case; it makes me special, someone who should not be tampered with! Or you could just be witnessing evolution right in front of your very eyes. You don't want Doctor Hedgehog to hinder progression, do you?'

'I don't think this is a case of evolution, Bank Vole,' Pine Marten says shaking his head. 'Your life would be improving if you were evolving; you would be adapting to your environment in a way that suits the present. You, however, have told me you feel incomplete. You feel lonely. You have feelings that are unrequited, that are never going to be met with mutual affection. That's not making you feel better. That's not making your life easier! It doesn't match the definition of evolution. We need to do something. We

# AN ULTIMATUM

don't have any other choice. You can't expect me to sit back and watch you suffer, Bank Vole. You're my friend.'

'But I didn't confide in you as a friend, I confided in you as a therapist,' Bank Vole replies.

'Fine. My professional advice is that you try to end this suffering immediately. I urge you.' Pine Marten touches his nose and extends his paw to illustrate his sincerity and diffuse any hostility.

Bank Vole doesn't place his on top. Instead, with his head down, he muffles, 'I may be feeling incomplete without her by my side, but that yearning is better than being numb of real feelings, lost in the notion that because we don't love, we're only here for our future species' gain. Not to be fulfilled, not to be different... just to keep our species going. If I can't love, well then, I might as well just be a body without a mind, without memories, without a soul. You say we evolve to improve our lives, but surely, if our life is as empty as this, then evolution is a farce.'

Pine Marten was concerned for him before, but now he's really worried. To speak in this way, with such passionate revulsion for the life he has, it's nothing short of disturbing. It makes him think the worst has happened. His wretched mind with its warped thoughts has taken over. It's ravaged him. He's allowed it to have complete control. If left untreated, it could turn him against everything. It could stop thoughts of socialisation or hunger, so Bank Vole leaves the council, abandons his friends, and stops eating. If Pine Marten doesn't act, Bank Vole's life could end prematurely, and he'll return into Earth, having spent his last few sunrises shrivelled under the weight of his own deception. Pine Marten knows he must be savagely honest.

Keeping his paw held out in front of him, he says, 'Bank Vole, listen to me. You do not have a hole in the back of your brain. What's happening is your mind is devouring you. Tricking you. It all started when you were breeding with Myodes Glareolus. You were fond of her then, as you should have been, but it decided to keep those feelings in your mind. Now, it's deliberately letting left iotas through. It's forcing you to think certain things and make wrong decisions. If you don't believe me, think about the incident with moving sticks recently. When you described what happened to us outside your burrow, didn't your mind make you lie about Thwack's involvement? It made up that she got you both dancing for our protection but that's not what she was doing, is it? See, your mind is controlling you and scheming for you to be dishonest, for you to say things you shouldn't. It's all part of its plan to dominate you.'

Bank Vole is about to argue that he hadn't lied. He had just been able to work out what had happened. Ok, Thwack hadn't told him. Perhaps it had been assumptive, but he had wanted to view her favourably. He was trying to save her from banishment. Free her from the loneliness she's crippled with. He had good intentions. That doesn't mean his mind is deceitful. Does it?

He tries to imagine what his mind would be like if it wasn't controlling him and consuming him with thoughts of Myodes Glareolus. What he conjures is a dull space, one that's bleak and bare like tree branches mid-winter. Everything, all that matters and is meaningful, leads to thoughts of her. She is his purpose, his focus and his beautiful distraction. He realises he doesn't care if his mind is tricking him. It's offering him a boundless appreciation for her, and he can't think of a better way to live.

'Pine Marten, as I sit here with you now, I can tell you there are many things I don't understand above Earth, but one thing I am sure of is that I want to love her until the

## AN ULTIMATUM

moment I close my eyes, takes my last breath and my heart pumps its final beat.'

'I have to give you an ultimatum then, Bank Vole,' Pine Marten says sternly. 'Either you see Doctor Hedgehog, or you tell Myodes Glareolus. It's one or the other. If you choose the latter and she tells you to leave, we'll miss you terribly. You know that. But I don't think it'll be bad for you in the long run. I believe without her there, your mind will move her into your memory, hide her away, never to resurface. You'll create new orbs that will be met with healthier iotas. You'll never feel lonely again. Or, you can stay here, and Doctor Hedgehog will try to force these thoughts to go. The decision is yours. Either way, Bank Vole, this torture must cease.'

Bank Vole, sombre, asks to be lifted down the tree. He feels trapped, and sitting inside a small semi-enclosed cavity is making the claustrophobia worse. How can he decide? He doesn't want his brain to lose his love for Myodes Glareolus. He also doesn't want to leave and never see her pretty berry-stained face again.

When they reach the tree's roots, he jumps off Pine Marten's back and tries desperately one last time to prove he's rational with a healthy mind. 'This really could just be bank vole evolution. We all have to start somewhere. I could simply be the first bank vole to love, and we could quietly leave it as that. I can stop bothering you with my feelings and keep the void to myself. I'll love Myodes Glareolus secretly and not disrupt any traditions. Pine Marten, I'm not causing any harm. Please don't cause harm to me.'

He walks away without saying goodbye. Pine Marten sighs with sadness as he watches his friend leave. Not all animals are meant to love. The bond is real; he knows this, but only a few tenacious, resilient species can do it.

Effectively, it's a mutual entrapment, filled with compromises and duties. Love is for those who can see past flaws, who know their partner isn't perfect but want to spend each moment with them anyway. This isn't Bank Vole. He claims it's love, but he has never said a bad word about Myodes Glareolus. When he talks about her quirks, he laughs at them as if they amuse him. It's clearly a delusion, Pine Marten decides. A trick of the mind. An obsession with wanting what others have. A desire to evolve. It's a myriad of things, but it's almost certainly – no, unequivocally – not love.

# ~ CHAPTER THIRTEEN ~

# Letting the Heart Speak

At first Bank Vole's offspring refused to let Tripper go anywhere near Thwack. She was outraged at Bank Vole for even suggesting it. Her opinion changed, however, when Tripper revealed she'd already paid her a visit and had done so alone. She realised she'd relinquished absolute authority over her pup the moment she'd allowed her to roam on her own. So, with the little control she has left, she has now agreed to let her go with Bank Vole.

He craws out of his home to go and collect Tripper. He's still flustered from therapy so could really do without visiting Thwack. He doesn't want to have to confront her about the contentious relay rumours. He just wants to sleep, even though napping has so far not eased any of his tension. Neither has eating. *Hopefully Tripper's company will cheer me up*, he thinks.

Before they depart, his offspring asks to speak to him alone. They walk slowly inland, away from the river and from Tripper, who is busy stalking a ladybird. When out of earshot, they stop and face one other. Bank Vole instantly knows something is wrong. His offspring is scrunching up her features and she only ever does this when she's bothered. He waits quietly for her to speak, forcing his ears outwards to show that when she talks, he'll be listening. She takes her time, fidgeting with her paws, then her tail.

'I want to talk to you about Pup or Tripper, I suppose I must call her,' she says faintly. 'I don't want to sound overly protective because I know she'll leave soon, and her and I, well, we'll have nothing to do with one another. Just like you left your woods to come here, she'll do the same and that's fine. It's expected. But I think she can be gullible. I think she could be led astray if she thinks something sounds different or interesting. She must get that from you, Bank Vole.'

She smiles weakly and strokes the top of her head as she draws herself closer to him. Now she can whisper and barely hear her own embarrassing words. 'I... I... I'm worried she's going to be influenced by Thwack, an animal far bigger and stronger, with teeth and a tail that can be used as weapons. If Tripper thinks Thwack is cool, which I'm sure she does, she might get carried away and forget the boundaries voles have to live by. She needs to be realistic... I'm not sure she is. I think she could be a bit of a fantasist.

'I know it's odd to ask anything from you, but can you please help look after her and make sure she stays with you at all times?' She steps back and hopes that on this occasion, Bank Vole will put his radical views aside and understand.

Despite now knowing her use of fantasist is a negative one and that she wants to steer her descendant away from his traits, Bank Vole vows to help. He resists telling her that most boundaries are made up, that if they start training their tails, they might become weapons. He wants to placate her, so instead, he rubs his nose, holds out a paw and promises to watch out for Tripper. She places her paw on top while her lip quivers with gratitude.

## LETTING THE HEART SPEAK

'There you both are! Can we go now please? A ladybird just dropped some disgusting yellow stuff on me, and I want to wash it off right away!'

This news makes Bank Vole and his offspring laugh. They too remember the first time a ladybird peed on them and told them to back off. Tripper's emergence puts an end to their conversation, so they say their goodbyes. Bank Vole's offspring watches her ancestor and her pup walk to the bottom of the hill. Truthfully, she thinks there's something sweet about them together, something wholesome. Her cheeks expand slightly as the corners of her mouth rise. Nobody sees her small, subtle smile. And that is just the way she likes it.

'Robin made us all form a line, like the lines we see ants do, but unlike ants, we had to stand very still.' Tripper fills Bank Vole in on choir practice while they scan the river to try and locate Thwack. 'Then she made these different noises and we had to repeat them. I was able to copy her high sounds but not the deep ones. So, she paired me with Cub because Cub is very good at making deep noises, and Robin said we can balance each other out. Cub is now my friend, she's really nice. She'll be called Badger soon, like your friend Badger. She said another word for him is Grandpa – no one calls him that, though. I'd never even heard of it. She said it means he produced the female that produced her and that he cares for her like the rest of the clan do. I like the word Grandpa. It sounds big and impressive! Anyway, overall, I would say choir was ok. Not as bad as I thought it was going to be.'

Bank Vole doesn't hear the last bit. He's thinking about his friend Badger also being a grandpa. He can only imagine how incredible that is. He wonders if Tripper's realised that this is what he could be to her if their species allowed it. By the way she's talking, it doesn't sound like she made the connection.

'I've found her! There she is! She's sitting with the other animals – look, can you see her relaxing on their riverbank?'

Bank Vole follows the direction of Tripper's pointed claws and sees Thwack is indeed getting very chummy with their – her – competitors. This is getting ridiculous! He shouts over to her but realises there's no way his quiet voice is going to travel across the water, especially while the birds are making such a racket. The sun is setting, so they're fluttering around, chirping, chatting, and wishing each other a good sleep.

Believing it to be impossible, Bank Vole flops onto the ground, deflated. He begrudgingly tells Tripper she should get comfortable too because they could be waiting a long time. This news doesn't bother Tripper. She begins clearing the area around her so she can lie down, squealing 'Green Leaves', the song she learnt in choir, as she smooths and pats down the soil. Her voice is charming, albeit slightly strained. Hearing her tugs at Bank Vole's heart, and he asks if she knows his favourite bird song, 'Beauties in the Sky are Dove Birds' because he wants her to continue. Without responding, Tripper stands up and places her front legs by her side. Lifting her head in the air, she opens her mouth wide and belts out the first verse. Bank Vole hums along contentedly, enjoying the moment, until they reach the chorus and Tripper asks him to join in.

'It would be great if I can practice singing in a pair,' she says.

## LETTING THE HEART SPEAK

Bank Vole's never sung before. It's never been of interest to him. 'Um, I won't be of any help. It's better if you sing on your own,' he says to avoid it.

'Does this mean you have sung before and didn't like it?'

'Well, no.'

'Oh, Bank Vole, you need to give it a go!' Tripper insists. 'You might be better than birds! Come on, let's sing together.'

Bank Vole tries to put his shyness aside. He lets noise leave his mouth and attempts to make it sound musical but he keeps stumbling and stopping. His vocals get quieter and quieter. He's just too uncomfortable. When he's inaudible, Tripper scuttles over and asks him to stand like they do in choir. 'Robin said you have to enunciate your words. I think that word means you have to sing loud and clear. Am I right?'

Bank Vole nods. Now upright, he tries to increase his volume.

'No, this really won't do,' Tripper states. 'You sound flat. Robin said you need to sound like you're running up and down mounds. I think you're holding back. You need to go for it! Robin said you have to sing with meaning, as if you are letting your heart speak. She said it has to come from your chest. You have to think of something true to you and find the voice that's coming from deep within.'

Tripper's big eyes peer into his, searching for whatever it is he treasures. 'Oh, that's funny Bank Vole. I can see myself in your eyes. Hello! That's my paw waving! Your eyes are like the river, I can see my reflection in them. It's like I'm in you. Look into mine, Bank Vole. Can you see yourself in me?'

## AN EXCEPTIONAL AURA

Bank Vole looks into the shiny dark circles on Tripper's face and sees his image staring back. 'We're in each other,' he says softly.

The moment is far more profound that Tripper intended. It's all Bank Vole needs. Clearing his throat, he gets ready to project his voice. What Tripper has done is show him what's true to him: it's their unofficial, innate bond.

'You look up and what's that white thing you see
Flying over your head?
It looks like a pigeon from high above
But it's not.
The beauties in the sky are dove birds,
Beauties in the sky are dove birds'

He gets louder. He imagines himself running through the woods, recreating the varied surfaces and textures with his voice. They squeal. This morphs into screeching, but Tripper doesn't stop. Neither does he. Now he's allowed himself to sing, to expend his breath and vibrate his vocal cords, aligning them with Tripper's, he realises how precious this moment is. It's making him embrace the vulnerability and brush aside his pride.

Thwack is still engrossed in conversation when the song is over, so Tripper begins singing 'Fill me up, Buttercup.' When birds sing this song, it usually makes Bank Vole think of food. Not this time. He joins in, even though he doesn't quite know all the lyrics.

The penetrating noise they're making becomes so loud it eventually manages to carry across the river. Intrigued and mildly impressed, Thwack leaves her new friends to paddle over. She lays on her back, paws behind her head and watches them. Her amusement dissipates as soon as she senses something from Bank Vole. She thinks he's emitting a weightlessness, like he's been freed of something. Overcome with sentiments she doesn't want to think about, she starts applauding loudly, whistling, and splashing so they stop. Complimented by her rowdy praise, Tripper asks Thwack if she'd like to join in.

'No, no!' Bank Vole yells. 'Thwack can't! She only likes singly loudly and it would get her in trouble.'

'Yes, I wouldn't be able to sing as quietly as you both were,' Thwack says sarcastically with a smirk spread across her face. 'Should have tried a lullaby, not a ballad, folks!'

Bank Vole tugs a whisker. Although, their voices don't rumble and boom like Thwack's, he gets her point. He gives her his best apologetic look, crouching so he appears extra small and pitiful.

They move into a bush so they're inconspicuous. Tripper dominates the conversation, telling Thwack all about choir practice and how much she's enjoying having her own name. Cooly Thwack tells her individual names will soon become commonplace. 'I've suggested the animals who live opposite do it too and they liked the idea.'

Bank Vole takes this as his opportunity. 'Yes well, while we're talking about them, we've noticed you striking up a friendship and—'

'Oh, don't say I can't do that now too, bud? I thought it was six rules only?'

'It's not that—'

'Why don't you live over there with them anyway? They're a lot friendlier and moving sticks rarely visit. You wouldn't have to hide all the time.'

'It would be too busy if we all lived there. This is our home.' Bank Vole responds gruffly, irritated the conversation is drifting in a direction he doesn't want it to.

'And even if moving sticks didn't come here, we'd still have to act appropriately.'

'Was your singing just now appropriate?'

Bank Vole refuses to answer. Instead, he picks up a leaf and rips it into little pieces. When the last shred hits the ground, he says, 'We've heard you've agreed to help them in the relay. Is it true you're planning on carrying Shrew across like you're planning to carry me?'

'Yes, it's true,' Thwack says casually. 'I figured I'm neutral. Look at where I'm positioned in the woods! Right in the middle of you both.'

Tired from both therapy and singing, Bank Vole puts it bluntly, 'You're wrong, Thwack. You have to pick a side. What if Shrew and I get to the water at the same time? Who would you carry across first? It doesn't work. I thought you, with all your knowledge and experience, would be able to see that.'

'Well to be honest, I thought you'd just be glad to get across the water. To know that with me there, your team will actually finish the race for the first time.'

Thwack's tactless remark turns Bank Vole's frustration into indignation. He pulls down hard on his cheeks so the red vessels underneath his eyes are on display. 'We wanted to *win,* Thwack, to be victorious!' he shouts. 'We thought you were on our team! What about the speech you gave in the Thicket? You said you would make us an invincible force! Was it all just a lie? You put your paw out in front of you! That makes it a heinous crime! And do you not think you should be showing your gratitude to the animals here? We're the ones who have allowed you to stay and found a way for you to take part in the race!'

He hopes having the truth laid out for her will cause her to reconsider. While Thwack slides her teeth across her bottom lip, Tripper, not part of the dispute, is biting fresh chunks out of a leaf. As she's so captivated by the drama however, she's forgetting to chew, so now has soggy morsels down her front.

'I'm not going to decide between the two teams, bud,' Thwack states unremorsefully. 'It's important I'm on both of your sides. Let me think of a solution. I really do want to help both of you, but not to my own detriment.'

Flabbergasted, Bank Vole retorts, 'This will be to your own detriment, Thwack. The council are only just starting to accept you and our council precedes theirs across the river. We have had more exposure to moving sticks, so our built-up knowledge means what we say goes. If you back out of supporting solely our team, the council will probably just want you gone. You were offering them something. You don't belong here, so you have to prove yourself. You have to make them see you're worthy. Do you not understand that?'

'I understand, Bank Vole,' she says calmly. 'I know I am of value. I will think of a way both teams are satisfied. Leave it with me.'

At this response, Bank Vole wants to leave full stop, but doesn't want to upset Tripper by going so soon. He picks up another leaf and starts nibbling it half-heartedly. Tripper wipes her chest and tries to fill the silence by talking about choir practice again. The conversation dwindles quickly, however, as she has nothing new to say.

Now no one is talking, Bank Vole's other flares get louder. They're all thinking about Pine Marten's ultimatum. It appears they're veering towards telling Myodes Glareolus, reasoning that it would be better to love her from another woods than forget to have ever loved her at all.

## AN EXCEPTIONAL AURA

Bank Vole glances over at Tripper while he ruminates. He sees disappointment sadly etched over her face. He knows this isn't the fun she would have been hoping for. He decides to make sure it is. For the sake of the little pup, Bank Vole decides to momentarily put aside his differences with Thwack. 'I would like to confide in you both and seek your help.'

Tripper is gobsmacked when she hears how Bank Vole feels. She squeaks with excitement; she had never even considered love a possibility. She listens carefully to his predicament and the decision he has to make.

'I'm sure I'm an outlier and Myodes Glareolus won't feel the same, but I'm going to tell her that I want to form a bond with her,' Bank Vole says. 'One where we always love and protect each other.' He sits down and rests his back against a fallen stick. 'Before I say anything to her though, I have to rehearse it. I need to make the idea sound attractive. I must think what a partnership can offer her. You see, she mentioned reciprocal relationships to me before, it was because…' Remembering it was to do with Thwack, Bank Vole doesn't finish his sentence. 'She thinks the best kind of relationships are the ones where you both provide for each other. So that's what I need to work out. What can I offer her that no one else can? I need to be able to give her something worth her while, that only a life partner can give. Can either of you think of anything?'

Tripper jumps up and down straight away, claiming she has the answer. 'I've got it! You should offer her a new, improved-looking Bank Vole!' she says.

Bank Vole screws his face up. This isn't the kind of suggestion he was after.

'I think you should do your fur like how I do mine,' Tripper continues. 'Push it all forward. Ooh, then make your voice different. Try and copy someone else in the woods. Something I've wanted to do recently is ask a bee to stick a leaf on my back with honey. Why don't you try that as well? Then you can purposely bump into Myodes Glareolus and pretend you've never met her before and try to woo her like you did the first time you both met. Maybe if she thinks you're a different bank vole, she'll be interested in getting to know you. It means you'll be able to spend time together, which is what you want.'

Bank Vole doesn't think Tripper's properly understood his objective, so he reiterates a few points. 'What I really want is a life-long partnership with her, not a blossoming friendship with a bank vole she thinks she's never met before. Besides, she says her body is too tired to breed, so I doubt she'll be interested in another.'

Tripper shrugs, standing by her suggestion. 'Maybe her mind would change once she gets to know this new bank vole, the one with the cool fur and leafed-back?'

A little insulted, Bank Vole hopes this isn't the best idea they can come up with. He turns to Thwack. He's counting on her, she must have some inspiring partnership knowledge.

Thwack's not really been paying attention, she's just been listening to little snippets. So when Bank Vole directs a question at her, she quickly deflects it by asking how he originally courted Myodes Glareolus. Her wet fur has formed another pool of water, so before answering, Bank Vole grabs the stick he's been leaning on and sits on top of it. Then he instructs Tripper to do the same. Together they drift around in circles on the puddle. The gentle ebb and flow enables Bank Vole to unlock and share his first encounters with Myodes Glareolus.

## AN EXCEPTIONAL AURA

'We met when we were young. I suppose I must have lived around 80 sunrises. I was new to the woods and Pigeon befriended me. She took me to the Thicket and introduced me to everyone, including Myodes Glareolus. I remember being incredibly short of words, far too nervous, but Myodes Glareolus, well, she talked enough for the both of us. At one point, she asked me what my favourite thing to do was, and I said it was to tell jokes. At the time, I told her one about moles having to cover their mounds because their noses protrude too much – it's not of the quality I tell now, but she had laughed and told me I should show off my good humour.

'We kept meeting up after that; we really enjoyed each other's company. Before we knew it, pups were on the way, and two more litters followed.'

'Well, that's quite uneventful if you ask me,' Thwack says bluntly. 'I think Tripper's on to something. You need to impress her. She must be enamoured by you, then you can tell her how you feel. Once she's fallen for you, it won't matter what you can offer her because your wooing will have won her over already. So, I suggest you try courting her the way other animals do. Sounds like bank voles aren't the best at it. You know the kind of rituals I'm talking about. The bowing, the dancing, the pecking. When it comes to mating, it's actually the female in my species who makes the first move. We let the males know when we're ready to mate by excreting on nearby mounds after we've ovulated. Males go around sniffing them all the time to check for the signal.'

This might be the most Thwack has ever divulged about her species. Bank Vole latches on to the moment and asks if they have relationships that last their whole lifetime. Thwack nods.

'Where's yours then?'

## LETTING THE HEART SPEAK

He could be getting somewhere here!

'I've got more important things to think about.'

Maybe not.

'I thought you wanted us to help you with Myodes Glareolus? Let's concentrate on that. So, are you going to go ahead with what we've suggested?' Thwack asks.

'I think I might. I could try to woo her by improving my appearance and then, with this new look, court her the way other animals do. After I've done that, she'll hopefully be charmed by me so much that when I tell her it's me and reveal how I feel, she'll say she feels the same!'

Excited, Bank Vole asks Thwack if there are any other courting techniques she can tell him about. He wants to gather as much information as he can so he can tell Myodes Glareolus as soon as possible. 'What about meese, the animals who have five names to choose from? Do they form life bonds? Or chupmicks?'

'You mean moose? No, they don't. And it's chipmunks, not chupmicks! Grey wolves have a mating ritual. Remember I told you and Pigeon they still exist? They approach each other, making quiet whining sounds and rub their noses together. Sometimes they might even bite each other's fur. Gently, of course.'

Bank Vole's mouth forms an upside-down smile. So far, none of these sound like something Myodes Glareolus would enjoy.

'There's also a vole actually, like you, who mates for life. Well, I say that, but some males do stray. Are you acquainted with the prairie vole?'

Dizziness suddenly consumes Bank Vole. He has to pick up his tail and slap his face with it to stop himself losing balance and slipping into the water. Thwack's done it! She's shown him his feelings are normal, that love is possible.

Vindication surges through him and he moves to sit upright, bolstered by the conviction.

'Wow, Thwack, wow! So there is a vole who has evolved the way I want us to. If they can love, then it's almost certain my species can too! Thank you, Thwack.'

'Sure thing,' Thwack says cooly. 'Have absolutely no idea how they court, though, bud.'

Bank Vole doesn't care. All that matters is they can love! He squeals with joy. Tripper joins in and asks him when he's going to tell Myodes Glareolus.

'At the next star-sky,' Bank Vole declares confidently.

'Speaking of which, I'd like to go to sleep now.' Without asking, Thwack pushes the stick Bank Vole and Tripper are sitting on until it reaches dry land. She's tired and thinks they've talked for long enough about a topic she's not interested in. Realising they have now been out for a long time, Bank Vole tells Tripper they should go home.

The three of them make their way through the thick leaves and into the open. Tripper, shuffling behind, asks if she can meet moose and real wolves. 'Will they visit here too?'

'Not everybody can come here, Tripper,' Bank Vole responds, laughing lightly. 'Thwack said it's a long way to travel and, also, there has to be room. You have to belong. Thwack is trying to fit in. She's trying to be accepted, but it's not easy.'

He looks up at Thwack and sees her eyes have glazed over. As nothing he's said has been upsetting, he figures the bright moon must just be making them appear wet. Before departing, he asks if she's worked out how she can participate neutrally in the relay. With her eyes still shiny,

## LETTING THE HEART SPEAK

Thwack gives him a beatific smile. She says she's thought of an idea and will reveal it at the next relay meeting.

'But that's physical practice,' Bank Vole protests. 'Rabbit has had her babies, so we're starting at sunrise! It doesn't give me any time to ask the others if you can attend. It means you'll be breaking the customary behaviours!'

Clasping her paws together, Thwack tells him her surprise will have them discarding the rules. In fact, her fantastic solution, she says, will have them begging for her to take part.

## ~ CHAPTER FOURTEEN ~

# The Bridge

Bank Vole has many neighbours, but none of them are wood mice. This wasn't always the case. Around 400 sunrises ago, Wood Mouse lived here and was part of the Copse Council – Bank Vole's predecessor in the relay, in fact. She was tiny, with unusually large features. She had long, dark whiskers, big, bright black eyes, huge round ears, and a tail that was a similar length to her entire body. She also had impressive and unrivalled grit. Similar to Bank Vole, she would try all sorts of crazy methods to get across the water, one of which was asking the animals to throw her. Nobody believed they had the strength or power needed to get her landing on the opposing riverbank, but she was adamant they gave it a go. Suffice to say, she crashed into the water after every toss, hurl, and fling.

You might be thinking, hang on – I thought the animal who crossed the water had to be one that can't swim? With Wood Mouse, an exception was made. Yes, her species generally can swim, but Wood Mouse hated the water so much, she'd avoid it whenever possible. Her fear made her a poor swimmer, and because of that, she was eligible to take part in the relay.

Unfortunately, wood mice only live for a maximum of 365 sunrises. So, not long after the relay, she started to grow frail, and her walk became unsteady. Her death heavily impacted the woods, and it was after eating her that Owl spoke to the council for the second time. He felt it was incumbent upon him to show his respect and praise for an animal he very succinctly described as 'small but mighty.' At least, that's what Bank Vole heard. Muntjac Deer, however, was convinced he'd said something else. He believed, and didn't hesitate to spread, that after devouring Wood Mouse, Owl returned to the group and described her as 'small but meaty.' For a while, Owl was viewed by many as vulgar and insensitive. Now that Bank Vole reflects on it, he's not surprised Owl doesn't talk much. If you don't say anything, nobody can put their words in your mouth.

    Wood Mouse hadn't been the only one of her kind living in their woods. There had been another, and they had been partners. When Wood Mouse perished, her partner was asked to fill her role in the relay. She politely declined. She wanted to find another companion, so left in search of one. Her departure was a defining moment for their woods. It meant that for the first time ever, they were without wood mice.

    Bank Vole was approached next. At this point, he had started breeding with Myodes Glareolus, so was close to turning down the invitation too. It was Myodes Glareolus who persuaded him to accept. She really wanted to see their species represented in the council. She'd coaxed him into it by assuring him that he'd be the funniest member and said they probably needed his humour. This was a good enough reason for Bank Vole to assume the position.

    It wasn't a smooth transition though. At first he resented the meetings. All the time congregating in the Thicket just meant time spent away from Myodes Glareolus and their pups. The animals didn't seem to find him very funny either, which was a huge blow. Eventually, after countless attempts and lots of new material, that changed, as did his feelings. His confidence grew and the animals became his friends. He was a good fit, just as Myodes Glareolus had predicted.

She also got something out of Bank Vole's membership. He would share stories with her, non-confidential of course, and these made her gasp and giggle. Most importantly, they made her think about matters her mind normally wouldn't. She enjoyed it immensely.

When they stopped breeding, a lot changed for both Myodes Glareolus and Bank Vole. One of the most devastating changes for her was that Bank Vole shared less. Now, on the few occasions they meet, he rarely talks about council conversations. He focuses on evolution instead, which she doesn't have a lot to contribute to.

Bank Vole was affected by their separation as well, clearly, but not in this regard. He's still a part of the council so gets to continue having interesting conversations. This part of his life has remained the same. In fact, the council has sort of become a refuge for him and he's grateful to be in it. He likes the trivial side to it as well. After he moved back into his own burrow, he became particularly fond of the game Sniffers. This is where one of the council members hides something in the woods in a place it wouldn't usually be found. The winner is the animal who sniffs it out first. For some reason, this activity makes Bank Vole laugh a lot, and whenever Pine Marten hears a giggle, he vocally encourages it to continue. He would sprint over to Bank Vole and tell him to keep his laughter going for as long as possible. Apparently, laughing is like a disease you should want to catch. Pine Marten says the more you laugh, the more you get used to finding things funny. Your brain gets conditioned into passing comedic, satisfied iotas, and these

## THE BRIDGE

are able to find most orbs funny. Bank Vole knows this hasn't happened to his brain yet, but he isn't too bothered. Unlike everyone else, he can always make up a joke if he fancies a chuckle.

Sitting in the Thicket, Bank Vole thinks he should probably take himself up on that more often. He doesn't lean on his jokes as much as he should when he's down or lonely. The thought of comedy makes him regret what he said to Pine Marten in therapy about evolution. He was wrong. It isn't a farce because having an advanced brain means he has the ability to find things funny, and surely no one would want to give that up.

It's sunrise, and the council are about to have their first physical practice. Bank Vole's been thinking about all sorts because he's alone. He's arrived extra early in the hope that he'll catch most of the team before Thwack joins. He'd ideally like to forewarn them about her attendance. Given that she's only been shown around the woods once, he's hoping she gets lost and arrives late.

He's feeling anxious. Thwack is breaking the rules by joining and if her new idea gets rejected, he's going to have to think of another way to get across the water. He sighs heavily. To stop himself from panicking, he tries to use Pine Marten's method of distraction… but this only gets him thinking about Pine Marten, which causes further apprehension. They hadn't left each other on very amicable terms. What will they be like with each other now?

'Ok, focus on something else,' he mutters aloud.

A tickling along his tail attracts his attention. He lifts it up to find out who is crawling over him. Hmm. Nobody's there. He keeps his paw gripped around it, nevertheless, to see if his tail can help him. Any stories about his tail he can distract himself with? Are there any tail jokes to make up?

## AN EXCEPTIONAL AURA

He draws it close to his face so everything around it becomes blurry. No. It doesn't work. He can't think of any. He sighs and drops it forcefully onto the ground. He guesses tails just aren't good at being the butt of jokes.

The diversion his mind needs finally comes in the form of Rabbit. Hopping energetically into the Thicket, she exhibits an unambiguously clear message: she is no longer pregnant. The parade isn't missed by Bank Vole, who asks how the kittens are doing.

'Marvellously, thank you,' she says with a smile plastered across her face. 'Nice to get the weight off me, just in time for practice! Those 30 sunrises felt like a long time. Now I just need to avoid getting pregnant until after the next relay. Wish me luck!'

Bank Vole squeaks in amazement. Rabbits certainly make sure their species' existence stands in good stead. They are prolific breeders. He's about to tell Rabbit that he's expecting Thwack to accompany them when she unfortunately trundles in. The other council members are right behind her. They're following so closely, they're practically stepping on her tail. Squirrel immediately asks what's going on. Thwack opens her mouth to explain but someone else's voice speaks.

'Hello! It's great you've all arrived promptly and congratulations, Rabbit.'

Everyone's eyes move from Thwack to the roof. Pigeon, hovering in the air could not possibly let Thwack talk before she did. It's her prerogative to address everyone first. She knows they all want Thwack to answer, though, so in quick, controlled succession, she passes the limelight back to her.

# THE BRIDGE

'I'll cut right to the chase,' Thwack says, extending both paws out in front of her. 'You're all wondering why I've told the other team I'll help them in the relay too, aren't you, eh? It's because I'm loyal to the woodlands, folks. All of it. You, them, both worth helping, I think. And to prove that, I have come up with a plan. Can you remember when I first arrived, I had started hacking down trees and y'all asked me to stop? Those logs are still on the riverbank. I'd like to make use of them. So herein lies my solution. Let me build a bridge. I will move the logs so they extend from your woods to theirs. It won't take me long and it'll be a safe and secure way for both Bank Vole and Shrew to get across the water. It's pretty darn brilliant if you ask me!'

Pigeon asks everyone what they think. No one responds. There's silence because no one wants to admit it could work. That would mean praising Thwack. She decides to single Bank Vole out, seeing as he'll be the one using it. Bank Vole doesn't hesitate to make his feelings clear. Moving to stand next to Thwack, he places his paw on top of hers.

'Right,' says Pigeon. 'Bank Vole is evidently in favour. Does anybody think differently? Someone must have something to say! Any objections... questions even?'

Muntjac Deer feebly stamps his hoof. 'I know certain animals believe Thwack is trying to make the river water spread into our woods, they think that's why she always splashes. So, on behalf of them... not me, I don't think this... I'd like to check whether this bridge could cause a flood?'

'Please assure these fretful animals they needn't worry. I can confidently tell you that water will travel easily beneath the bridge,' Thwack responds.

# AN EXCEPTIONAL AURA

Now, Squirrel kicks his paw to the ground. 'Neither Bank Vole nor Shrew thought of this, so doesn't it break the rules? I thought it was down to them to work out how to get across.'

This question is directed at Pigeon, so she deliberately places herself in front of Thwack to show that only she needs to answer. She elongates her neck and puffs her chest, endeavouring to appear bigger than she actually is. She realises there and then how puerile Thwack makes her act. 'That was an intelligent question, thank you, Squirrel,' she says. 'I believe it could be argued that this method *is* the result of Bank Vole's idea. It was him who thought to get Thwack involved in the first place and it will still be Thwack carrying him across. The only difference is that she won't be using her body, she'll be using a structure she's built. The fact that the other team are going to benefit from what was originally Bank Vole's plan is frustrating. However, Thwack has made her position clear. She wants to help both teams. We either agree to it or don't let Thwack participate in the relay at all. It is, of course, totally our decision. We never confirmed Thwack could take part. We haven't promised anything and by allowing her, it will break the rules you created. If we say no though…' She pauses here, wishing she didn't have to say the next part. It flatters Thwack too much. 'If we say no, it means Bank Vole will have to think of another approach. One that seems fool-proof and safe. I guess we have to decide what's best for our team.'

'Unless Bank Vole already has a backup plan, it looks like we are *forced* to go with Thwack's proposal,' Squirrel says reluctantly.

The rest of the team respond in a similar way, grunting and nodding with deliberate unenthusiasm. Thwack accepts their dispassionate response with alacrity and dashes

# THE BRIDGE

off to make the bridge. Bank Vole, pleased, doesn't think he's ever seen her move so fast.

The council leave the Thicket together and travel to Squirrel's starting point at the bottom of an ash tree. It has to be said that the first practice is often long and drawn out. It's like an extension of their analysis meeting. As a team, they walk through the race, stopping at each position to watch one another perform. By doing so, it allows for live scrutiny and feedback. It is helpful, albeit a little wearing. All the practices after this require them to rehearse as if it were the actual relay and this, they feel, is where the real fun begins.

For now, Squirrel works his way to the top of the tree to collect the leaves in the exact same way he'd done before. The animals can't really judge much because he's very quickly out of their view. Somehow, though, someone does find something to comment on.

'Stop! It's all wrong. He's doing it all wrong.' It's Thwack. She's soaked and waddling towards them, wagging a paw.

'Stop!' she repeats as she gets closer. 'You're wasting time going all the way up there, Squirrel. The leaves at the top are too exposed to the sun. You need leaves with more moisture. They'll tie to the chain better. Aim for the middle of the tree, deep within the crown. They may be a little harder to pull off but will be the most durable.'

Apoplectic, Squirrel scurries down the trunk and marches over to Thwack. 'Who said you could intervene? You're not in our team. Go away, go and build your bridge and stop watching us!'

Pigeon rushes over to stand in between the two of them. She spreads her wings so they both have to take a step back. 'Listen to me,' she commands. 'Squirrel, return to your starting position and try to calm down. Thwack, you *should* be staying out of our business. You've decided not to be in our team, and these are the consequences – you cannot watch us practice and you most certainly cannot contribute feedback. I'm sure you've got plenty to be getting on with.'

'I've finished the bridge already! I am a quick worker. It's done and ready to be tested!' She whistles in celebration, but only Bank Vole joins in with a squeal. 'Oh, and about returning to the water... sure, I can do that. You should know though that I'm going to be helping the other team. They've asked me to as they know I have great tactics.'

Upon hearing this, Badger charges forward. He will not have the other team gain any advantage over them. Unashamedly, he pleads for Thwack to stay. *So Myodes Glareolus was right again*, Bank Vole thinks. Thwack's becoming of use; they're beginning to understand her purpose. She, on the other paw, gets to be involved and feel like part of the group. Reciprocal relationships. He must remember to thank her.

He likes having Thwack accompany them to each stage of the first trial and doesn't mind that she's making the whole process longer by critiquing every approach. As far as Bank Vole's concerned, her suggestions make sense.

'And if I may, I have a tip that'll counteract the potential wind. Owl, when it's your turn, I think you should swoop down at the beginning and fly low over to Mole rather than flying high and only diving down right when you see her. You'll be dealing with less of a gust then. I know I have already said this, but I want to reiterate again, folks, that I think you're all tremendous. Your methods just need some tweaking. We'll get there!'

# THE BRIDGE

Unlike Bank Vole, the other team members are finding Thwack extremely patronising. It takes a lot of deep breathing and in some cases, physical restraint for them to not argue with her.

Eventually, they get to Bank Vole's turn. Thwack's bridge is outstanding. It really does start on their side and end all the way across the river on the opposing team's land. The shape and colour of it reminds Bank Vole of a long and wide mole mound. To prove how strong and sturdy it is, Thwack asks Muntjac Deer to kick the tip of it with his hoof. 'See, it didn't move at all,' she says.

She can tell they're speechless, all amazed by her creation. This is what she expected. She points to the stones she's stacked for Bank Vole and he gingerly walks towards them. Knowing his friend can't climb, Pine Marten kindly rushes over and lends his paw instead. Relieved, Bank Vole walks on to it and smiles up at Pine Marten as he lifts him to the top of the log. He's glad to see that neither of them are holding a grudge.

As soon as he lands on the bridge, Bank Vole grabs a protruding layer of bark and pushes his back legs away. He's checking for friction so wants to see if they slide. The bridge looks magnificent, but he still feels apprehensive. Yes! It's a rough surface, plenty of bumps and scales. Even if it rained, he doubts it would become too slippery. A little bulb of confidence anchors inside of him.

Next, he focuses on where he's got to run to. The distance looks overwhelmingly far. He picks up each paw and cautiously places them down in front of one another. His balance seems good. He's not wobbling around, not tipping towards the water. His mind starts to quieten; thoughts fade away. It's like it has registered that he's safe, so his body can take the reins.

## AN EXCEPTIONAL AURA

He sucks air in and begins to run. With each stride, he gets a boost of adrenaline. He lets his legs take charge. He runs and runs until he reaches the other side. Jumping off the bridge, he keeps running. His heart is racing, his sore paw is hurting but he doesn't stop running until he's right by the water, facing his woods. He hears the roar of his teammates before he sees them. They're jumping, spinning, digging, revelling in this monumental moment. Now Bank Vole stops and does the same. Knocking his head back, he lifts his nose to the sky and squeals with all the strength he can muster.

He's crossed the river. He's going to make it to the race. For the first time, they're going to complete it. They might even win it. All thanks to the newcomer. His friend, Thwack.

## ~ CHAPTER FIFTEEN ~

# Love is a Choice

Lying out in the open, Bank Vole's staring at the glowing moon. It's reminding him of the middle of a daisy. It's so perfectly round. In the woods, they believe this is a good omen. When the whole of the moon is on show, they think it's purposefully giving you extra light. It's telling you to do something, find something, go somewhere. Whatever you need to do, it will be there to guide you. Even the diurnal animals act on this belief. If the moon is full and there's a task they've not achieved, they abandon sleep and go do it. The bright luminescence can't be ignored. Bank Vole has waited for a cloud to cover it. He's tried to force a nap. What with all the relay excitement, he should be able to drift off. He can't. Avoiding it isn't possible. The moon knows he pledged to tell Myodes Glareolus this star-sky. It is round for a reason. It is time.

He scurries towards the water and splashes his head. The cold whips away his nerves and stimulates him to push forward the fur around his face. He glances down and waits for the rippling water to become still. His warped and wonky reflection turns steady. The look staring back at him, it's… something. Certainly bold. Hopefully striking; potentially outrageous. He decides one alteration is enough. Anymore and she might think she's talking to a dishevelled rat. This is plenty.

Now, with the moon's help, he has to find her.

Approaching her burrow, Bank Vole quietly recites the courting rituals Thwack told him. He's come up with some of his own too, believing she might find them more appealing.

She's not home. *Not the best start*, Bank Vole thinks. He observes the light above once more and tries to relinquish control. He must relax. It's going to happen. The moon will lead him to her.

Running up the hill, Bank Vole finds his guide has moved and settled in front of him. Following it, he ploughs through long grass and carefully weaves his way around Muntjac Deer's snoring, never-ending body.

He's tested when he arrives at the chestnut tree. The moon is still ahead, but he knows that to the right of this tree, there's a big blackberry bush. She could easily be in there. He decides to sprint over to it. Diving inside he sniffs for evidence of her and calls her name. The only response he gets is from a badger who tells him to quit squealing because it's ruining his meal. Myodes Glareolus is not there.

Out in the open, Bank Vole faces the moon once more and tells himself not to yield to temptation. The moon knows what he wants to do. It will take him to her; he must trust it.

He really does try hard to maintain this belief and stays on track, even when the journey becomes monotonous. Eventually, not having a clue how much further he has to go gets the better of him, and he succumbs again to his own impatience. He spots a strawberry bush to his left and strays, scurrying into it to see if she's there. They were surprisingly tasty when they tried them recently, so he can imagine her coming back for more.

He inspects the ground to see if she's built a secret burrow. He picks up leaves in case she's fallen asleep underneath them. No. There aren't any remnants or markings, nothing to indicate she's there. He stamps on an already squashed strawberry to let out his frustration. Now that he knows he's going to tell her, he wants to do it immediately. Pull that splinter out of his paw, chuck the ants down his mouth. *Where is she?*

He quickly eats an unscathed berry for luck and goes back to the moon, promising to keep his eyes focused on it. Marching onwards he bypasses all of her favourite places. The moon is a circle for a reason, he repeats internally. It's taking him to her.

Suddenly, everything in front turns black. Bank Vole is enveloped in darkness. He looks up and sees the silhouette of an elder tree. The moon must be directly behind the elder's bush-like crown, he figures, so its light is obstructed. He trudges over and rests his back against the short trunk. Doubt is creeping in; defeat feels close by. Surely, if the moon is helping, it should always be viewable. He yawns and massages his aching paw. The moon was probably guiding him to something else. It's his fault, he got it wrong.

Hang on.

There's faint rustling and crunching coming from the other side of the trunk. Lifting his nose in the air, Bank Vole tries to work out who it is. Their scent is powerful. It's sweet, very sweet. He jolts upright and re-pushes his fur in the wrong direction. It's her. It's Myodes Glareolus. The moon really is round for a reason! It's brought him to her.

He hastily darts around the tree but freezes the moment her figure appears in the corner of his eye. She's crouching down and eating the elderflowers. She's stuffing them in her mouth with such voracity, as if she's afraid the wind will blow and sweep them all away. He scoops a flower up from the ground and swirls it around and around his own mouth, deliberately trying to make as much noise as possible.

'Bank Vole, is that you?'

Gulp. He didn't think Myodes Glareolus would know it was him right away because of his messy fur. It startles him and causes a flurry of nerves to erupt from his stomach and gush into his ears, his legs, course down the tip of his claws and bolt towards the very edge of his whiskers. She scampers towards him so he stands as tall as he can, hides his injured paw, and takes a deep breath.

'Oh, hello! Yes, it's me. What a surprise to see you here.' He's putting on an accent as he wasn't meant to admit it's him yet. He's attempting to mimic Pine Marten's smooth and alluring voice but his imitation is embarrassingly poor. His vocal cords lack the necessary depth and softness.

Smiling is proving to be a difficult task as well. He's so nervous that he's only managing a slight lip raise from the left side of his mouth. Although he's choosing to look around Myodes Glareolus instead of at her, he can see she is giving him a silent, intense stare. This look causes him to fall apart. The muscles in his face unexpectedly run amok. The half smile suddenly comes and goes as it pleases, and both eyes begin to twitch randomly too. Panicking, he shakes his body and flicks his tail hoping the movements will distract her from his rogue facial spasms.

The magnitude of what he's about to do overwhelms him. The messy fur suddenly seems subtle. He wishes he'd made more of an effort to look striking. He's meant to be trying to intrigue and charm her after all. Looking his normal self isn't enough. To overcome this mistake, as well as take charge of his riotous face, he inhales and holds his breath in his cheeks. He doesn't know if a puffed-up look is attractive, but he needs to do something.

'Bank Vole, what are you doing? I don't understand the game!' Myodes Glareolus asks, giggling through her words.

Usually, her laughing pleases Bank Vole. Not this time. It shows she's not picking up his signals. *Ahh, I must bow*, he thinks. Bowing is a popular courting ritual in the woods. It's bound to make his intentions clear. He rises and falls at her paws repeatedly until dizziness forces him to stop. Holding his head still to regain balance, he glances over at her and sees she's now frowning and covering her mouth. His exertion was evidently in vain.

He doesn't give up and moves quickly on to the next act. This is one he's made up himself. He jumps in the air, waving with one paw. The manoeuvre should impress her, he's showing he has enough energy for the both of them, is skilled, and able to multi-task.

'What are you doing?' Myodes Glareolus asks again. 'Talk to me! Say something!' The longer he's mute, the more she's regarding his behaviour as unfunny and strange. 'You need to say something, please! Are these ideas you're practising for the relay? Are you wanting to distract the other team?'

Bank Vole shakes his head. She's completely oblivious. Should he try anything else? He really doesn't want to resort to biting her cheek like a grey wolf. He looks miserably at the ground. It's not working. Despite the new look, the different voice, and the rituals, she still sees him the same way. Just Bank Vole, an animal she's no longer attracted to. He exhales (finally) and his cheeks and chest collapse. He decides to stroke his fur downwards. As she knows it's him, he might as well look like his ordinary self.

'Have you heard one of our descendants has started calling herself a different name? She now answers to Tripper. She was inspired by Thwack. Do you think you would ever have your own name?' Bank Vole's trying to ease himself into the conversation, hoping his nerves will calm. He is using his normal voice now. It's wavering and exposing his jitters.

'I don't need another name,' Myodes Glareolus replies matter-of-factly, sniffing and licking leftover food off her paws. 'I know what I am. I don't need to be called anything else.'

Bank Vole lifts his face, and their eyes meet. Their gaze lingers on one another, and he feels his heart come alive, doubling in size and beating hard against his chest. To regain focus, he concentrates on the scattering white blanket of petals surrounding them.

He wants to show her that not everything comes down to need. Ultimate satisfaction, he believes, comes from choice. Need is derived from necessity, desperation and duty. Choice is freer. It can be whimsical and playful. It can also be meaningful and earnest, much more than need can ever be. It shows what it is you really desire. It's choice that can make you happy. He tries to express this with something he knows she holds dear.

'Our diet, it's varied, isn't it? We eat leaves, nuts, fruits, seeds. Sometimes we enjoy flowers. Occasionally, we dine on insects. At least I do!' He lets out a small laugh. 'Don't you find the best meals are those where you're eating what you really fancy? When you wake up from your nap and find the food you crave?'

'Definitely.'

'Well, that's because you chose it. You needed to eat, but you picked the food you wanted. Other aspects of life can be like that too. Your name, for example. We all need one, but you can choose what it is.'

'What makes choice so important? It's self-serving,' she retorts. 'There's much more value and benefit in working as a team, being part of a collective. Not putting yourself first. Aren't we all happier when we play our part, when we all act how we should? Our woods stay harmonious because we all cooperate together. Besides, changing my name could make me look ashamed to be a bank vole and I'm not. I don't want to be disloyal to my species and I'm no better than anyone else, so I don't need to be set apart.'

'You've used the word need again!' Bank Vole points out. 'This isn't about thinking you're superior. It's more like… appreciating who you are. Awarding yourself with your own identity. You are a bank vole, as am I, but no one can ever replace us. Millions of bank voles have been born and there'll hopefully be millions more in the future, but not one of them will be an exact replica of either you or me. Marking yourself with a separate name, it just honours you with that little distinction. Gives credence to the fact we're all special.'

He knows he's going off on a tangent, but if she doesn't recognise choice as a concept, she's going to find it even harder to comprehend the prospect of a life bond. 'I guess what I'm trying to say is that choices don't always appear obvious because they're not always presented to us as one,' he continues. 'When we're little pups, we're moulded and conditioned to live in the constructs we're taught. The few choices we have are laid out for us. But if we remove the limits that are placed upon each species, life can be so unique and varied. So much of what we're told doesn't apply to us or isn't available to us seems made up when you think about it. Who says we can't eat sticks or sleep in a nest, for example? It's enlightening to see what's really out there, what's really possible once these invented restrictions are removed.'

'I have made choices, Bank Vole, as have you.' Myodes Glareolus's calm tone doesn't match Bank Vole's excited one. 'You chose to leave your woods. We both chose to breed with one another. You're making out like we've got it really tough. I am trying to get to grips with what you're saying. I really am. I just don't see how my life needs any of these extra elements that you're classifying as choices. What would I really gain from any of them?'

By now, Bank Vole's breathing has stabilised. He's still nervous, his heart is still pounding, but her question encourages him to confess. 'My flares are forever talking about you. You are always in my mind. Everything I do, see, smell, I connect it to you.'

Myodes Glareolus is shocked. The disclosure seems to have come out of nowhere and it isn't something bank voles say to one another. She places a paw over his mouth to stop him from revealing any more, but he gently moves it away.

'Please, let me continue. Since we stopped breeding, we've seen so much less of each other, and I've missed you. Your kindness. Your forgiveness, your patience. Your advice. The way you cheer me up. I've been trying to explore, prod the edges, check the boundaries, see what else our species can be. There's been this huge hole in my life as

## LOVE IS A CHOICE

of late, and I've been aching to fill it. I stand here now, certain I can't. What we had together, it's the best life can offer. No other reward or situation can replace it. We may have stopped breeding, we may have been living apart, but all my joy, all my love, never left you.'

He touches his nose and offers his paw, holding it flat in front of her. 'We both know the life of a bank vole is a relatively short one and that there are things we need to do during that time. We need to eat, we need to dig a burrow, we need to sleep. We must breed to sustain our species. We have to serve the future. We're tied to these necessities. Then, after around 730 sunsets, we perish, leaving only our aura, which hovers unseen above those who miss us the most. We know how it all works. But what if we go out of our way to make our lives more fulfilling? What if we make some scandalously wild choices that actually make us very happy?'

Myodes Glareolus is too stunned to react, so Bank Vole moves his paw and places it on her shoulder instead. 'If we act on the adoration I feel towards you, the tenderness I know we share, then we won't have just breathed, we won't have just fulfilled our bank vole duty. We'll have created a new energy, spiritual chemicals that will float above the two of us. We'll be forming our own air. It will be like an exceptional aura that only you and I feel. Now I know we don't *need* one another. But I *want* us. I want us to spend the rest of our sunrises together. I know it sounds crazy, but I think you and I should live like badgers and pigeons. Like prairie voles, a relation of ours. We have a bond; let's make it everlasting like they do.'

He squeezes her shoulder affectionately and keeps talking, hoping some of what he's saying makes sense to her. 'You know when we see moving sticks in the rain, they pull out these things and duck underneath them? Pigeon told me they're called umbrellas. She said they stop moving sticks from getting wet. Our bond will be like that, you see. It will be our own invisible umbrella. When we stand underneath it, it will protect us from the raindrops of loneliness and shield us from storms of pain. Please, let's not waste any more time. Let's not deprive ourselves any longer. Let's determine our happiness, and perhaps even the happiness of our species. Let's choose us.'

Although Myodes Glareolus doesn't speak, so many flares have sparked in her mind. The fondness they have for one another, yes, she knows that exists. She cares for him, she always has. She thinks he's handsome, funny, brave. Producing and raising young together has been the highlight of her life. She doesn't expect anything will beat it. She's ok with that, though, she enjoyed it while it lasted. She's accepted life may not be as stirring or busy as it once was. She knows she's at another stage in her story. One where she's slowing down, doing less, being solitary. How can he suggest they still act as lovers when they won't be trying to produce offspring? It's absurd.

He's hoping bank voles will evolve to have life bonds. She had thought he wanted them to grow wings or bigger ears. He wants them to love! How will this make their species happier considering most usually have numerous partners? She doesn't ask.

He loves her! All this time, she worried he resented her for not breeding anymore, for weakening his lineage. She'd been thinking he was forgetting her stories and not wanting her advice. She thought he'd been seeking therapy to dispel his bitterness and seek refuge in innovation. What does this mean for therapy – has it been successful? Was

## LOVE IS A CHOICE

Pine Marten trying to get him to stifle these feelings or express them?

The questions keep coming. Does she feel this void he's describing? Does she need protecting from raindrops of loneliness? She steps away from him and sits amongst the blossoms.

Unless they're actively breeding, bank voles don't have a partner. They don't. She's seen it. They do everything alone. She's never questioned why. Should she? Her mind, for the first time, begins to churn and chug at this notion. What has determined their singular lifestyle? Is it something Earth decided upon, or is it some made-up rule like Bank Vole thinks? *Why do some animals get to form bonds that last forever?*

Cradling the fallen flowers, she closes her eyes and allows memories to propel into her mind. Memories she's treasured and wrapped delicately away. Bank Vole taking her to the furthest blackberry bush in their woods just so she can discover if they taste different. There's palpable excitement, laughter, lightness.

She sees them marvelling over their newborns and feels the elation, slight delirium, the bliss, the fervour. In quick succession, she watches Bank Vole teaching these pups how to build a burrow. He's digging and talking at the same time and a load of mud ends up in his mouth. She watches as he makes a big deal spitting it all out. Then she sees the pups demonstrate what they learned and laughs out loud when they chuck clumps of mud into their mouth and hyperbolically splutter and cough it straight back out. It was funny then and it's still funny now.

She observes Bank Vole sitting with her while she was in labour with their second pups. He's stroking her face softly and telling her anecdotes from the Thicket to distract her from the pain.

The memories continue.

Her face draws downwards as she's reminded of the time their last pups left the burrow. Bank Vole was by her side when their offspring waved goodbye. He remained standing with her long after they disappeared out of sight. It was raining. She remembers feeling the raindrops on her fur. The woods had turned dark and there were echoing cries for shelter. No, no, actually that's not true. Her memory corrects itself. She had looked up and been surprised not to find dark clouds. There was, in fact, a clear blue sky, gloating immodestly between the trees.

Her mind plays the moment Bank Vole climbed out of her home to return permanently to his own. The space suddenly looked huge! Too big. She remembers lying down to nap and feeling a throbbing pain pierce through her chest. Sliding her paws across her front, she'd tried to locate the injury. She'd suspected a thorn had buried into her skin and felt around several times but couldn't find it. Everywhere was soft. There weren't any cuts or grazes. No sign of blood.

She's shown the many times she would scurry to the top of her burrow because Bank Vole was calling her. She'd hear him yelling her name, telling her he had news to share. How upset she'd been when she'd poke her head out and find no one there. She'd wasted energy. She'd been silly; her ears had deceived her. They were the reasons for her sadness, for her misery. Only those.

Her brain acts like water in the wind. It writhes, swells, and collides. It swishes her thoughts, feelings, and memories and crashes them into each other. Something keeps surging towards her. Something is making sense, but whatever it is recedes and vanishes before she can grip onto

## LOVE IS A CHOICE

it. Resembling a wave breaking and retreating, the bubbling foam, her truth, is getting submerged time and time again back into the rolling water.

She's not understanding anything.

She thinks about her life now. That's easier to process. She sweeps, visits Wren with Goldcrest, looks for the best fruit, and sometimes sees Bank Vole. She, on the whole, is ok. Maybe she had been sad, maybe her life had fallen apart, maybe she'd been lost. Not anymore. She's found new sparks of pleasure. Different modes of joy. She's fought through a struggle she didn't really acknowledge she was having. She's surpassed the worst of it now. So, what shall she do?

She opens her eyes and sees Bank Vole has sat himself down beside her. Usually, she can feel when someone has moved closer so is surprised she hadn't felt his advancing presence.

'I... I'm completely overwhelmed, Bank Vole. I don't know what to say.' She lets her flares speak freely. 'What we had, it was sincere and honest affection... fleeting, I think... but it existed. Love, however, the whole concept of it, I've only ever witnessed. To have it be offered to me... it's bewildering and surreal. To even consider accepting it would be, quite frankly, mad.'

She releases the petals, lightly pats her nose and holds her paw out to him. 'I'm sorry. I only want to be honest with you. This... this isn't something I can do. I can't love Bank Vole. I wouldn't know how to.'

Bank Vole slowly places his paw on top of Myodes Glareolus's. After a short while, he turns his around so their palms meet. He presses into her skin padding and feels the contact apply pressure to his limbs. He welcomes the force, holding on to this tangible connection. Gradually, his paw slides backwards and falls to his side. He gets up in silence and leaves to go back home, clobbered and crushed. He's indescribably distraught.

Myodes Glareolus is now on her own underneath the elder. She picks up a flower but realises as she lifts it towards her mouth that her appetite is strangely suppressed. She drops it, wipes the fur around her nose, combs through her whiskers and decides she too will go. A little whine coming from behind makes her stop.

'Just so you know,' the quavering voice says, 'when I'm older, I'm going to find a partner to be with forever. So, if it's tradition you're worried about, it's going to be broken anyway. My descendants – your descendants – will form life bonds. Our species can love. You just have to let yourself believe it.'

She turns around to see who is speaking to her but she's too late. The animal has already run off. All she catches is a glimpse of a small figure with bushy fur that's styled outrageously over a round head. Round, like the moon. *Round*, she thinks, *just like the middle of a daisy*.

## ~ CHAPTER SIXTEEN ~

# *An Unexpected Discovery*

Each animal has its own unique way of psyching itself up for the race, and Pigeon likes to observe them all. She flies over to their starting points and watches everyone prepare. Muntjac Deer always walks slowly with a stick on his head; Rabbit runs on the spot and Pine Marten stretches, manoeuvring his body into various positions. Bank Vole, she's noticed, has taken to scratching his ears. The most amusing for her is, indisputably, Squirrel. He throws himself onto an ash tree trunk, jumps off it, flicks his tail, hurtles around the base (often tripping over his own manic paws), and repeats this routine over and over. Compared to everyone else, it's a little over the top and Pigeon enjoys it very much.

Balancing herself on a low, wonky bough, she too starts getting ready. Birds could fly past at any moment now to signal the crown they've created is complete, which will mean the race can begin. She dips her neck and coos, warming her voice so it's set to commentate.

Pigeon is laying all of her hopes on a win for Bank Vole. She's viewing the bridge Thwack's made as his passage to victory. It's got to be! He deserves it after his accident and for being so patient with the arrogant newcomer. Pigeon isn't sure what will happen to Thwack once the race is over. She can tell the others still haven't taken to her. She's too patronising and at the same time, too complimentary. Simply put, she doesn't belong. She anticipates an awkward and unpleasant conversation is on the horizon.

She starts to wobble and lose grip. The birds are swooshing by, and their speed has produced a sudden gust of wind. She immediately orders all her other flares to be silent. The race has begun!

Squirrel is already sprinting up the ash tree, so Pigeon drifts in the air and peers through the foliage. Shouting as loud as she can, she lets all the animals dotted around the racetrack know what's going on. 'Squirrel, with ferocious speed, has climbed up the trunk. He's made it to the centre of the tree and is now sitting picking the leaves… he's making the leaf chain, piercing little holes with his nails. The leaves he's picked look very green, a much darker green than the leaves he picked last time. Ok, it looks like he has four leaves tied together. Four more to go.'

She yells for quiet whilst overzealous spectators beg for Squirrel to hurry up. Their heckling doesn't trouble him, however. He's feeling confident. His paws are steady and the knots he's making are really tight. He's just pulled hard on two leaves and the stalks didn't loosen. They remain tied together, sturdy, and tough.

'Squirrel is doing a wonderful job.' Pigeon boosts his self-belief. 'He has now picked the last four leaves and is bounding down the tree. Well done, well done!'

She watches as Squirrel places the string of leaves around Muntjac Deer's antlers. She should be describing this to the crowd, but the intensity of it silences her. Any slight movement of Muntjac Deer's head could cause the chain to slip off. As he's such a fretful and fidgety animal, it could easily happen.

## AN UNEXPECTED DISCOVERY

'Oh, thank goodness!' she says aloud, blowing out the air she'd been unconsciously holding in. 'Right, everyone. Muntjac Deer, who was waiting at the bottom of the tree, now has the chain. He's walking along with it – oh!'

One of Muntjac Deer's legs gives way and his body sways from side to side. His nerves are getting the better of him. 'Calm your jitters!' Pigeon whispers as she glides above. 'You can do this!' She says the latter again, shouting for the benefit of the crowd. 'He's very capable of doing this! Yes, that's great, he's picking up speed… come on faster… watch out for the big dip right in front… great, you're not so shaky now. Muntjac Deer, crane your neck slightly to the right, the chain is off-balance!'

Muntjac Deer doesn't listen. He's seen Pine Marten ahead, standing by the hollow, dead tree trunk. He's galloping towards him, desperate to get his part over and done with. Pigeon quickly flies over to Pine Marten, giving him a concerned look. If Muntjac Deer is too hasty, he might not pass the chain over properly. She tries to use her role as commentator to guide him into sliding it directly onto Pine Marten's paws.

'Ok now, Muntjac Deer must *very* steadily lower his head. Easy, *easy!* Oh no, the chain is a little tangled. It's entwined in Muntjac Deer's left antler. He's going to have to shake his head so it falls off, and Pine Marten is going to have to react quickly when he sees it dropping. Muntjac Deer is turning his head… Pine Marten is following the motion with his cupped paws… yes! The chain has been caught successfully!'

The animals watching from the sidelines burst into cheer. Pigeon dives down to momentarily rest her shaken wings. That was close. It was almost over for them. She feels a light push coming from behind and believes it's her partner forcing her to continue with the commentary. She glides over to the end of the fallen tree trunk and pokes her head in. She sees Pine Marten enter the hole with ease.

'Pine Marten is crawling swiftly, dragging the leaf chain along with him. He seems to have a good grip on it,' she says.

Really, Pine Marten would like to take his time travelling through so he can soak up the sound of everyone roaring his name. After the ordeal with Muntjac Deer, the crowd is enlivened. Pigeon's words help him to hurry. She keeps shouting inside the hollow and her echoing voice is drowning out the charming chant. Just as Pine Marten reaches the end she stops commentating, steps back and makes way for Owl, who is now hovering by the tip of the trunk. Shortly afterwards, Pine Marten emerges into the light. He savours hearing the last cry of his name as he throws the chain up for Owl to catch mid-air with his beak. This is the part where Owl has to take extra care not to clamp down with his mouth so as not to break the chain. Thankfully, he manages to collect it and keep it intact. Calmly, he makes his way towards Mole and Pigeon flaps beside him.

'Owl has beat his wings 15 times so far. He has 35 more to go till he can drop the chain to Mole. He's flying very low to avoid the wind, although there's not much of that, luckily. Oh, there's Mole… Owl is going to release the chain in three… two… one.'

Scooping the chain up with her long nails, Mole holds onto it with one paw and begins digging a hole with the other. It's at this point Pigeon realises she herself has swooped down too low as she's getting whacked with flecks of soil. Rising into the air, she tilts her body so the mud

## AN UNEXPECTED DISCOVERY

sprinkles off and counts how long it's taking Mole to travel underground.

'Mole needs to speed it up slightly. It seems like something is irritating her snout; she keeps rubbing it. Ignore the itch, Mole, keep digging!'

Mole bends down to assess the depth of the hole. She's disappointed to find it's still too shallow. She wants to get in there quickly so she can get away from Pigeon and all the bystanders' glares. She has a foreboding, pessimistic feeling about the race and it's making her agitated. She's never felt like this. Time and time again, even after a history of losses, she's always been optimistic. She doesn't understand why she's feeling differently.

'Mole is still digging,' Pigeon informs the crowd. 'Ok, her head is back in the hole... and it looks like the rest of her is going in too. I can now only see her short tail. She's out of view now, inside Earth. I can no longer see her. Remember, Mole has to keep digging and travel underground for 40 breaths before she can re-emerge. Rabbit is waiting patiently, trying to figure out where Mole will reappear. She's pacing... Rabbit has stopped pacing. It looks like she thinks Mole is going to reappear right behind the daffodils. Let's hope Mole doesn't pull them up! What a dazzling yellow! It's hard to stop looking at them when you start... but I must! Right, Mole would usually have appeared by now. I've batted my wings 50 times so far. She had finished her part in 45 before... Rabbit is looking stressed. Mole must still be digging. Surely not long now... Wait, wait, here is Mole! But she's coming back up the hole she's already dug! She has the leaf chain with her. She's saying something. She looks frantic. She's gesticulating wildly. It looks like something has gone wrong. Hold on, everyone!'

# AN EXCEPTIONAL AURA

Pigeon stops commentating and rushes down to see what's happened.

'I can't, it's not working! I can't do it,' Mole yelps.

Rabbit bounds over and asks Mole to elaborate.

'Something is blocking me, Rabbit. Something is preventing me from digging any further!'

'Let's not panic,' Rabbit replies, looking quizzical. 'Can't you veer slightly? The rule states that once you dig a hole, you can't start digging another one, but there's nothing about you changing direction whilst you're underground!'

'I can't, I've tried!' Mole wails. 'I've obviously never dug this specific patch before as I'm facing a blockage from each direction. I can't get past whatever it is. I've scratched, pulled, pushed it, but whatever it is, I can't move it.'

Rabbit, shocked, lifts her paws to her cheeks. She tries to console Mole by telling her obstructions could happen to anyone, but her supportive words fall flat. Mole is full of guilt and humiliation. She returns underground to continue prodding the strange impediment, even though she knows that, at this point, the race is indubitably over.

Pigeon has reached this conclusion too. She soars into the sky and calls for the remaining council members to abandon their positions. Flying round and round, she orders them to convene directly under her invisible circle.

They struggle to believe it when she breaks the news.

'You have to be wrong, Pigeon,' Badger says despairingly. 'This was our chance! Everything was in our favour. The lack of wind, the bridge, even the sun! It's been shining a flaming warm orange on us, like the kind you see on a leaf in autumn. It felt like it's been basking us in a blaze of belief. This just can't be happening!'

'Why would something block Mole?' Pine Marten asks rhetorically. 'How can we be so unlucky?'

## AN UNEXPECTED DISCOVERY

Pigeon has to announce it to the crowd next, so she advises they block their ears. Hearing shrieks, or worse, boos, won't make them feel any better. They do as she says, but that doesn't stop Badger from looking at the river and spotting Shrew. He nudges Squirrel, bobbing his head towards the water at the same time. Together they watch the mammal zooming across Thwack's bridge, her leaf chain trailing behind her.

The others would miss this heart-shattering moment if Thwack, who is sitting in the water, didn't whistle so loudly. The high-pitched sound she makes manages to penetrate their covered ears and they immediately turn to see what it is she's celebrating. Appalled at how happy she is, Muntjac Deer decides she was never impartial.

'It wouldn't surprise me if she buried something deliberately to stop us from winning,' he says. 'I have heard rumours about her having a real nasty streak.'

Bank Vole disagrees. He thinks Thwack would be just as jubilant if they'd won too. She wanted her bridge to be successful, and it has been. It's helped a team win and that's all that matters. She doesn't pick sides, as she said. She's just loyal to the woods.

When Shrew reaches the crown, Pigeon lands next to Bank Vole and opens a wing to deliberately block his view but he rejects her offer of protection. Ducking underneath it, he watches the celebrations as they unfold. Those who can swim jump into the water and those who can't balance themselves on the bridge. Joyous chants seem to be coming from every direction.

'How can I have been involved in two relays yet not raced either of them?' Bank Vole asks Pigeon with his eyes fixed on the winners. 'The most frustrating part is that I worked so hard, but that won't be remembered after I'm gone. The details never are. I'll just be known as the bank vole who let my species down.'

Pigeon holds Bank Vole's face in her wing. She drags it away from the revelry and forces it to look up at her. 'We all wanted this for you, Bank Vole. We really did. I urge you to please remember that victory takes many forms. Maybe you didn't win because you've already won enough. Think about it! Who accepted their injury like a champion? You. Which legend tamed the strange beast by the river? You. What hero interacted with moving sticks twice and lived to tell the tale? You. Maybe the other team won because that's the best story their descendants are ever going to be able to tell of them. Your descendants will never stop sharing yours. There are so many and they're all far more impressive. You're the real winner because your life is so full and varied – and I'm sure it'll continue to be too!'

The council leave to go to the Thicket and Pigeon suggests they follow them. She purposefully lags behind in case there is anything else Bank Vole wants to share. She can sense a heaviness emanating from him that can't just be coming from losing the race. Bank Vole isn't planning on divulging anything, but their walk is interrupted anyway by a certain odour. It invades their nostrils and gets more and more pungent. Eventually, after turning around numerous times, Thwack appears. She's waddling towards them.

'I've been running, so excuse me while I catch my breath!' she pants. 'I just came to say don't worry, Bank Vole. This loss... y'all be ok. You'll feel like a winner soon. We all will, buddy.'

Pigeon's chest immediately expands. She's unable to conceal her irritation. Her friend is upset; now is not the time for Thwack to give one of her silly, cryptic speeches. She walks on, hoping it'll prompt Bank Vole to end the

# AN UNEXPECTED DISCOVERY

pointless conversation and rejoin her. To her dismay, he does the opposite.

'Your words are comforting, thank you,' he says. 'At some point, everybody has to feel like they've won. You cannot lose all your life. For now, though, we're going to sink our sorrows with sticks and leaves. Care to come with us?'

Pigeon shoves her beak into the ground and pushes it in deeply. It's the only way she can force herself to stay quiet. She doesn't understand how Bank Vole's arrived at that interpretation. It baffles her! He's misunderstood Thwack. He's somehow spun her words into something sympathetic. He's got to be wrong. What she was saying was empty, devoid of meaning. For how can every animal in the woods collectively feel like winners?

When they get to the Thicket, Pigeon flies straight over to the council corner, leaving Bank Vole and Thwack to trudge through the crowds. For Bank Vole, it isn't an unpleasant experience. He's greeted with pitiful expressions and paws that are being held out to face the sky. The same cannot be said for Thwack, who's walking behind him. The extended paws are all retracted as she passes. She's met with sneers and chides instead.

She's also not greeted warmly when she reaches the council corner, but neither is Bank Vole. The atmosphere is stale, and conversation is minimal. Believing they need a few jokes to lighten the mood, he studies them all for inspiration. As their faces are miserable, however, his brain struggles to pass a funny iota. He decides to look outwards beyond the brambles. Here, trees dominate his view. Funny thoughts immediately form in his mind, so when their talk of fish dwindles, he jumps right in.

'What tree is always yearning for more? The Pine!' As it's a simple joke, he doesn't wait to deliver the punchline. It would be ruined if someone guessed the answer before he announced it. He sees smiles spread on their faces the same way cracks do on drought-infested soil. They all seem to welcome the humour. *If they liked that*, he thinks, *the next one will really tickle them.*

'Two trees are in a battle over maturity. What trees are they?' He pushes his neck forward to scan the group. This one is harder, so he believes he can pause to create suspense. 'The alder and the elder!' he shouts gleefully.

There's hooting, howling, snorting. Badger's shoulders shuffle up and down while he giggles away. He knew his jokes would help! He scratches his ear to try and come up with another.

'Ok, I have one,' he declares. 'What tree is always ill?' He's laughing himself now. 'The sycamore! Do you get it? Sick more? And I have another! What tree is the favourite?'

Again, he waits a moment. This time, unfortunately, he leaves too long a gap.

'The poplar tree?' Rabbit guesses.

'Nope!' Bank Vole replies, relieved that she's got it wrong. 'It's the yew tree because it's so attentive. All it does is concentrate on you.'

They aren't any squeaks or roars.

'I've got to say, I think Rabbit's punchline was better,' Squirrel remarks. 'Poplar tree sounds like the popular tree.'

Others nod their heads, agreeing with Squirrel's comment. Bank Vole, disgruntled, refuses to tell anymore. To suggest Rabbit was funnier, well, they've shunned the comedy now, ruined it. They can sit in silence and resume

## AN UNEXPECTED DISCOVERY

their misery for all he cares. He crouches down on all fours and huffs.

'It's a shame Mole isn't here,' Pine Marten says, attempting to placate Bank Vole. 'She would have liked those.'

Bank Vole hadn't noticed she wasn't present and neither had Thwack, who asks where she is. Rabbit says she's still at the racetrack digging, determined to find out what it was that was blocking her. 'I told her to leave it. I said I suspect it's something moving sticks made and buried a long time ago. Mole is convinced it's natural, though, because it smells of mud. I think she's dealing with a curiosity affliction.'

Not wanting Mole's mind to be analysed without her consent, Pine Marten swiftly changes topic. 'Thwack, your fur looks so thick and is consistently silky. Do you have any tips you can share?'

Fur always gets them chatting and Badger instantly chimes in, saying he's desperate for advice because he's started to lose fur on his back. He said his ancestor pointed it out to him and told him it's a sign of ageing. He turns around so the animals can inspect it. They all crowd around and see noticeable bald batches.

'Thwack's just left,' Pigeon announces when they return to where they were previously standing. 'She must not realise I have almost 360-degree vision and so can still see things that are happening behind me. She tried to do it discreetly when she thought we were all looking away.'

Everybody, including Bank Vole, is confused. *Why has she suddenly gone?* Muntjac Deer asks Pigeon why she didn't question her.

'I didn't want her here in the first place, so was glad to see her leave,' Pigeon says honestly.

## AN EXCEPTIONAL AURA

Bank Vole stops listening. Pigeon's comment is hurtful and he doesn't want to hear it. He just wants to concentrate on why Thwack's left. He invited her to join them so she could feel like part of the group, so she could feel like she belonged. He's trying to stop her from being lonely. Isn't that what she wants? He runs through the order of events to try to work out what could have made her leave without saying goodbye. He'd seen her laugh at his jokes so it wasn't those. Afterwards, they spoke about Mole's absence. Thwack herself had enquired about that. She didn't follow up with any more questions, so he doubts her departure is to do with Mole. Then Pine Marten complimented her fur. A-ha! That's it! Thwack doesn't like talking about fur. She was adamant she didn't want him to call her anything that related to her fur and she's previously said fur jokes aren't funny. It's got to be that. He avoids disclosing this to the others because he knows they'll think it's odd and use it as another reason to not accept her. Instead, he tries to shift their thoughts by telling them about chipmunks. He drones on and on, repeating the same facts Thwack's told him until Mole cuts into the circle. Her paws are covering her mouth and she's shaking her head. Her evident distress causes them to gather around her and ask what's wrong. Slowly, very slowly, she removes a paw from her face and points a long, sharp nail back in the direction she came in. 'Dug up... blocking... unbelievable... come... this way...'

They all scramble out of the Thicket at once. Upon exiting, they bump into Doctor Hedgehog. Pine Marten isn't sure if Mole's discovery needs medical attention so he urges her to join them. She does so willingly.

Mole leads them to her starting point in the relay race. It's now a total mess. Mud is splattered everywhere.

## AN UNEXPECTED DISCOVERY

Pigeon notices the daffodils she'd been admiring are wilting, suffocating from the many mounds Mole's created. She scans the area, hoping Mole isn't expecting them to travel underground.

'Look at this.' It's instantly made clear that any ventures into Earth will be unnecessary. Mole has positioned herself next to her excavated object.

To Bank Vole, it looks like a white and orange rock. There doesn't seem to be anything special about it. Pine Marten thinks the same until he bends down to get a better look. 'No! It cannot be!' he cries.

At his reaction, the rest of the group hurry forward. Their responses all mirror Pine Marten's when they too work out what it is. They gasp, they gulp. Not Bank Vole. He's still none the wiser. He scuttles around it and tries to inspect it from all angles, tilting his head one way and the other. It just appears to be a white stone with holes and sharp orange edges. He doesn't get it. Pine Marten thinks viewing it from above will help so gets Bank Vole to walk onto his paw.

As soon as he's elevated, Bank Vole screams. Now he sees it. The discovery is so astonishing it causes him to lose balance and Pine Marten has to push him back onto his palm quickly before he topples off. He lies still for a moment with his eyes closed and takes light, rapid breaths. Then he spins onto all fours and pulls two of Pine Marten's claws apart. Clutching onto them tightly, he's able to study the thing that knocked him and shocked him. The thing that's made all other surprises seem meagre and mild. For staring back at Bank Vole is a skull. A skull with small holes for small eyes. A skull that arches upwards at the top and curves inwards at the bottom to fit large, sharp teeth. Four orange, jutting teeth, to be exact. That's right. This skull, these fused cranial bones, look just like Thwack.

## ~ CHAPTER SEVENTEEN ~

# Indelible Traces

'We must tell her!' Bank Vole exclaims. 'She must be told that someone like her has been here before!' He's now speaking to everyone from the ground, having walked off Pine Marten's paw.

Mole is glad to finally hear someone talk. Doctor Hedgehog is massaging her head to settle her shocked mind. She's not enjoying the circular movements at all, though, despite being told repeatedly how soothing it will be. She's been looking for a way to make it stop, so now Bank Vole's spoken, she latches on to the conversation. 'I think there's a whole family down there. I was able to dig this up, but there's a lot more blocking me. I doubt it's just one animal. Doctor Hedgehog, please, I really think you should study it intensely so we can find out more.'

Her craftiness has actually worked in Doctor Hedgehog's favour too, who readily obliges. She removes her paws from Mole's head and lays them eagerly on the skull. As she's not a council member, she'd been patiently waiting for someone to grant her permission and was hoping a calming massage would do the trick! She examines the skull thoroughly, sliding her paws around all the surfaces and in all the crevices. She loops a claw around the eyeholes and pulls gently on the teeth.

'It's a clean, healthy skull,' she declares. Her voice is sharp and authoritative and she's placing a heavy emphasis on each adjective. 'Solid and smooth. I can't see any damage to it, so I don't believe it was suffering from cerebral issues. The condition… yes, I think this animal was alive around 145,000 to 150,000 sunrises ago. I'd need to confirm that by comparing it to my cranium collection, of course.

'So, what does this tell us? Well, our brains were less advanced back then, as we know. Travel existed to find food, but no one was able to cross the biggest river like Thwack claims to have done. No one had the skills or intelligence to do that. So, based on that fact, I would presume her species once existed here. How they all ended up in a mass grave, well… I'd need to do a thorough examination on all their other bones to properly determine that. There are many reasons why these sad circumstances could have happened…'

Squirrel cuts in. Standing upright and flicking his tail energetically, he says, 'This isn't making any sense to me. My mind must be confused. Are you really suggesting Thwack actually belongs here? That she is one of us?'

Doctor Hedgehog nods as she surveys the teeth that are wedged behind the four larger ones.

'Well, we shouldn't tell her. It makes us look stupid. We're meant to know everything about our woods, as it is now and how it's ever been, who has lived here and who hasn't. As council members, it weakens our authority. Besides, we'll never get rid of her if she thinks she has a right to be here!'

A snigger escapes Pigeon before she has the chance to suppress it. She stamps her claw on the ground so she can speak next and explain her reaction. 'Squirrel, don't you think she already knows and that's why she came here? She's not innocent. I guarantee it. She's aware of her species' past. I've always thought she was strange. I mean, what animal travels across the biggest river imaginable to come to a place she's never been to before? Who arrives somewhere and refuses to reveal their species? It's absurd, all of it. Now, with this discovery, it's beginning to add up. It's obvious her species has something to hide. That's why she's sickly sweet with us one moment and trying to put us down the next, forcing her "brilliance" down our throats... her erratic behaviour shows she's safeguarding something, that she's living a lie.'

Pigeon is speaking with such conviction it would be easy to forget she's merely giving her an opinion. Bank Vole feels inclined to point this out. 'Well, that's not what Thwack told me. She said she came here because she'd heard how special our woods are. That she travelled a great distance because she wanted to see if the rumours were true. And she's been pretty consistent with me. She's just friendly and inquisitive.'

'Bank Vole, sometimes you seem so naïve. Hearsay alone wouldn't inspire you to come here! I think you could be on to something, Pigeon,' Rabbit says, wagging a forefoot.

'Now, now, Rabbit. Bank Vole was only repeating what Thwack told him, and she could've been telling the truth. There might be something precious about the skull and whatever else is down there. Her species might view our woods as extra special because of that,' Pine Marten suggests. 'They might worship these bones. I've heard of this kind of thing before. I just wish she'd been honest with us as soon as she arrived. It's hard accepting that we didn't welcome one of our own. But she just caused so much chaos!'

'Yes she did. She was very disruptive. I wonder if we've heard of her species then, if they've been here before? Perhaps we'd recognise the name,' Badger adds.

Bank Vole is getting impatient. To him, speculating is pointless when they could just get answers from the animal they're all talking about. 'If we show Thwack the skull, she's bound to open up!' he says.

'I understand she's your friend, Bank Vole, and you don't want to keep this discovery from her,' Rabbit says gently, sorry for calling him naïve before. 'But, it means there are two different opinions floating amongst us. Squirrel wants to keep it between us; you, Bank Vole, want to tell her. We're going to have to hold a vote. If the results lean towards us telling Thwack, then I agree with your urgency. We should do it as soon as we can. Someone may have seen the skull while Mole went to fetch us from the Thicket. We need to be in control of the situation.'

Pine Marten stamps his foot so he can propose something else. 'Why don't we hide the skull for now, find Thwack and force her to answer the questions she's avoided? She's had one up on us by not revealing her species. Now we too have a secret, so we are playing on even ground. I think we should use this skull to our advantage. We don't have to be hostile, but we should demand she's frank with us. If we believe she's really coming clean, that she's divulging it all, then we can reward her with the skull and welcome her, truly and fondly, into our home.'

There's no need for a vote. Pine Marten's idea is a popular one and they all travel down to the riverbank to summon Thwack. As it's star-sky, they expect to find her sleeping. She's not in her usual spot near the bank vole burrows, so they split up and search all along the water's border, with Pigeon and Owl flying over to the winning team's side of the river in case she's curled up somewhere there.

They reconvene without any luck. An unusual stickiness is now hanging in the air, which is accompanied by a muddy rain smell. Bank Vole doesn't notice it, as he's consumed by a dominant flare. It's worried Thwack's left for good because Pine Marten asked about her fur, as ridiculous as that sounds. Every animal takes pride in their fur, feathers, scales, or spines. Having your outer layer be praised, well, that's the biggest compliment. He knows it isn't for Thwack, though, and wishes he knew why. He keeps quiet while the others work out what to do before seeking shelter. They decide the skull, which they had temporarily hidden in a mound, should be looked after by Badger because it's unlikely anyone would dare invade his home. Then, they agree to continue looking for Thwack once the weather has cleared up. Before they separate, Rabbit, fretful and concerned, wants to get some questions off her chest. 'Why do you think Thwack's species became extinct, Doctor Hedgehog? I'm worried the same will happen to rabbits. Do you think they just didn't breed enough?'

'Perhaps. Or they might have caught a disease that wiped them all out,' Doctor Hedgehog says.

'And Pigeon, what about the moving sticks' conversation, the one you overheard with the flames? Is there any connection to the skull there?'

Using a wing to sweep the mud off the drowning daffodils, Pigeon has a think. *Could there be a link between the skull and the "old flame coming out of the woodwork" comment?* She doesn't ponder for long as she's distracted by Owl. He had been his usual still self but now he's suddenly rotating his head and looking behind him. When he returns his face to its frontal position, he blinks twice, slowly. Then he spreads his wings and rises up. Gliding directly above them, he makes very subtle, measured movements until something catches his large, dark eyes. He swoops back down and rigorously inspects the ground. Without looking at anyone, he, for the third time since joining the council, opens his mouth and speaks. 'Thwack has been here.' His voice sounds like it's coming from his bill rather than his throat, but it's steady with confidence, nonetheless. 'I can see very faint, wet flipper marks. I bet you'll be able to detect her scent if you sniff where I'm standing.'

He notices another marking and follows it, his face close to the soil once more. 'She was not alone,' he says affirmably.

As Owl cannot smell, Rabbit hops behind him to try and help. She does do this, but not in the way she intended. As she's inhaling and wiggling her nose, a tiny strand of fur shoots up a nostril. She sneezes it out and holds it up in front of her.

'Pup fur,' Owl states before Rabbit's even had a chance to properly look at it. 'Most likely a bank vole's.'

At the mention of his species, Bank Vole's stomach pops and gurgles. He wraps a paw tightly around it to try and settle it. He's instantly troubled. If Thwack's been here, that fur could only belong to one pup.

'Let's not think the worst,' Pine Marten says to lessen his anguish. 'Thwack and Pup may have not even seen the skull. It was buried, after all. They'll probably appear at sunrise, and we'll have worried over nothing.'

Squirrel, tired, carelessly blurts out another scenario. 'Maybe Thwack saw the skull, abducted the pup and fled? Us finding it could have made her angry. Pup could be in real danger.'

## INDELIBLE TRACES

Bank Vole's little body lets out a fretful squeal. Squirrel's words haunt him. They're too much for him to bear. He slides into a trance, displaying a wide-eyed stupor. His frame sways from side to side and his ears are so pricked, they look like they could touch the black clouds that are looming overhead. Unbeknown to him, he's mumbling aloud. 'Tripper, her name is Tripper. Tripper, her name is Tripper,' he repeats over and over.

Later that same star-sky, Bank Vole crawls into his offspring's burrow. He sees the pups asleep, snuggled up together and his offspring sitting on her own. Upon hearing him, she removes the paws that are covering her face and silently scurries out of her home. Bank Vole, ashamed and upset, trails behind. They sit right next to the entrance with their back to the water.

'I'm sorry, I'm so sorry,' he whispers. 'I promised you I'd protect Tripper while she was around Thwack. She must have gone to see her alone...'

His offspring takes a short, sharp breath. The dread she's been shoving away plunges and leaks inside of her. It causes both aches and numbness. 'Is she dead?' she asks. 'Have I let my first litter down?'

Bank Vole watches a centipede scuttle merrily past, its hurried legs always in a rush. Right now he wishes he could sit on top of it and let it carry him away.

'I don't know,' he sobs. 'They're missing. They've gone somewhere together, but we don't know where. I'm sorry.'

Strangely, as if out of nowhere, his offspring feels the dread smatterings reduce. They're being hosed down and curtailed by a surprising spray of serenity. 'They're probably on an adventure. Tripper wants to be like you, Bank Vole. I bet she's asked Thwack to take her downriver so she can experience what you did. I know I've been worried about Thwack influencing Tripper, but I don't think they'd run away together. Tripper in tow would only be a hindrance for Thwack. I'm sure they'll be back soon.'

His offspring's stoic attitude only pains Bank Vole more. He can't tell her about the unearthed skull, about the fact Thwack may have been keeping secrets. The council has deemed it confidential, and he promised he'd keep quiet.

'There is more to it, isn't there? Your eyes have sunk into your face; you look drained.' Her body slumps. The dread she'd felt diminish boils over, spilling into her foolish optimism, engorging it to its death. Quite quickly, this too gets sucked up and desiccated. It's replaced by a pummelling of angry rocks. 'Didn't I tell you she's a wild one? She's just gone, hasn't she? Doesn't even care to say goodbye after everything I've done for her. I should have never let her spend time with Thwack, regardless of whether you were there or not.'

She breathes heavily and speaks emphatically, sputtering and squealing. 'Although what difference would it have made anyway? She would have still gone. She was out to defy me. She has this zest to be different and there's nothing I can do to stop that. It's embedded in her, just like it's embedded in you.'

Bank Vole cowers, unsure how to handle her understandable but rapid rage.

'I've tried. I wanted to show her how pleasant life as a traditional bank vole is, but her brain works differently to mine. It's more like yours. It rebels.

'I hate feeling guilty. I don't want to feel bad. I don't want to feel this is my fault. That I'm ill-equipped to raise young.'

She takes a long, weary breath and looks around the woods. 'You know what, this is Tripper's life. If she wants to leave and live somewhere else, she can. That's normal for bank voles, so how can I disapprove? She knows how to find food, how to make a burrow. It's premature for most pups, and I wish she had stayed a little longer, but that's for my own assurance. I wanted to be certain she was ready. But if she's gone, I must let go. And you must too. I should never have asked you to look out for her. Neither she nor I are your responsibility. It was wrong of me to ask anything of you.'

She gets up, shakes mud off her fur and forces an imperturbable, calm manner to manifest within. Bank voles don't have loving feelings for one another, so she renounces all the maternal feelings she had for Tripper. It's done; the part she played in her life is over. She goes to enter her burrow and be with the pups that need her. Before her face disappears into the hole, she nods to Bank Vole and signals for him to join her. He follows, unsure what is happening. Inside, he stands on the edge, as usual. He sees his offspring settle next to her huddled pups. Then, she pats the space beside her. He gingerly makes his way over and takes a seat, confused and dubious, until she leans against him and rests her head on his body.

She knows what she's doing may seem very daughter-like, but that's not possible for their species. No, to her, what is happening is simple. A caring, kind animal, who just so happens to be her ancestor, needs comforting and she, merely another of his kind, is there by chance to do it.

## ~ CHAPTER EIGHTEEN ~

# Chaos and Candour

When you think about something a lot, it can develop an omnipresence. Whatever you're thinking about can consume you and start appearing in places you've never seen it before. Have you noticed this? For example, you, moving stick, let's pretend you haven't gone swimming in a long time and start doing so at your local pool. After a few visits, you're enjoying yourself. You look forward to dipping your feet in the cold water and eagerly await the childish giddiness you encounter as your body gets lower. You like snubbing the goosebumps that appear all over your skin, warning you not to go any further. With a mischievous grin, you push your legs down and spring yourself forward. You want to feel your body move, get pleasure out of making odd shapes and revel in the all-consuming tiredness you experience afterwards.

Then the takeover commences. You see an advert on the train showing a child wearing armbands. You're in the supermarket and overhear someone talking about a recent diving trip. You walk through your town and see countless shops selling swimming paraphernalia. You pass two separate art galleries, both of which have paintings of the sea on their window displays. You switch on the TV and the screen shows two actors writhing about in a lake.

Is it a coincidence, or has swimming always been so ubiquitous and you're only noticing now because it's on your mind? Pigeon is questioning this about moving sticks. They are everywhere to her. She could be in the woods or in the air, and somehow she manages to connect things to them. She feels like they've seeped into every corner of her brain, every fraction of her life. It's not an exaggeration either. Moving sticks have even entered her dreams. She's now wondering if her original distraction is becoming an obsession.

Currently, Pigeon is sleeping. In her dream she's resting on a warm house roof, seeking respite from the bitter chilliness. Perched there, she's watching some moving sticks in the adjacent building, most of which are seated with white hair. She notices that if any stand, they move slowly or need assistance. It's clear to her they are old and will be returning into Earth soon, if this is still what moving sticks do.

She sees one shift forward in her seat, grip the arms of the chair and hoist herself up. Her bent frame is very wobbly, but she is able to walk unaided to the window. Looking out of it, she stares directly at Pigeon and waves at her. Pigeon dips her neck to wave back. Then, pulling the same hand inward, she motions for Pigeon to come closer. Pigeon does so without hesitation. She flies towards the house and stands on the windowsill. She studies the moving stick through the glass and when it speaks, Pigeon is miraculously able to understand every word.

First, she shares her opinion on birds, saying she's always believed them to be wise because they can view everything from above. They see it all, so she imagines they assess situations holistically, unlike those living life on the ground. The latter only ever see things at one level so they develop poor judgement and warped beliefs.

# AN EXCEPTIONAL AURA

Rather randomly, she goes on to talk about her fascination with horses. She states that nothing encapsulates freedom more than a running horse. Pigeon senses envy. She's correct. The moving stick tells her she wishes she were a horse because then she wouldn't know what it's like to throw up. Vomiting, she divulges, is a huge fear of hers.

The conversation shifts again. A clear liquid spills out of the moving stick's cloudy and troubled eyes and rolls down her face. She's weeping. Her tears are making her tremble. Her hands are visibly shaking as she tries to wipe them away. She's sad, she says, because moving sticks are stuck. They're miserable and tormented; they want to abandon the stress that's tying them to the Grey, but they don't know how. She begs for Pigeon to help them return to the woods.

Pigeon, excited, hops from one foot to the other. Speaking the moving stick language perfectly, she reveals that this is her life's mission, that she will absolutely do her best to make this happen.

After hearing Pigeon's declaration of support, the moving stick unlatches the window. Pigeon steps back to allow it to open, but while she hovers in the air, the moving stick ushers her to come closer again. She's smiling, her pupils are dilating and the lines around her eyes, cheeks and mouth intensify. Pigeon lands on the outer corner of the window base and looks up at her new companion with enthusiasm and affection.

But now she has Pigeon where she wants her, the moving stick's smile fades. Her face droops and the texture of her skin transforms. The wrinkles, which had looked like soft, striped, delicate markings similar to that found on a leaf, look cracked and cragged, like the edge of a rock.

In a deep, rumbling voice, she tells Pigeon the woods are ugly, that Grey is better than Green and that all the animals in the woods need to die. She purses her lips and strains her eyes, forcing their blue iciness to gleam menacingly. Then using a hand which is of a similar hue, she grabs the window handle and slams it shut. Pigeon, unable to flee in time, is squashed. The blow smashes her bones, cracking them instantly. She collapses, lying weak and defenceless, wedged between the opening and closing of the window. The moving stick's arm reaches out above her. *Whack!* The window is pushed away and then violently pulled back in again. Feathers are ripped out of Pigeon's body. They shoot out in shock before drifting down slowly, gracefully succumbing to their fate. The lacerated holes they leave behind drain Pigeon's blood. She feels the wetness gush across her broken wings.

She's gasping for breath; her eyelids are heavy. She knows it's almost the end. She turns her head sideways to take in her last moments above Earth. In the distance, she can see a grey building that is making a chiming sound. The shape of the structure becomes blurry. She's unable to focus.

Slowly and painfully, she rolls her neck so she can face the sky once more. But the sky isn't there. Neither is the moving stick. Instead there's a distorted figure that's hurling abuse at her. Through the haze, she sees a familiar brown head with big teeth and a round body. It's Thwack. She's spitting and screaming, ordering Pigeon to die.

Pigeon's eyes open suddenly. Squirrel has been shoving his tail in her face to brush her awake. She had been swaying rather drastically on the branch, and Wren, who was resting near her, had called for help. She'd been worried Pigeon was going to slip and get an injury like Bank Vole.

## AN EXCEPTIONAL AURA

Being forced out of dream-woods leaves Pigeon disorientated. After thanking Squirrel and Wren, she flies off to hide in a horse chestnut tree. She wants to dissect what just occurred. Doctor Hedgehog hasn't been able to find out how dreams work yet, but she knows they move quickly into the memory and when they get there, they can't always be retrieved. Pigeon tries to run through everything at speed.

The moving stick who appeared in her dream, she knows who she is. She's seen her in real life on a few occasions, although they've never interacted. This moving stick is one of those who doesn't seem to notice Pigeon at all. It's always rather expressionless. Once Pigeon landed right near to her, within touching distance, yet the moving stick carried on sipping her drink, unaffected. This pleased Pigeon immensely. She likes to think those who don't react to her presence see her as part of the Grey. They view her as one of them. She thinks they'll be the moving sticks who will listen to her when she finally devises a plan that'll bring them home. Her dream now makes her think otherwise.

Digressing slightly, she tries to work out how much longer she's likely to live. The answer should help her measure whether she can keep tottering around, trusting her mind to eventually come up with something, or if she needs to somehow apply pressure to it. She knows her species usually see around 2,190 sunrises and that she's lived over half of that number already. After briefly assessing her health, what she's witnessed and how long her partner's been gone, she calculates that she has about 1,160 sunrises left. *Not imminent*, she thinks, *but it will probably come round quickly*. She lightly claws the wood she's sitting on. She wishes the trees were being more helpful. She'd hoped by coming back, they'd have a plan in place for her, one that made so much sense everyone else would get on board, too.

## CHAOS AND CANDOUR

So far, they've just been talking about spring. She lets out a big sigh. It would be better if she wasn't on her own in this endeavour. Out of pure desperation, she decides to give them another chance.

She begs Crow and Crow, who have annoyingly appeared beneath her, to stop bickering. If it wasn't for them, the place would be silent. Typically, they ignore her, squawking and cawing, until one flies off in a huff. The other follows it, evidently not wanting the argument to end.

The hush Pigeon desired descends upon the woods. She inches closer to the trunk and, in the same manner as before, clasps the branch, shuts her eyes, and breathes methodically. She feels the vibrations resound through her and waits patiently for them to transcend into voices. When they do, however, they're convoluted and echoing because they're not speaking at the same time. Pigeon holds her body still in anticipation. She's hearing f's, she's hearing r's… Eventually she hears it all. The trees are finally shouting in unison. Their chant has become clear and pronounced. They're saying one word, *'foydurar.'* Chaos.

Her eyes shoot open. Chaos, that's exactly how Pine Marten described the turmoil Thwack caused when she first arrived. The trees must have heard and are repeating it, so they all take heed. She hadn't analysed Thwack's appearance in her dream yet, but realises that's clearly where she should have been focusing her attention. She uses the branch she's on to gain extra elevation. Pressing down heavily, she lets go and springs into the air. Flying high in the sky, she surveys the ground beneath her. The others probably haven't been listening to the trees' cries. She needs to find them; she needs to immediately inform the council that Thwack's disappearance is temporary. They haven't seen the last of her.

'Chaos,' she utters the word again. *What kind of mayhem will the strange beast cause now?*

It is the council's duty to keep the Thicket in good shape. Now that the relay is over, Rabbit, Muntjac Deer, Owl and Squirrel are busy tidying it up, cutting twigs back with their mouths and levelling the ground out with their feet. It's arduous but infrequent, thanks to animals eating the edges of the Thicket whilst chatting, therefore giving it an unintentional yet helpful trim.

Bank Vole and Pine Marten are standing nearby. They are planning to join in with the clearance once they've caught up with each other.

'I did as you asked. I told Myodes Glareolus how I feel. I haven't seen her since. She was very shocked,' Bank Vole says.

The therapist in Pine Marten is relieved to hear this news. He believes this is the first stage in Bank Vole's recovery. The normal Pine Marten though, the one who sees Bank Vole as a friend, is sad. He's going to miss Bank Vole a lot when he's inevitably asked to leave. Keen to escape his sorrow, he offers a few commendatory words before hurrying them into the Thicket so he can hack at sticks and busy himself. As soon as they clamber in, however, Rabbit pounces on them. She, like everyone else, wants to know if they have any news on Thwack and Tripper.

'We don't have any updates either,' says Squirrel after Bank Vole and Pine Marten shake their heads. 'I just hope the pup is ok…'

Muntjac Deer starts trotting in a circle. They all know this means he has something exciting to share. 'I've heard things. Toad, who lives quite a few woods away, told Carp she passed a weird furry animal in the water. What else? Ahh yes, someone, I can't say who, is sure they smelt her in their home recently. Another told me Thwack has wings and they saw her fly off with the pup on her back. It's all very worrying.'

Pine Marten rolls his eyes at Bank Vole and whispers, 'I think we can take those rumours with a pinch of mud.'

Much to Muntjac Deer's disappointment, everyone else thinks the same. The clear-out resumes without any questions being asked. After a period of quiet, Squirrel remembers something. He has a message he needs to pass on.

'Oh, Bank Vole,' he shouts, making the little rodent jump. 'I almost forgot to tell you. The bank vole you bred with came by earlier. She was looking for you. She said if you would like to speak to her, you'll find her in the furthest blackberry bush. Bit early for blackberries, though, isn't it?'

Scuttling across the woods, past the juniper, the oak, the pine, into the wildflowers and the long grass, around leaves and over mounds, Bank Vole spots the furthest blackberry bush. It's right at the edge of their home, where the woodland meets the Grey. It's here that moving sticks enter the woods, and after they've walked around in a circle, it's here they leave. He'd told Myodes Glareolus about the bush just before they started breeding. Eager to find out if their proximity to the Grey made them taste different, she'd asked him to take her there. Bank Vole hasn't returned since and is surprised to find she has. It's a long way to travel and there are plenty of blackberry bushes closer to the river. He stops in his tracks, pulling on a whisker. She probably doesn't come, he realises. She's probably lured him here so he can leave quickly and quietly without any long, drawn-out goodbyes.

He reaches the tip of the bramble. The leaves' jagged edges look razor sharp, and he's convinced they're warning him not to enter, to turn back, and to pretend Squirrel never said anything. But he can't. He has to climb in. He has to accept her decision and suffer the consequences. It was the risk he took. He nervously crouches down and squeezes his body into a small entrance.

He sees her instantly. She's sitting down, unknotting her fur. He makes his way over, astounded not to find a trace of food on her despite the fact she's surrounded by flowers and small green berries. She's never been able to resist before. He stands opposite her and looks closely at her paws. He can't believe it. They really are completely clean.

'Have you decided the berries are too infested with moving sticks after all?' he asks. 'That they do indeed taste different by being so close to the Grey?' He knows they're not there to speak about food, but her abstinence intrigues him.

Hearing his voice makes Myodes Glareolus realise how nervous she is. She can't keep focus, her eyes dart from his to the ground. She gives herself a moment and then takes one deep breath, stiffening her back and expanding her chest. 'No, Bank Vole,' she replies firmly, her voice steady as she fixes her gaze upon him. 'I haven't started eating because I've been waiting for you.'

Bank Vole feels his heart slide upwards into his head. It shrinks his brain and thumps loudly against his ears. *What does she mean?*

She dabs her nose and then holds the shaking paw out in front of her. 'I'm a lucky bank vole. I had ancestors who looked after me well. They filled me with all the confidence and knowledge I needed to make it above Earth, and when I came of age, I felt ready to put everything they taught me into practice,' she says.

'As you know, I didn't travel. I stayed in these woods, and it's here I tried to build my adult life. It wasn't easy. I had been so used to having my siblings around. I guess it's normal to feel jittery when you leave each other, but the cold, it seemed freezing, and the silence was deafening. It was almost unbearable until you came along. You, with your kind face and funny jokes. Something about you felt strangely familiar. I can't explain it.

'I had been looking forward to finding someone and acting upon my bank vole duty. I had yearned to impart my ancestor's knowledge and wanted to raise young pups. So, I was relieved when we met. It felt like things were falling into place. Happening how they should. But what I experienced ended up being so much more.'

Bank Vole is sure his heart has swollen; he's worried it's dangerously close to bursting. He places a paw on his chest to check it's where it should be. It really does feel like it's moved upwards and will soon be leaking out of his ears. *Thank goodness*, he thinks. Crisis averted. It's there, beneath his neck, galloping away like Muntjac Deer did when Thwack first arrived.

'You mentioned the moving stick umbrella when we last spoke,' Myodes Glareolus continues. 'You said our bond would be like an umbrella, that it would protect us. It made me think of something. When we're out foraging, far away from our burrow and we suddenly smell moving sticks, we panic, don't we? Often, I forget where I had planned to hide if they appeared. I'm so scared I can't think. I have to try really hard to remember it and when I do, I, of course, run to it as fast as I can. What happens next, though, always surprises me. The moment I reach my hiding place, all the worry, the fear, it vanishes. As quickly as it takes for a frog to stretch out its tongue and catch a fly, the terror that was crippling me, it just evaporates. I lie there quite peacefully and wait for them to move. And I know why. It's because I'm inconspicuous. I trust they're not going to discover me. I know I'm going to be ok. I relax simply because I feel safe. I think that's the best feeling anyone can feel and the best gift someone can bestow upon another. Safety. When you feel safe, your mind can be free. You can think about whatever you like. The weight of worry isn't pushing you down.'

She pauses aware that what she says next will change their lives forever. 'Bank Vole, this is how you make me feel. I always feel safe when I'm with you. Safe from moving sticks, safe from judgement, safe from hurt. I'm at peace.'

Her extended paw becomes shakier, so Bank Vole puts his on top, hoping it will offer her some comfort. He feels the pads of her paw press hard against him as she steadies herself with his touch. She places her other paw on his cheek. She looks at a face she's come to know so well, and her eyes start to dance as if her favourite song is being sung.

'I know what I said before; I told you I couldn't do it. That wasn't true. And I know by making this decision, everyone will talk. They will say we're strange. I guess, to the masses, we are. But thanks to you and a certain little pup, I've realised my happiness is my own. Together we can all make sure the woods are clean and healthy, together we can share food... but my happiness, it's mine to look after and feel.

'The things you said about me and the way I make you feel, Bank Vole... to know I can bring as much joy to you as you do to me… it's too precious to ignore. I can, I have been. But I don't want to anymore.'

Myodes Glareolus breaks eye contact and looks down. Bank Vole sees her eyelids move from side to side. She's trying to work out if she's missed anything, if anything has been left unsaid. When she looks back up, her favourite song seems to have ended and been replaced by one that is sad and troubling. She wraps her tail around his, interlacing it and bringing him closer.

'If we both get to live through winter, it'll be our last. Certainly mine. Can you believe that, Bank Vole? It's gone so fast! When did two young pups get old? Coming towards the end, you really see how fleeting everything is. This is it. This is *really* it. What we've seen happen to others is going to happen to us, sooner rather than later.

'I've started to think about the aura I've created and who it's hovering above. I've been considering what I've done well and if there's anything I should have done differently. Should I have been more outgoing, more sociable? I've wondered if I should have gone on more adventures.

'Can you remember bringing me here to this blackberry bush? It's the most daring thing I've done. And I would have never done it if you hadn't agreed to take me. I remember returning to my burrow afterwards and it taking me ages to sleep. My mind was racing, unable to believe the risk I'd taken and how exhilarating it had been. It was such a wonderful adventure.'

She starts stroking his cheek, the sensation of which tickles Bank Vole and causes a relaxing shiver to run up his body.

'I dared myself to travel here alone. To test how brave I can be. To see what boundaries I can push. I made it

# AN EXCEPTIONAL AURA

– here I am! It was thrilling to make my way through the woods. But should I have had more adventures like these? Well, I believe, really, I've had the best one anyone could ever ask for. My greatest adventure is standing in front of me. You, Bank Vole. You've taken my mind to places it has never gone before. You've taught me things, made me think, got me to see the woods above Earth in different ways. You, you are my greatest adventure.

'And what you said last time we spoke… it made me realise that our incredible memories had been submerged deep, deep into my brain. Thoughts had been numbed. Your confession felt like an awakening, a release. It made me see that I never truly wanted our adventure to be over.

'I too want to continue our bond, Bank Vole. You and me, until Owl swoops down to collect us. Let's be together.'

She stops touching his face and reaches for his injured paw, tenderly cupping it in hers.

'I… I… how…?' Bank Vole is struggling to speak. He tries several times but stumbles over the right words. What can he say that will encapsulate how lucky he feels and how grateful he is? What can truly express his euphoria?

He racks his brain. He scratches his left ear.

It turns out nothing can. The extent of his ecstasy simply can't be conveyed through words.

He pulls Myodes Glareolus towards him and hugs her tightly, passionately. With this embrace, he hopes she senses the depth of his attachment to all that she is and all they are together.

'I feel it, Bank Vole,' she says quietly as she squeezes him back, gripping on to his waist. 'I feel it.'

## CHAOS AND CANDOUR

The happy couple amble towards the river in a sweet daze. Bank Vole's delirium is still affecting his speech. Myodes Glareolus, on the other paw, cannot stop talking.

'There's something else,' she grins. 'I've decided I will have another name. In addition to our species, I'd also like to be called Pristine. It's an ode to cleaning, an activity that's helped me cope. Plus, when something is pristine, it means you're keeping it in its original condition. That's something that's been worrying me, the thought of feeling like – or being seen as – rejecting my bank vole origins. Now I can see that's not the case. I can be in love, I can have a new name, but nothing will stop me from being a bank vole.'

Bank Vole thinks her new name is magnificent. He grapples to tell her, but his vocal cords remain unreachable. Pristine, knowing him better than any other, brings up something she believes is guaranteed to help him speak again. 'I've really missed your jokes, Bank Vole. Do you have any new ones you can share with me? I would love to hear them!'

Well, it appears Bank Vole can be in any state; he can be sad, lonely, shocked, nervous, and so overjoyed that it renders him speechless, but his mind will never let him forego the chance to tell a joke. He's not sure how it works, but his voice is delivered back to him, and he uses it to ask Myodes Glareolus why ants crawl up Muntjac Deer.

Although Myodes Glareolus has no clue what the punchline could be, she starts giggling, excited for the answer.

'Because they're making their way to the ant-lair,' he replies, pleased to hear his voice again.

'That's brilliant, Bank Vole. Ant-lair and antler!' Now that he's talking, Myodes Glareolus cuts right to the chase and brings up where they should live. 'How shall we choose between my burrow or yours? Hmm… mine is undoubtedly cleaner, smells better and is deeper, which is very important. You know how much we both hate the cold and the further underground you are, the warmer you feel. Do you think you should move into my place?'

'You make some good points,' Bank Vole says, enjoying the jesting. 'I think you're forgetting what my burrow has to offer, though. Firstly, it's closer to the water—'

'Marginally!'

'Well, marginally still counts! So that means mine is in a more desired location. Secondly, it's wider, and, in my opinion, that should be the main criteria when co-habiting. We want it to be spacious!'

The river is now in view as they climb down the hill. They decide to thoroughly inspect both of their burrows, but before they begin, they bump into Pine Marten, who has just been enjoying a drink.

'Hello, Bank Vole. Hello, Myodes Glareolus. Well, that was nice! I didn't realise how parched I was! The water tasted very pleasant. Now excuse me, but Bank Vole, may I please speak with you?'

Pine Marten's face has turned serious, leading Bank Vole to believe he must have news about Thwack and Tripper. Pristine leaves them alone and rushes home to make sure her burrow is the best it's ever looked.

Pine Marten and Bank Vole walk towards an ash tree. When they get to the trunk, Pine Marten stops, crosses his legs, and pulls his bushy tail forward. 'Oh, Bank Vole, this is awful, isn't it? Even when you think you love someone, it can't be comfortable sticking around and making small talk after they've ordered you to leave. I thought I'd rescue you! Just then, I saw you both and thought, eek, I must help! I wish we weren't in this situation, I really do. But, as I've said before, I do think this will be good for you. Has it not really hit you yet, Bank Vole? Or did you know it was coming and so are prepared? I thought you'd be devastated!'

Now Bank Vole knows why Pine Marten asked to speak to him, he's able to liberate the smile he'd been trying to stifle. 'Pine Marten, she feels the same as me!' he blurts out. 'Can you believe it? My mind is only just starting to process it. I have been mute until very recently. Yes, we're going to be in a life bond. In fact, we're just deciding whose burrow we should call our home.'

Pine Marten never predicted this outcome. The surprise makes him sway slightly with dizziness. If this was anyone else, he'd want to shout 'yuck' from the top of his lungs. He cannot imagine anything more torturous than sharing his exquisite life with another. For Bank Vole, though, he's delighted. Not only does it mean he'll no longer feel lonely, it also means his friend gets to stay! He wants to celebrate but first issues an apology. 'Truthfully, I had not believed this to be plausible. I'm sorry I was trying to move the iotas.'

'Please, do not apologise,' Bank Vole replies. 'I know therapy has worked tremendously for others. Look at Pigeon! She needed help and you were able to guide her mind towards a more positive path. You've helped her heal. You're a brilliant therapist. But for me, well, I guess I'm not your usual case. Perhaps all I needed was a friend to listen and push me to take action. Now, you can't say I didn't get that,' Bank Vole laughs. 'Thanks to you, I am no longer alone. I'll be forever grateful.'

## AN EXCEPTIONAL AURA

His mouth is aching, yet somehow the beaming smile prevails. He pats his nose and holds his paw out. Pine Marten places his on top.

'So, the two of you are choosing a home now huh? Why don't you connect your burrows underground so you can keep both? Be like rabbits; take over the place!'

Bank Vole thinks this is a brilliant idea and steps back to tell Pristine. Pine Marten detects his haste but feels compelled to share something before they depart. 'You must listen, this is very important. Now that you're going to live together and be around each other all the time, it's likely you'll notice she has traits that bother you. You rate her "wonderful" now... soon that'll change to "fine." You mustn't worry, Bank Vole, this is normal. Most couples experience this disappointment. It's one of the many weird things about these bonds. Just know you can always speak to me about it if you want to get things off your chest... as a friend or therapist... in whatever capacity you'd prefer.'

Bank Vole's already scuttled off so shouts his thanks with his back turned and Pine Marten chuckles at the rapid change in his demeanour.

'Stay where you are!'

His eyes shoot upwards. A silhouette diving down from the sky is ordering both him and Bank Vole to freeze. He can tell by the figure's shape and size that it's Pigeon. Her tone is alarming. When she lands, she crashes into the ground chest first. Either unscathed or too preoccupied to care, she lifts her short legs and gets right to it.

'I've just spoken to the others in the Thicket and now I must speak to you two. It's about Thwack. Look, I know I've always been cynical about her, but you must listen to me. She's up to no good – even now! Did you manage to hear the trees earlier? They were repeatedly chanting "chaos," Pine Marten, the word you used to describe Thwack's arrival. They know something and they're warning us, I'm sure of it. We need to find her. We need to take charge; otherwise she's going to come back and ruin the harmony we've harnessed and treasured.'

Pine Marten starts patting Pigeon lightly on the back to try and calm her. 'Look, I regret the way we handled certain things with Thwack. Bank Vole, for example, had too much responsibility. We should have all carried the load, should have cornered her together, pressed her for the truth. I know you did try to do that at some points, Pigeon, and I wish I'd supported you,' he says. 'But it's been a while now and we've looked everywhere. You've got to let it go. She's gone, Pigeon. She left our wood as mysteriously as she came in. I know the prospect of that alone is unsettling, but you can be reassured that if anyone new ever turns up here, we won't make the same mistake again. I hope that brings you comfort. And let's be honest, after we imposed the rules, she wasn't too bad. The bridge, for example, was a great idea.'

'What do you think the trees are referring to then?'

'I'm not sure, Pigeon. Did anyone else hear it? There's a chance you misheard them. The consensus we've all reached here is that Thwack and Tripper have sought fun elsewhere. You don't need to worry yourself.'

Bank Vole doesn't say anything. Unless there's been sightings of Thwack, he doesn't want to talk about her. He feels irritated that Pigeon has swooped down and demanded his attention over this. He wants to get back to Pristine. Pigeon, however, is riled up and continues uninhibited.

'I didn't mishear them, Pine Marten. They kept saying *"foydurar, foydurar."* If the search for her has stopped, then I at least ask we keep guard. She can't just float in on a log like she did before. We have to all be on watch. Our woods must be on high alert because…'

Weirdly, she stops talking mid-sentence. Her gaze is averted. She's looking at something in between them. Confused, Pine Marten and Bank Vole spin around to see what it is. Like a performing trio, all three mouths open and drop simultaneously.

Thwack is pulling herself out of the water and stepping onto their riverbank. The sun is radiating on her wet fur, revealing streams of red, orange, yellow. The colours of fire. Everything suddenly clicks for Pigeon. The trees, moving sticks, they all knew. She watches this old flame, this animal whose species has been here before, who Earth's wanted to return, and sees her hunched body blend in with a place that has always been hers. Pigeon's feathers instantly move outwards in fear, becoming markedly tousled. Thwack has come back home. And, she realises upon hearing Bank Vole's piercing squeal, that she's alone.

# ~ CHAPTER NINETEEN ~

# All is Revealed

Sitting upright, Thwack shakes her head to get rid of the excess water in her ears. She scratches her body, drying it and freeing it of any knots. When all is untangled, she lifts her tail up and collects a yellow goo into her paw. She lathers this all over her fur.

She's not said a word to Pigeon, Bank Vole or Pine Marten. The latter two have been relentlessly hounding her with questions, but she's not looked in their direction once. She's not even flinched at their voices.

Their probing stops with the goo's emergence. Its odiously pungent smell, a combination of sweet and musky, is too much for Bank Vole and he has to step back to stop himself falling ill. Pine Marten, on the other paw, is too transfixed to utter another thing.

Their sudden silence doesn't seem to affect Thwack either. She carries on inspecting her fur, now checking to see if there are any dry spots. When she finds some, she rubs her oily gunk over them.

Looking from her friends to Thwack, Pigeon decides enough is enough. She puts her fear aside, spreads her wings and marches staunchly towards the soaked, round animal, not stopping until she feels the water dripping from Thwack's fur directly on her head. 'Tell Bank Vole where

Tripper is right now! You have no right to keep this information from him. She's his descendant!'

A large spherical droplet has amassed on the tip of Thwack's chin. Pigeon looks up just as it detaches and it plummets directly into her eye. 'Also, on behalf of the council, I summon you to an emergency meeting. We're not fools, Thwack. We know you came here with a motive. We know you've been harbouring secrets. That slime you've just paraded being one of them!'

Now Thwack is sure she's covered her whole body in oil, she lifts her head, turns it sideways and gazes at the fast-flowing river. 'Back away, birdy. Back away if you know what's good for you.'

Despite numerous blinks, the water isn't properly draining from Pigeon's eye. Her vision is blurred and this, on top of Thwack's clipped and threatening voice, resurfaces her dream. She hears the same anger, the same brazenness. Her assertion diminishes and she hops back immediately.

All three animals, bemused and apprehensive, wait. They keep their bodies tense, ready to defend, and watch Thwack as she surveys the river. They see her focus on the water hitting the bank and hear her grunt faintly as it recedes, leaving its imprint on the soil. They spot a fly landing on Thwack's sticky chest. Unlike their questions, she can't ignore it. She looks down at the bug and lets it struggle. When she feels it's learnt its lesson, she flicks it free and massages the affected area. Then, after wiping her paw clean on the ground, she slowly raises her neck and faces her inquisitors.

'Gather as many animals as you can from both sides of the woods. Bring them here to the riverbank. I have indeed been hiding things. Until now.'

## ALL IS REVEALED

Pigeon and Pine Marten set off instantly. Bank Vole, however, stays put. 'Why aren't you talking to me, Thwack?' he asks in a quiet whimper. 'Haven't I always believed you and wanted the best for you? I treated you as a friend. I confided in you... I thought we were the same. I thought we were both lonely.'

Pine Marten hears Bank Vole's plea and turns back. He tries to persuade him to move, telling him the sooner they collect everyone, the sooner they'll find out what Thwack has to say. He knows imploration is futile and that Thwack wants to reveal her secrets in front of a crowd.

Bank Vole still refuses to budge. He's staring at Thwack now, taking in the sinister look on her face. He knows he's seen this expression before, but it would always disappear so quickly that he'd think he imagined it. It's unmistakable now, lingering long enough for him to analyse it. He sees her mind like an impending storm. It's a dark, grey cloud filled to the brim with rain. He wonders if the seal will break, if, after gathering everyone, she'll permit it to burst.

To Pine Marten, Bank Vole seems frozen, too distressed to stir, so he scoops him up in his mouth. While he carries him to the nearby burrows, Thwack shouts that she wants them to bring the skull as well.

Bank Vole is shivering when he's dropped outside the entrance to Pristine's home. He isn't sure if it's Pine Marten's saliva or Thwack's command, but something is making his fur stand on end.

Assuming it's a mixture of both, Pine Marten apologises. 'I'm sorry you're so cold. I know you don't like going in my mouth. I hope you can see I didn't have much choice! Now, let me tell you the plan for rallying everyone. I'm going to prioritise finding the rest of the council and will round up those who live in the opposite woods. Pigeon is concentrating on tree dwellers, and you, Bank Vole, have to work on everyone else. Seeing as Pigeon has had a head start, she'll no doubt help you if you need her to.'

Although Bank Vole is still in close proximity to Thwack, he's able to concentrate much better now he's not absorbing her gloominess. He springs into action, quickly telling Pristine and the rest of his species about Thwack's return. His offspring he speaks to last. The news makes her wail; Tripper's absence, she believes, can only mean one thing. Bank Vole tells her to not think like this, he tells her to believe Tripper is still alive, but she continues to squeal. Upon hearing her cry, Pristine comes out of her burrow. She knows Bank Vole needs to continue assembling the others, so she assures him she'll take care of her. He reluctantly leaves them both and goes to shout down every hole and hollow. He manages to find Mole and asks her to spread the message underground.

Pigeon, meanwhile, is not simply adhering to Thwack's request. She's also making sure it's done with efficiency and order. Positive a commotion will ensue with so many animals congregating to hide in the same area, she instructs the birds she's gathering to take charge.

It's a good call. The melee that descends upon the riverbank causes anarchy, and birds have to work hard to disband the scuffles. They flit about, shoving as many animals as they can in bushes or up trees and when those spaces are filled, they cover those remaining with leaves or debris. The desire to be inconspicuous isn't as extreme for them, so when it's their turn to settle, they all squeeze onto exposed branches.

Nobody knows what they're meeting for, but they can all see Thwack sitting by the edge of the water. By the time Bank Vole, Pigeon and Pine Marten come back, rampant rumours have spread, and they hear whisperings of them as they make their way through the concealed crowd. They hear that "the beast" can make a fire and is going to burn the woods down. That she's ravenous after her long swim and wants to eat them. They even hear that she's going to throw them in the river and drown them one by one. Bank Vole would bet precious hazelnuts that Muntjac Deer has invented these silly stories to add to the hysteria, yet his mind simultaneously considers their plausibility. *Who really is Thwack?*

    Pine Marten counts all the different species he can smell. As some animals like hedgehogs are pretty odourless, he's aware he won't have captured everybody. The numerous scents he has calculated, though, inform him most are being represented. He looks at the council members from his woods. They're out in the open, strategically spread around Thwack. He nods at them, and together, they stamp their feet. A hush rapidly ripples through the crowd. Soon, all that can be heard is the light whooshing breeze, the babbling water, and Thwack's heavy breathing. She was keen to avoid further questioning, so has deliberately sat with her back to everyone. Now there's silence, she twists around dramatically and stands.

    She scans the area. Her face, taut from clenching, suddenly breaks into a smile. The smile becomes a laugh. The sound alarms Pigeon, who is still associating Thwack with the version she saw in her dream. She registers all the scattered stones by the water's edge and lets out a snivel. The Thwack in her dream would use those as weapons. She leans forward in the tree so only the tip of her claws touch the branch. She may be scared, but if Thwack really is a monster, she wants to be ready to defend her neighbours.

## AN EXCEPTIONAL AURA

Thwack's laughter stops and she speaks mockingly to the predominately hidden crowd. 'So, I see a lot of y'all have chosen to disguise yourselves. Afraid moving sticks will see you and harm you. I really do find that funny. Better than any of your jokes, in fact, Bank Vole. It's the irony of it. Y'all think you're following a woodland rule, one you've set amongst yourselves, so you're safe from the nasty furless beings. You think it means you're in control. But it's not really a woodland rule, is it, eh? It's a moving stick rule. You're keeping out of their way, being submissive, doing what they want you to do. You let these non-animals dominate your home. It's ridiculous! You hide and they win.'

She bends down to lift part of the bridge out of the water and rests it on the bank. Climbing on top of it, she stands elevated, presiding over the majority. Feeling powerful, she decides now is the time to see the skull. Badger, who has been looking after it, willingly brings it forward. He assumes that because he backed Thwack's involvement in the race, she will address him amicably. To his surprise, she doesn't. She snatches the skull and rebuffs his smile, leaving him feeling like a disgraced little cub.

Holding the skull in front of her, Thwack analyses it in a similar way to Doctor Hedgehog. She presses it against her nose and inhales it. She slides her paw across every detail, touching each feature before touching that part of her own face. She studies the back of it and looks at it from upside down. Then, when there isn't a part of the structure left for her to examine, she throws it down on the ground. It rolls backwards and splashes into the water, briefly bopping up and down before sinking out of view. The council are astonished. They hadn't expected Thwack to dismiss it. The act, to them, verges on sacrilegious.

## ALL IS REVEALED

'Thwack, we think we worked it out. We think we know what the skull means—'

Pine Marten attempts to start a conversation, but Thwack, now on all fours, has turned away from him. She doesn't want anyone else to lead this, so she is walking along the bridge to shut his speech down. Halfway across, she gets what she wants. The silence resumes, and she stops to work out her next move. When the direction becomes clear, she manoeuvres herself around and crawls back towards the edge of the log. She looks ahead and says gravely, 'Here's the tremendous truth.'

Ears become erect, and bodies lean forward as Thwack rises once more. She's practiced this speech many times, so although it's momentous, she's able to execute it with ease. 'As y'all are aware, many sunrises ago, moving sticks used to live here. They were animals back then, they were called hapo simneos and like everyone else, they were controlled by their stomachs. That was a big connector you know, trying to satisfy the incessant growling and groaning that came from within. Most animals would try to achieve this by copiously eating the same food. Others though, including hapo simneos, experimented. And *this* was the biggest differentiator. To fill *their* stomach, they sampled all sorts of organisms. They took risks, and mark my words, these really were risks. With our evolved brains, we pretty much know what can and can't be eaten. They were without this knowledge. Their brains were a lot smaller, so for them, it was a case of trying and potentially dying. However, if an animal didn't perish from poisoning, the gamble was worth it. Their species diet expanded. They had more and more to eat, and were, they believed, on the path to satiation. Instead though, they experienced something else. Bodily changes. Some found their limbs grew longer or their stamina increased. Others discovered a new strength. The hapo simneos, they felt a weird sensation in their head. These extra nutrients had caused something incredible to happen. Their brains developed and formed an internal voice. Y'all know about this. We now all have it. But at the time, it was completely new. They didn't know how to handle it. They still don't actually. They're completely governed by it.

'Each and every one of them listened to what their internal voice told them, they yielded to its authority. When it convinced them they could be superior, better than all other species, they didn't question it. When their internal voice told them that other animals were lesser and that they could supersede their skills, they accepted it. With certain changes, their internal voice told them they could reach total domination and be the best at everything.

'And you can, in a way, see why they listened. Their internal voice taught them how to make a fire, a phenomenon only lightning could create. What a feat that was! A real show of supremacy. So, when their internal voice also instructed them to get rid of their fur, they did. Having been told fur slowed them down, that it was an unnecessary weight, that they'd never be the quickest at hunting with it, they ripped it off and endured the pain. Without it, they'd be nimble, able to climb trees better, run faster... besides, now they were able to build a fire, what use was fur? Their internal voice said if they kept tearing it off and proving to Earth they didn't need it, Earth would let them evolve without it.

'The plan worked. Eventually, young hapo simneos' were born furless. And you know what? For a long while, they were thriving. But then everything changed. They hadn't anticipated the big freeze. The sun, Earth's heart, was angry that an animal was able to create what it provided. It had believed the power to emit warmth, to join forces with clouds to create lightning, had only rested with them. It was outraged this gift wasn't theirs alone, and to show just how furious it was, it refused to burn. The sun would push its smouldering flames round and round its spherical realm and prohibit any rays from effusing outwards. It meant those living above Earth only got the sun's light.

'The cold... it was inconceivable. Everything was either covered in ice or became it. Most animals didn't know what to do. Shelter was scant. Food was sparse. Some didn't survive. The harsh conditions drove them to extinction. As for the hapo simneos, well, they looked out for themselves. I guess you could admire their brute determination to sustain their species at whatever cost. They struggled to build fires, but their internal voice told them to be resilient and find other ways to cope. It reminded them that if anyone deserved to withstand the cold, it was them. Now, it's this moment, even after they've lost their fur, that I believe they stopped being animals. They become vermin.'

Thwack pauses to bend down and drink some water. Her mouth is getting dry, and it is making her speech slower. While she submerges the lower half of her face into the river, she notices how still everything is. Her audience aren't moving. She's not seeing tails flick; she's not hearing itches be scratched. They're captivated, as she thinks they should be. Picking up a stone to fidget with, Thwack hoists herself back onto her stage. She rolls the solid mineral around her claws and picks up where she left off.

'When hapo simneos first discovered they had an internal voice, it was helping them reach food from the furthest and highest places. But when the ice fell, their internal voice became fixated on warmth instead. It made hapo simneos jealous of all the other animals around them.

Unlike them, they'd kept their fur. They believed they couldn't be experiencing the same suffering. Being so cold, it made them feel weak. They were meant to be superior; they couldn't allow this. So, they started to see other species as weaponry. They had the warmth they coveted. They began stripping them of their fur, ripping it off them as they had once ripped their own.

'And that was it. As soon as the first hapo simneos wrapped itself in fur, they knew the battle had been won. They knew the ice wouldn't be their demise. From then on, they wrapped themselves up in as much fur as possible and relished the warmth.

'When the sun realised what was happening, that hapo simneos were no longer being punished, it released heat above Earth again. It had been wanting to prove a point and hadn't predicted the consequences that would stem from that. It didn't want hapo simneos to be the last living thing in existence.

'Soon colour came back, plants grew, food was in abundance. The hapo simneos' internal voice, though, remained fearful, terrified they would encounter something horrific like that again. So, despite having the sun's rays beaming down on them once more, hapo simneos continued wrapping themselves in fur. They continued to be cuddled by other animals' modesty, by their decision to keep what Earth had given them.'

Thwack is momentarily distracted by Rabbit who is taking a seat, tired from standing for so long. Unlike everyone else, she's not finding the story very riveting and would like to get back to her kittens. She wishes Thwack would hurry up and reveal why she's gathered everyone. She lets out a big sigh to show she's bored, but it doesn't seem to have any effect. Thwack carries on.

## ALL IS REVEALED

'You see, the ice may have melted but hapo simneos had changed forever. They couldn't relax; they were traumatised. They couldn't enjoy life's little treasures, like picking berries or playing games. Now they had an internal voice, all they could think about was their own survival.

'They were encouraged to live on their own and fend for themselves. Their internal voice told them to section off a part of the woods and build something that could resist extreme weather. So, they did just that. They set up the Grey. And along with the Grey, they made guns. Long, cruel weapons that kill instantly. Armed and protected, it became a real case of them against all other living beings. And any time they did return to the woods, it was just to ravage and ransack – they only cared about themselves. They believed the only value we held above Earth was for their use.'

Thwack takes a deep breath and squeezes the stone she's holding. This is the part where her species enter the story. Everyone is soon going to know who she is and what she's here for. All of a sudden, she feels hot and clammy. 'Now, you call them moving sticks. Quite an apt name considering they sure do move,' she tries to maintain the same pace and volume as before but her voice is quavering. 'In a bid to sustain their species, they travelled and explored new lands. They wanted to gather as much fur and resources as they could. One sunrise, they arrived at the place where I used to live. Hapo simneos already resided there but they still lived amongst other animals. They did kill, but not like the newcomers.

'The newcomers arrived having travelled on a boat, that's a moving structure hapo simneos settle on when they move over water. And joining them on that boat was Cat. When she ventured across the new land, she was particularly surprised to see my species. She said where she'd previously been living, all of us had been culled. We had been murdered for our fur and none of us were left. We had been killed to extinction. We didn't have any descendants left. We couldn't outbreed their guns.'

Bank Vole is glad they're surrounded by plenty of air as everyone, including himself, suddenly sucks a load in. The gasps are short and sharp and remind him of the ones he makes before he's immersed underwater. He's beginning to understand Thwack's look of anger now. She's starting to unravel and make sense.

'That's right,' Thwack says affirmably. 'My species came from here too. That's what the skull was. A dead member of my species. Could have been an ancestor of mine. Anyway, Cat said hapo simneos, what I'll now refer to as moving sticks, were running rampant. She said they needed as much fur as they could get to warm their skin, to warm their cold minds and their cold hearts. They started to torture and massacre my species in the new land too, but luckily, that land is a lot bigger than this one, so my species were able to swim to areas moving sticks couldn't get to. So, thanks to my ancestors, my species still exists. We're fighters, we're survivors. We are beavers.'

Nobody is able to keep quiet any longer. The name beaver echoes from the burrows to the trees, spreading through the woods like wildfire. Badger locks eyes with Mole. He can tell just by her expression that she too has been told about beavers and the terrible extinction.

'My ancestors told me about them. I just hadn't thought it possible for them to still exist!' she says to him.

'Neither had I!' Badger replies. 'And to think one has been living amongst us all this time… an old neighbour. My ancestors spoke so fondly of them.'

## ALL IS REVEALED

Thwack waves a paw in the air to get everyone to be quiet. She still has a lot more to say and doesn't want to lose their attention. When that doesn't work, she whistles as penetratingly as possible.

'Good, now remain quiet. Where was I... ahh, yes,' she clasps her paws together and grates her top teeth across her lip, deliberately making everyone wait. 'After a while, beavers had had enough. My species yearned to live freely, the way they had before. A few started to swim where they wanted, openly and confidently, in front of moving sticks. They decided they'd rather live freely for a short while than live a long life oppressed. This audacity shocked moving sticks. In fact, it impressed them. Word got around about how courageous, brave, and bold beavers are. Moving sticks realised what a mistake they'd made. They wanted beavers to exist in all the places they had before.

'And this is where I come in. They chose me to move here and well, I didn't resist. I walked onto the boat because... actually, before I get into that, let's talk about my arrival, shall we, eh? Well, that was a shock! Not one animal welcomed me. Not even when I meekly and briefly ventured inland did anyone from either side of the woods say hello. I knew you were all around. I could smell you. But why were you all hiding from me? I eventually found Bank Vole, and he told me why. No one recognised me. I was a stranger, a beast.'

'That was your opportunity to reveal who you really are! If you had just said you are a beaver and explained this whole story when you arrived, things would have been so different,' Pine Marten says.

'Oh, and you would've all believed me, would you? You'd have trusted me, taken my word for it? I don't think so. You only believe me now because I have tangible evidence. The skull proves I belong here. If it wasn't for that, I think y'all would have always seen me as an outsider and you know there's such an irony to that…'

She jumps off the log and paces up and down the bank, the stone still rolling around in her paw. 'Remember I said Cat listed all the animals who lived here? Well… not all of you were named. Yes, not all of *you* really belong here. Who shall I start with?'

She strides over to Squirrel. He's leaning against the base of a tree trunk, trying to camouflage his frame.

'One of my biggest opponents, a member of the revered council, and such a treasured relay racer… you're such an integral part of these woods, aren't you, eh, Squirrel?' Thwacks says glaringly.

Squirrel lowers his head shamefully.

'Your silence speaks volumes! I take it then that you know. Yes, when Cat listed all the animals who lived here, there was a squirrel on the list… but it wasn't your species, was it? It was the red squirrel. Your species were brought here by moving sticks. In fact, they aptly call you the *grey* squirrel. You're really from a place not too far away from where I travelled from. And what's shocking about your species – do you want to tell them, or shall I? Actually, let me do the honours…' Thwack steps back to project her voice. She doesn't want anybody to miss this. 'When grey squirrels arrived here, they started killing their cousins with a deadly disease! And they've continued doing so ever since! They are trying to eradicate the animal who really belongs.'

Thwack smirks when, for the second time, she hears gasps all around her. Squirrel looks up at his species. They're crouched down low in the dark tree hollows. All he can see are their jet-black eyes, which are filled with fear. This was their secret, never to be disclosed. He tries to think how he can protect them. Thwack's sadism, however, weirdly works to Squirrel's advantage. Rather serendipitously, her desire to humiliate means he doesn't need to fret. She makes it known there are others to mortify.

'Who else was adamant I didn't belong? Rabbit, I can see you now. Moved to hide inside the brambles, have you, eh? So you're a coward as well as a hypocrite. As with Squirrel, you obviously knew you weren't originally from here. Disgusting how you were willing to treat me with such contempt! Guess my story isn't so boring now, is it? Let me hear you sigh again! No? Not so brazen now! Oh, I'm ticking these council members off, aren't I…'

Thwack waddles over to Muntjac Deer and starts walking in circles around him. 'Let me spin around you, as I'm the one with gossip now!' she sneers.

Muntjac Deer is shaking, his teeth are chattering. He's always been one step ahead of rumours, always wanted to keep on top of hearsay so he'd be able to quash any rumblings about his origins. Now, Thwack is going to carelessly spill it, rendering him unable to twist or alter her words.

'Why are you so terrified of me?' Thwack asks. 'It should be the other way around! You're not native, so who knows what damage you're causing to our woods. I dread to think what harm you're doing!' She releases a short, forced laugh and then shouts for Pigeon. 'Where's that judgmental bird?'

'I'm here, Thwack, and I know what you're about to say.'

Pigeon has moved to sit comfortably on the branch. She no longer feels the need to be on high alert. She is very aware of her species' beginnings and doesn't think either she or anyone else needs to be embarrassed about it.

'I know I originate from a hot, dry place south of here. That is one of the reasons I like going into the Grey, actually. I like to perch on their warm rooftops because my species had been used to heat, and that's passed on to me. Pigeons have been here a long time now, though, and I don't feel bad because—'

'You should, Pigeon. Where's your humility? You all should feel sorry for how you've treated me. After everything beavers have been through, I should have been welcomed, revered…'

'But we didn't know who you were!'

'You assumed I was beneath you all. You took one look at me and decided to slap me with rules. You didn't even respect me after I obeyed them.' She climbs back onto the log. Her posture is stooped and her eyes are dark. She'd been looking forward to that bit, to putting everyone in their place. But the fun and games are over. Seriousness, condemnation, must prevail.

'So, back to moving sticks. It's apparent they can see the value in beavers now, but what about all my ancestors? What about their suffering? Their lives were needlessly cut short. Shall I just move on? They're dead, after all. Well, I'll tell y'all what I think. The stories about them, they live in my brain and are being stirred and blended with my own experiences. They may be dead, but what happened to them is very much alive. I think their memories are my memories. I don't have to have been there to understand the cruelty. That pain has been implanted in me, it's shaped me, made me who I am. And let me tell ya, it's cumbersome. The thought of passing this on…I don't want my descendants to carry this oppressive weight. I don't want them to get upset at the mere mention of their precious fur. I need to make changes; I need to alter this shape we beavers make.

## ALL IS REVEALED

'I know there's too many to defeat, but I need to inflict pain upon wretched moving sticks. I need to get them to see they are not superior. That we still possess features, skills, knowledge they don't have. To do this, I'm going to need help. Tripper has gone into the Grey to find the animals who have dared to encroach on moving sticks' territory. Animals they're afraid of such as rats and foxes. She's also going to look for bats, adders, and other deer. I'm going to form an alliance with them and develop a plan that will torture moving sticks in a way they've never experienced.

'As for this place... I know many of y'all are decent, you will want to show contrition. Here's how you do it. You accept me as your leader. You follow and obey my orders. And look, I can see your value. Squirrel, I know you're cunning. Pine Marten, I know you're a good facilitator. Badger, you may be older, but you still have great strength. Believe me, you will all benefit from my leadership. With me at the helm, you will feel powerful. You will be inundated with feelings of gratification. Together, we will show moving sticks we are not to be reckoned with. Together, we'll get justice!'

Pandemonium breaks out as the animals take in what Thwack's saying. There are squeals of horror and growls of dismay. Many grab the nearest animal and pull them close for comfort. Others leap out of hiding and run home, unable to hear anymore. Surprisingly, though, there also are a few cheers. It appears that some want to join Thwack and seek revenge.

Badger walks over to where Thwack is standing. His eyes are heavy, his mouth is curved downwards. 'I am sorry, Thwack,' he says amidst the noise. 'Would you have ever told us you're a beaver if we hadn't found the skull?'

Thwack throws the stone she's been holding into the river and doesn't speak until the ripples it produces disappear. 'I thought you'd all know the moment I arrived. I'd been concerned about it, to tell you the truth. You see, I came here knowing I wanted to get revenge on moving sticks and knew I'd need backing. I'd thought that my being a beaver might make y'all think I was weak because of what they'd been able to do to us. So, I was loud and destructive initially, to show y'all we're not. Then when Bank Vole said no one recognised me, I used that to my advantage and changed tactic. I thought I could temporarily bypass my species name and garner your support by showing my worth and getting y'all to like me. Obviously, it wasn't easy because I also needed to interact with moving sticks to show them I'm not afraid of them and this annoyingly went against the rules. But, nevertheless, I tried to please y'all. I stayed neutral, I built the bridge. I figured once everyone was fond of me, I could reveal who I was and it wouldn't change your opinion of me or hinder my cause. But it didn't work out how I wanted it to. You were all adamant I didn't belong and that was that. It got to a point where I thought even if I did reveal my species, none of you would believe me. I was quite stuck to be honest. Then Tripper showed me the skull and well, everything fell into my place. I confessed all to her and off she went.'

'That's why you called her Tripper in the first place, isn't it? Because you knew she'd leave and do your dirty work for you.' Neither Thwack nor Badger had realised Bank Vole had been behind them listening. 'You've taken advantage of a young pup,' he squeals, his voice raised and angry. 'One who was eager to learn and be different. Where exactly is she? Tell me! Someone else can do this job for you, not a little pup whose life is bright and bountiful. How dare you try and darken it! Let me bring her back!'

Pigeon pushes a terrified chaffinch off her chest and flies down to stand next to Bank Vole. Catching the end of his speech, she adds, 'Yes, Tripper needs to come back, and you need to forget about being our leader, Thwack. Everything needs to return to normal. Moving sticks have done terrible things in the past, absolutely, this is true. But those exact moving sticks have returned inside Earth. You'd only be punishing innocents. You'll be a hypocrite, inciting pain on those who don't deserve it.

'If anything, they need our help. Their internal voice is wrecking with them. Ever since the big freeze, they don't know if they can trust it. It told them to shed their fur and it shouldn't have. But it dominates them, it still insists it knows what's best. Moving sticks are lost. We should all be thinking of them as sick creatures who need looking after. They need to be nursed back to the woods. They're still animals, even if their internal voice has made them forget that. They can still be one of us.'

'Enough!' Thwack has been desperate to shout that at Pigeon ever since they met. She riles her up the most with her pathetic support for vermin, who she doubts would place any value on her or any other bird's life. 'You're the hypocrite, Pigeon, not me! You're so keen for moving sticks to feel they belong, but what about me? Why didn't you treat me the same way? I am also from here!

'And you say they are suffering, that you think they're sick. But what do we do with those that are sick? We return them back into Earth. Moving sticks are of no use to us. They don't make life above Earth any better for anyone, not even themselves. They don't even suit being here! They have to cover themselves up because they're always cold.

## AN EXCEPTIONAL AURA

They suffer. Really, the kindest thing to do is end their pain. They'll be begging for it anyway by the time I get my army on them. They'll be cursing their very existence.'

Thwack, stirred and excited, is yelling for everyone to hear. Afterwards, she's bombarded with questions. Animals are keen to know what part they'll have to play and if the new arrivals will want to eat them. While she answers, the council furtively gather and whisper in a circle. Their discussion, however, doesn't last long. As soon as Thwack notices, she stops talking and barges into them, pushing Mole to the ground. 'Don't outcast me more than you already have!' she shouts. 'I'm your leader now!'

Pigeon is appalled at the sight of her friend lying injured. She tenses her claws and points them in Thwack's face. Flapping her wings repeatedly, she attempts to block Thwack's view and thus stop her from hurting anyone else. The move conversely irritates Thwack, who ruthlessly slaps her away with the back of her paw. Pigeon falls back, unconscious. Bank Vole, Rabbit and Muntjac Deer all rush over to see if she's ok. Gently, Bank Vole peels her eyelids back and sees her pupils have rolled up towards her head. She's breathing but not stirring, so Rabbit suggests Muntjac Deer carry her to a safer place. Keen to escape anyway, Muntjac Deer gives in to his trembling legs, letting them buckle without resistance. His lowered body enables Bank Vole and Rabbit to push Pigeon onto his back. He rises slowly, feeling the stiff weight slide towards his neck. Then he zones in, focusing his gaze on the dark green canopy in the distance.

Bank Vole doesn't watch them leave. He's distracted by a hissing sound. It's coming from Pine Marten who he sees charging at Thwack, ready to attack. To his utter dismay, he gets shoved by Badger, whose push causes Pine

## ALL IS REVEALED

Marten to roll into the river. Rabbit, too, witnesses this betrayal. Furious, she hops behind Badger and uses her two hind legs to kick him hard in the back. Caught off-guard, he topples to the ground, bashing his nose. He roars dramatically, alerting Thwack, who is waving goodbye to the council from the opposite woods. Before running across the bridge she built, they'd sworn their allegiance to her. Realising she may also have an ally in Badger, Thwack challenges Rabbit to a fight. Rabbit, aware of how much faster she is, accepts. She picks up a stone and throws it at Thwack. Ting! It hits her front teeth and bounces onto her chest. Amused, Rabbit continues to goad her as she waddles over, hurling stone after stone fearlessly. Then, when Thwack is close enough to grab her, she runs. She darts round and round, reaching such a speed that her legs become a blur to onlookers. Thwack is trying and failing to catch her. Rabbit begins to laugh; she knows she's beyond Thwack's reach. Until there's an unexpected intervention. A murder of crows flock down to fly beside her. They beat their wings rapidly so they can get ahead and slow her down. Rabbit's view is now impacted. She keeps running, twisting and turning to try and trick the birds. They momentarily lag behind, allowing her to gain speed, but even so, she knows they're making it easier for Thwack to advance. She grits her teeth, getting them ready to bite. Any instant now, Thwack's going to grab her... swoosh! She jumps with fright. A big brown animal has indeed emerged, but she quickly discovers it's not Thwack. With his wide wingspan and silent, dramatic glide, Owl forces the crows away. Rabbit, now out of breath, watches him as he turns to fly serenely and intimidatingly over to her chaser. Thwack frantically waves her paws in the air to try and stop him approaching, but Owl manages to latch his beak onto her ear. He clamps down, applying enough pressure to make her scream and beg for him to let go.

Squirrel, up to this point, had been staying out of it. However, now that Owl is hurting Thwack, and Pine Marten and Mole are lunging towards Badger, he decides to act. He climbs one of the trees his species are piled into and uses the acorns they've stashed away to pelt Thwack and the council. Unsure what is striking them from above, they all stop fighting to find out.

'It's me! Up here!' he shouts. 'Let's not hurt one another! Look at what you're all doing! Let's listen to our leader, Thwack. She's right. If we work together, we can be the greater force! Let's target moving sticks! Us squirrels, we, too, want revenge. We were forced to move here – they didn't care whether we wanted to. We've been burdened with a secret we didn't want to have! We've made do and done the best we can, but the pecans our ancestors used to eat are legendary. We've heard they'd crumble into your mouth and melt like delicate snowflakes. We've been deprived for too long!'

His species cheer, supporting his desire for change. Pine Marten doesn't. He wrings his fur and feels a deep sadness course through him as he looks around. From this moment on, their woods will no longer be what it was. It will be filled with turbulence. It will be harsh, chaotic. He politely declines Doctor Hedgehog's medical assistance and walks over to Thwack, who is hunched over, caressing her bleeding ear. He touches his nose and holds his paw out to her. He does this not because he sees her as their leader but because he wants to show he respects her as an animal, and so, consequently, he should be able to speak to her honestly, like a peer would, on behalf of a very special friend.

## ALL IS REVEALED

'We were kinder to you than you make out, Thwack. You acted suspiciously from the get-go. You deliberately flaunted yourself in front of moving sticks. You were loud and secretive. Just because you've explained why now, that doesn't mean you weren't difficult to live with. We could have banished you. We were close to, believe me, but we didn't. Do you know why? Because of Bank Vole. He had the utmost faith in your integrity. From the moment he met you, in fact, he was certain you had a place here. He said you belonged. Thwack, Beaver, Beast, whatever you are, you harbour extreme anger and believe the only way to dispel it is to cause damage. Some, many even, feel stirred by your speech and will join you in your quest to inflict pain. I will not stand with you. I want to enjoy life and there's very little enjoyment to be had in another's suffering. I will stay away and mourn the stability we once had, even if that stability was based on us hiding from a species we considered unpredictable. For me, it worked. All I ask from you is to please show some kindness to Bank Vole, the animal who has always been by your side. He wants to know where Tripper is. Please, do the right thing. Tell him.'

Thwack, exhausted, moves backwards to sit on the log. Her fur is muddied and her ear is soaking. She lets the blood trickle onto her cheek while she calls Bank Vole over.

'I can't deny that you have helped me, Bank Vole,' she says quietly when he reaches her feet. 'I know you were patient and caring, that you had good intentions. The others in this woods couldn't take to me, but thanks to you, I was tolerated. Thanks to you, Tripper sought me out. I will tell you where she is. We'd been hiding just beyond the moving stick gates in an area with large erect stones and long grass. She'll still be there now, following the river in the direction of the Grey. I warn you, though, her mind is excited by this, it's enthralled. She wants to do this for me, for all the woodland animals. She wants to make her mark. So, you can go and find her, but she won't want to return. Your reunion will end in a parting. She will continue on her mission. It will, Bank Vole, be a goodbye.'

## ~ CHAPTER TWENTY ~

# Tripper's Mission

Bank Vole's offspring can't bring herself to look for Tripper. She's worried she'll unleash silly emotions if they find her, and that wouldn't be very bank vole-like. She still doesn't want to break with tradition, even if her ancestors have. So, she decides to remain at home. Her other pups still need her, and this is the excuse she gives Bank Vole.

Pristine, too, stays behind. Now that the fighting has stopped and they all know Thwack's plan, she's returned to her burrow and is keen to start digging. She likes what Pine Marten suggested, so is going to attempt to create a tunnel between her home and Bank Vole's. Safety underground now seems critical. She's asked to smooth out Bank Vole's burrow too. As far as she's concerned, it's unkempt, bordering on unloved. He unabashedly agrees.

So, it's Bank Vole, Pigeon and Pine Marten who leave the woods to look for Tripper. They set off at star-sky, so they're less likely to come across moving sticks. Pine Marten, especially, is nervous. He's never ventured out of the woods before and, having never planned to, feels ill-prepared. He also feels extremely vulnerable. Pigeon can fly off the moment there's obvious danger and Bank Vole can hide in the smallest little spaces; he can't do either of these things. He said he'd go because he wants to help, but as they step out of the woods and through the moving stick gates, he wonders if his presence is actually going to be more of a hindrance. He observes the grey path ahead of them that's split between flat, manicured grass. This dull landscape stretches out into the distance, as far as the eye can see. He takes a short, sharp breath as his fear increases. There are barely any trees to run to for coverage. He's going to be incredibly exposed and unsafe. He squeezes his lips together, securing them shut, and pledges to stay as quiet as he can for the whole journey.

Pigeon, meanwhile, much more familiar with the surroundings, chats away. Hobbling along, mildly wounded from the brawl with Thwack, she tells them she thinks Tripper's going to be ok. 'I mean, some of the things moving sticks have invented are dangerous, but they themselves really aren't too bad. Honestly, I think if any see Tripper they'd either run away and leave her in peace or react adoringly, like they do with Thwack. I don't think it's them we need to worry about. It's other animals. Thwack says we can all work together like one big pack, but outside of the woods, most just fend for themselves. Even Thwack. She's just thinking about herself in this situation.

'Moving sticks knew to be wary of her. Have you both made the connection yet? Like us, they would have seen her floating on that bit of wood, you know the log she arrived in the woods on? I'm guessing that as she was new, having just been brought back, they didn't know her name, so they looked at her brown, reddy fur, her yellowish cheeks and her bright orange teeth and called her a flame. Her fur even has bits of yellow and orange in it when it's wet. It's the same as us calling moving sticks "moving sticks," effectively. They just named her after what she closely resembles: flame in a fire. And I think they added "old" into the description because although they didn't quite recognise her, they had a sense she'd been here before.

'Anyway, can you remember what the other moving stick said when she heard about "this old flame"? She said it was awful and to be careful. They knew. They knew Thwack was trouble. If only we'd been able to work out the meaning behind their conversation sooner. Hopefully my understanding of their language will keep improving, so I can interpret it quicker next time. I don't want to become a gossip like Muntjac Deer, but there's a lot to be gained from eavesdropping.'

Neither Bank Vole nor Pine Marten want to talk, so they respond with a nod. This simple gesture is all Pigeon needs to continue.

'We must keep listening to the trees too. I don't think you all pay them enough attention. They have more foresight and wisdom than any of us could ever muster. They, too, clearly knew Thwack's species once existed here. Remember I told you they said, "Earth's patience has been honoured, life is being restored?" They said that because they knew Thwack's a beaver, a native, and that Earth had wanted her to be walking in our woods again. And that's not it!' she says excitedly. 'Remember I told you I also heard them chanting "chaos,", the word you had used, Pine Marten, to describe Thwack's arrival? They continued saying it because they must have known she has vengeful plans.'

Pine Marten momentarily forgets where he is and tells Pigeon out loud that she's right. Clearly, they should be listening to the trees more regularly. They could give them an insight into how things are going to pan out.

They reach a mass of grey upright slabs that are sitting on top of the short grass. The glistening river, lit up by the guiding moon, is flowing leisurely beside them. Realising he's dared to speak and got away with it, Pine Marten relaxes slightly and asks Pigeon what she thinks it is they're walking through. Pigeon had hoped no one would ask. She doesn't know the answer and doesn't like to be caught out. She picks her words carefully, endeavouring to come across informed.

'Well, as you can see, flowers are placed in front of the stones… moving sticks do this.'

'Why?'

Now Pigeon's in a dilemma. Should she just admit she isn't sure, or continue making out she does to save face? She decides to go with the latter.

'Well,' she says again, 'They place the flowers here to try and get it to become less grey. They're trying to bring colour back to this place. They want it to be like the woods it's next to.'

Pine Marten thinks that's believable. 'So, these are the moving sticks who are likely to listen to you, Pigeon, don't you think? If any are going to return to the woods, it's bound to be these ones.'

Pigeon feels rather guilty for guessing, but a short, shrill shriek wipes away her remorse. Bank Vole, terrified, runs underneath Pine Marten, who has slapped a paw over his mouth to stop himself from screaming.

'That'll be a fox. It's not mating season, so it must be marking its territory,' Pigeon says. 'Let's move closer to the river and travel along there. If the fox smells us, it may attack us, seeing as we're no longer in the woods. Our harmonious rules won't apply. If we walk by the river's edge, you both have a means of escape. Pine Marten, you'll have to jump into the water and take Bank Vole on your back. I doubt a fox would be desperate enough to follow.'

Pine Marten hates swimming because it messes up his fur. He knows he'll have to put his vanity aside, but he really hopes it doesn't get to that. The three animals rush towards the water. The fox's call has startled them all. Pigeon had been enjoying having her friends alongside her as she ventures back into the Grey. Now, she's reminded that this isn't a fun expedition. It isn't the opportunity for her to show off her moving stick knowledge. This is a perilous journey, and because she's acquainted with the area, her friends will be relying on her to protect them. She focuses on why they're here: they're looking for Tripper. The best way for her to spot something is when she's in the air. She is awarded with a much wider view and can detect movement better. She tells her frightened friends she's got to fly, that she'll look for both Tripper and the fox, and promises she'll be back as soon as she's done a thorough scour. Bank Vole and Pine Marten return to nodding silently and cling to each other for comfort.

Up above, Pigeon sees a crawling mole and smells a colony of sleeping starlings. So far, there doesn't seem to be any sign of the fox. She sees a leaf fluttering on the ground and watches the wind push it forward. Tripper too, doesn't seem to be near. *Whatever this place is, it's pretty empty*, she thinks. *There's not much sign of life.*

She turns around mid-air and begins flying lower. She's heading back to the river, sure there's nothing to see. Flying against the wind now, she beats her wings ferociously. A heavy gust pushes her backwards. She flaps on the spot to regain balance and looks down to prevent her eyes from watering. Holding herself in this position, she notices the leaf again. It's now resting directly beneath her. The fact it's no longer being thrown by the gale-force wind is odd. She swoops down to investigate. Even before she alights, Pigeon realises that what she'd thought was a stalk is, in fact, a tail. What she'd regarded as a colourful leaf is actually red, brown, and grey fur. It's an animal of some sort. Landing tumultuously right in front of the creature, the little being jumps and squeaks, shocked and scared in equal measure.

'Tripper, it's you!' Pigeon says breathlessly. 'I hadn't meant to frighten you! I've come to find you. It's me, Pigeon, from the woods.'

Tripper recognises the bird. Truth be told, she's happy to see a familiar face. 'It's nice to see you,' she says. 'Have you heard I have a very serious job to do?'

Pigeon can already tell that on this occasion, Thwack's right. It isn't going to be easy to persuade Tripper to come home. She's so determined, so proud of the task she's undertaking, that it's the first thing she mentions. 'Yes, I've heard about it,' she says calmly. 'Before you go, though, I was hoping to take you to someone. They're very close and it won't take long.'

Tripper hesitates. Thwack had instructed her to focus solely on what she needs to do. Sensing her reluctance, Pigeon blurts out that the animal waiting for her is Bank Vole. As soon as she hears his name, Tripper yields and follows Pigeon hurriedly.

After a short while, they see the two bunched-up animals standing by the water. Scurrying as fast as she can, Tripper bounds towards Bank Vole, nestling herself into his body. Letting out squeals of both joy and pain, Bank Vole strokes her head and immediately pleads for her to come back. He wants to do all he can to show his descendant how important she is to him and that this pursuit is unsafe. He tells her the Grey is dangerous, that animals there think differently. He tells her they're hostile because of their harsh environment. He tells her Thwack's anger is her own, that it's not Tripper's duty to heal her wounds. He begs her to abandon this adventure and tries to convince her something better will come along. Something fun that will help their species evolve.

'Our plan worked, Tripper. I messed up my fur like you advised and confessed my feelings. I'm now in a life bond. And my partner even has a new name. She wants to be called Pristine. See! You are already creating such an impression. You've got what it takes to improve the life of bank voles. That will be so much more rewarding for you than this. So much more meaningful.'

Tripper listens, pulling herself away from Bank Vole so she can look at him and take in everything he's saying. The smile that spreads across her cheeks when she hears his news is entirely unfeigned. So, too, is the crumpling around her eyes when he asks her not to go.

'I want to do this,' she says confidently. 'I'm Tripper, I travel. It's part of who I am. It's in my name. This is my opportunity to make a difference, to leave a legacy. I *am* thinking about our species. Beavers were treated terribly, and me, a bank vole, can help put things right!'

She tries to lift his mouth up with her paws to get him to look happy, but his lined lips drop back down as soon as she lets go.

'Please don't be sad. I'll be back before you know it! And when I am, I'm going to have the best stories to tell, just like you, Bank Vole! Then I'll fall in love as well and live the rest of my life with someone.'

Bank Vole has to look elsewhere. Any view will do. He just can't look at her little face. He knew there was a possibility of her eventually leaving to look for a breeding partner, but to go for the sake of another animal rips him apart inside. His throat is becoming increasingly tight and his legs are starting to weaken.

'Tripper, if you need to do this, if you feel you have to go on this journey, then I'll come with you.' Pigeon, her voice soft, breaks the devastating tension. 'I don't like Thwack. I think she's conniving and bitter, but your mind is clearly set on this. Let me come. I can help keep you safe. I know a lot about the Grey, about moving sticks, about where you can locate these animals you need to rally. Take it from me, Tripper, travel can be lonely; it can be daunting and scary. I'll be your guardian; I will help you achieve your mission so you can come back and live your life peacefully with another bank vole until your last sunset.'

Tripper is too young to understand exactly what she's taking on. The task that lies ahead of her doesn't seem as formidable as it should. She thinks she can do it alone. Besides, Thwack had told her this quest was their secret. She doesn't want to go against her orders.

'I can't, Thwack said—'

'Thwack has told us everything. We know what it is you have to do.'

Pigeon's statement surprises Tripper but if Thwack is ok with Pigeon accompanying her, she doesn't see any reason to be against it. Although she's sure she can achieve it solo, she'd prefer company. She responds with a shrug.

Bank Vole is overwhelmed with thanks. Usually, when he wants to sincerely express his gratitude, he, like the other animals, extends his paw. As birds can't respond in the normal manner, which is to place a paw on top, they sweep a wing across instead. To each other, however, they dip their heads. And this is what Bank Vole does now. He lowers his face to show Pigeon just how thankful he is. The gesture touches Pigeon and she dips her head back. Then, without wanting to prolong his pain, she gently leads the pup away with a nudge of her wing. As always, she is thrilled to be visiting the Grey. Her puffed chest may have regained its purple hue in the woods, but she's ready for it to dull in colour once more.

Pine Marten stands next to Bank Vole and crosses his front limbs. Together they watch the new companions head towards a place they've always considered scary and severe, somewhere they've proudly believed is drastically different to theirs.

'And so a new suffering begins,' Bank Vole sighs. 'I'm going to need you again, my friend.'

Unlocking himself, Pine Marten drapes a paw around Bank Vole's shoulders. 'I'm always here. And if our peaceful woods gets filled with hatred and blood, I'm going to need you and your jokes, too. I may not have love to soothe and strengthen me, but I can't think of any better armour than our friendship.'

\*

Walking past a cracked slab of grey that's sitting slanted on top of Earth, Tripper marvels at the moss that's draped around it. The colour is so green and bright, it almost glows against its drab surroundings. The plant seems infectiously joyous, like it's deliberately spreading its luminosity across the solid surface it's living on. Its bold, buoyant beauty reminds her of someone and makes her think of something. She turns around and looks back at Bank Vole, an ancestor who has helped her champion her differences, who has made her see how impactful and gratifying her little life can be. It's clear to her now that what her choir friend Cub has with Badger, she has too.

'Goodbye, Grandpa,' she shouts. 'I hope you can hear your new name.'

His bottom lip is curled, his shoulders are slouched.
He can.

*I feel your aura floating above, Grandpa, and this book is dedicated to you.*

Printed in Great Britain
by Amazon